SAGE ISLAND

Samantha Warwick

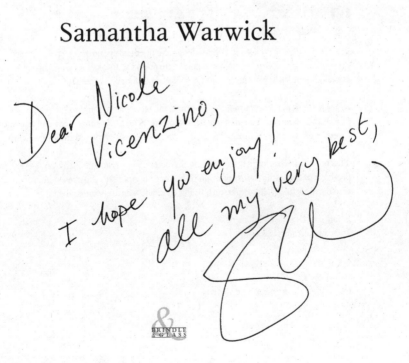

Dear Nicole
Vicenzino,
I hope you enjoy!
all my very best,

&
BRINDLE
& GLASS

LIBRARY AND ARCHIVES CANADA CATALOGUING IN PUBLICATION
Warwick, Samantha, 1977–   Sage Island / Samantha Warwick.
ISBN 978-1-897142-33-2

I. Title.
PS8645.A79S24 2008   C813'.6   C2008-903089-3

Editor: Lee Shedden
Cover image: Paolo Curto / Getty Images
Author photo: David de Vlieger
Epigraph: From *The Long Swim* by Richard C. Angell, copyright 1947 by Richard C. Angell. Used by permission of G.P. Putnam's Sons, a division of Penguin Group (USA) Inc.

Canadian Heritage   Patrimoine canadien   Canada Council for the Arts   Conseil des Arts du Canada

Brindle & Glass is pleased to acknowledge the financial support to its publishing program from the Government of Canada through the Book Publishing Industry Development Program (BPIDP) and the Canada Council for the Arts.

Brindle & Glass is committed to protecting the environment and to the responsible use of natural resources. This book is printed on 100% post-consumer recycled and ancient-forest-friendly paper. For more information, please visit www.oldgrowthfree.com.

Brindle & Glass Publishing
www.brindleandglass.com

1 2 3 4 5 11 10 09 08

PRINTED AND BOUND IN CANADA

This book is dedicated to

Gertrude "Trudy" Ederle (1905–2003)
&
George Young (1910–1972)

The feeling within you, the urge to crawl out of your skin and get away, get away, is so strong that it couldn't be uniquely personal. It must be a universal feeling, shared by all the others.

Richard Angell, *The Long Swim*

THAT FEELING when you first enter the water, straight as a needle; that underwater glide, the flying, weightless sensation of being suspended—free. You soar up to the surface and hit a rhythm, strike forward into a hypnotic swimming trance. That is where I feel right. The transformation of the hand, from palm and fingers to amphibious paddle. Back and forth, breathing every three strokes, pivoting through the turn, shoving off the wall, and recovering each new arm cycle with a smooth high-elbow technique.

The splashes of my arms, timing of my breath, and beating of my heart become my own personal song bag. Music drums, stretches, constricts; it undulates in time with my stroke, until there is no more music, and the rhythm is replaced only by breath, momentum, and the slosh of water in my ears.

There is something inexplicable, something intrinsic about the repetition in swimming. The regression that comes with moving through water—prehistoric simplicity. The idea of peeling out of myself and shedding my human, female skin, becoming wild, a drifting speck, divorced from the patter of thought and city scream, floating through some green river toward the open sea. That is the connection. The clearing out of everything, wipe the mind's slate clear—*tabula rasa*.

ONE

THE SS *CABRILLO* oscillates in rolling swells; wind whistles over the water. Salt water sprays my face, and I can't decide if the air is warm or cold—it's deadpan average. Swells rise and fall like giant, fluid hills. I am waiting for a thrill to shoot through me at the thought of being away from New York, out of the cheerless, anemic blaah of winter—but all I feel is fatigue and nausea. There was a time when excitement glowed in my centre and shivers crept through my bloodstream. Those shivers, that luminosity, are lost to me now—heaved overboard into the ageless chasm of unrequited dreams, replaced by Freud's theories on neuroses and an ever-present fear that I am cracking up.

The late-afternoon sunlight is orange on the water, and as I gaze out ahead, a chunk of craggy and sage-covered land becomes clear. A long curving row of mop-headed palm trees stands guard along the coastline. The air is balmy. I breathe in the fresh, salt-tangled wind and watch the island—Santa Catalina—grow larger as the steamer pitches toward a harbour filled with boats. With each pitch, I clutch the railing, bracing myself against the urge to vomit overboard.

I am arriving two weeks before the event to acclimatize to the ocean, as I am not especially familiar with salt water. I came here alone to adapt to the island in solitude, because there's nothing else I want more in the world than to slip away into a new place and swim

3

and explore and be natural. The city felt like a big, fat clot lodged between me and my spirit.

The spirit, according to Florenz Ziegfeld—as described in an issue of *Vanity Fair*—is a "definite animation indicative of personal power, resources and adaptability." Personal power, resourcefulness, and adaptability—all that stuff about shivers and life and excitement, I call it the *spuzz*, the human spuzz.

The boat takes up landing in Avalon Harbor, and I look down at the ocean, at the sandy bottom and starfish stuck to reefs, lucid and brilliant through many feet of water. I don't know anything about this strange purple island, except what I read in a leaflet on the rattler leaving New York: that it is a rugged, somewhat secluded place—full of salty coves, morning fog, and barking sea lions that lounge on the rocks when the sun is hot. I read that it was the Pimugnan Indians who first settled here, that octopus is harvested for the ink it produces, and that Catalina Island once served as a station for pirate contraband.

As the passengers disembark, the main street of town is humming with musicians, busy little shops, and people riding around on bicycles. The town is small, not exceeding a square mile or so, and is surrounded by hills that are tinted purple by bunches of sage brush. Fish is being barbecued on grills; smoke drifts down the street, and I hoof it with my satchel and duffel bag to the hill designated for swimmers preparing for the race. It is dotted with tents already.

I don't have a number yet, but I've heard that there are more than four hundred registered contestants. I will need to arrange for a convoy to navigate my course. This shouldn't be a problem; Wrigley has solicited many boats and pilots for the event. He has promised twenty-five thousand dollars to the fastest swimmer to cross the channel, and an additional fifteen thousand dollars will be awarded to the first woman finisher. Wrigley offered national heroine Trudy Ederle five thousand dollars to swim across the San Pedro, and even after he upped the ante to ten thousand, she still threw him over. And despite the fact that I have, in recent months, developed a loathing toward Ederle, never mind millionaires with too much money to throw around—entertaining ideas about burning down their ostentatious homes and freeing their exotic birds—I find myself here.

As I hike up an arid path, swimmers, trainers, and aimless hoboes have turned an otherwise barren, brushwood-covered hill into a nomadic encampment. Beside smoky fire pits, olive-coloured tents with celluloid windows have been assembled, complete with folding chairs and ice boxes, and, tied to tree branches, paper lanterns swing from side to side in the wind. Ukuleles, harmonicas, and laughter sound over the hill.

I stake out an earthy patch on the brow of a high, rocky shelf. There are small evergreen trees with white flowers blooming in clusters at the tips of the branches, and a twisted old cypress tree dangles over the edge of the shelf. Water crashes onto chalky bluffs, the ocean bulges and recedes. The sun moves slowly from sky to horizon.

I set up camp amidst several boulders that block out some of the wind, gather dried sage scrub into a stone-encircled pit on my lot, and try to build a fire. The tent and camping supplies came from my older brother, Michael—he left them to me when he decided to forgo a university scholarship in favour of what he called "the expatriate movement."

I sit away from the eye-smarting smoke on the biggest granite boulder and pull my sweater sleeves over my fingers. It is one of those sunsets that gives off the illusion of summer, of warmth—a smudge of red across the horizon. The wind veers and smoke burns into my eyes; they're almost normal again since the infection, or *incident,* whatever you want to call it.

The approaching sound of clanking glass startles me out of my despondency. I turn around and a skinny man is ambling toward me in the dimness, dressed in a tattered plaid shirt and corduroy pants. He is reciting a series of words to himself in a mumbling, sing-song way: *ack beer ink Johnnie king London Emma nuts orange pip queen yorker ʒebra.* Over his shoulder he carries a burlap sack that I can only guess is full of empty bottles. He draws closer to my camp, his bottles clink, and he peers at me through the twilit wash with small glassy eyes. "Good evening, young bint," he says. "Any more for any more?"

He brings his hand to his forehead and salutes. "Loot," he says, and it seems he's asking me for something—bottles or food or matches. I don't understand what he wants. Through his burlap sack, fluid is seeping out and dripping onto the ground. He smiles, baring a broad ridge of yellow teeth, and points to my tent, "Swell bivvy."

A ripple of panic undulates through me. I've only been here a few hours and the resident crazy man has already landed at my camp. I look into the flames, hoping that he will carry on toward the other camps. But instead, he seats himself across from me and holds out his long skinny fingers to the smouldering fire. His grey hair is lifted easily by the air, as though static electricity were gently pulling it from his scalp. He starts humming, but it isn't really humming—it's as if he's reciting something again—it sounds like *dah-dah dah-dah-dah di-dah-dit di-di-dit.* I consider him coldly as he clasps and unclasps his reedy fingers. He looks up from the fire, his fine blue hair framing a halo around his face, and stares at the side of my head.

"Palm?" he asks.

"What palm?"

He holds out one of his long dirty hands and displays the lines and creases that criss-cross his palm.

"No palm reading," I say. "How 'bout you carry on?"

My heartbeat rattles against my rib cage. His face—despite the white and blue hair that wafts around it—appears younger than expected, doesn't quite correspond with the rest of him. He points to his chest, "Loot," he says again. "Back to you."

He smiles his unsightly yellow smile, neurotically clasping and unclasping his hands, rocking a little toward the fire, and reciting a variation of his words again: *pip nuts yorker pip nuts X-ray pip nuts beer, Charlie: out.*

He stops, hums, and stretches out his freakish hands to the flames.

"You forgot," he says. "Shame."

Cold chills splash into my face and chest. "What?"

"Silly bint. You forgot it."

"What are you talking about?"

He is watching the air around my skull, turns to the fire, rocks back and forth, and brings his hands to his face to hide a muffled bout of ridiculous laughter that he appears to be sharing with an invisible person. He puts his hands to the fire again, and instead of reciting his words, he chants: *Red or grey bint does not know—red for friend and grey for foe. Red or grey bint does not know, red for fortune, grey for woe.*

"Leave!" I say sharply.

He blinks. "Palm?" Earnestly displaying his sooty hand once again.

"No. No palm reading. Go away." I poke at the fire with a thick branch, feeling my insides twitch.

His smile dissolves and he looks unhappily into the fire. I see that he is not wearing any shoes; his feet are weathered and black with dirt. "Goggle-eyed booger with the tit," he says.

I stand up with my fire-poking stick. "That's enough!" I shout, still nauseated from the boat ride. "It's time for you to leave!"

He bobs to his feet with a spring.

I wave my stick at him. "Carry on!"

He is not especially hurried, and ambles back down the hill toward the other camps, repeating words and *dits*, but in the dark I see that he diverts into a brambly trail.

Even if the island crazy man could read palms, I wouldn't let him near my hands with a forty-thousand-foot pole. I don't like to dabble in the mystic. I don't like to know what will happen, and I don't like the idea of a perfect stranger peering into my fate.

7

It was Maizee who fostered this paranoia of all things meta-physical, by adopting fate and superstition into her everyday routine the way younger soldiers abandoned the Church after the war. I sit for quite some time, uneasy, watching the fire. Beyond the sloping grassland speckled with swimmer-nomads, there is a marina where small lights flicker, masts creak, and halyard ropes vibrate and bang in the wind.

The wind begins to roar through the tops of high palm trees. In the twilight dark of an unfamiliar place, palm leaves rattle like bones, island ghosts shake in the branches. Nocturnal flower smells are potent and mixed into the smoke of cooking fish.

Freud says that biology is destiny.

I lean forward, wrenched by a pang of dread.

TWO

HIGGINS USED to say I had a physical intelligence. "There are different types of intelligence," he said. "There is the intellectual kind," and he tapped his head with a loose fist. "There is the emotional kind," he tapped his chest where his heart would be, "and there is the physical kind. A person with physical intelligence should never underestimate his gift."

This was the statement that lit a fire in my rib cage and sent tassels of electricity through my bloodstream. Swimming became a *place* as opposed to a simple activity—a refuge of glassy tile and watery echo where I could lose myself in the underwater world of movement and rhythm, where I could hear the tinkling of water in and out of my ears. In the water, there was far more to being alive than greasing double-papered pans and curling strips of pastry.

That said, my training was not all smooth, meditative poetry but a racket of breaking water and muffled echo, a tumble of ache, throbbing shoulders, and smarting red eyelids. Swimming was my wild place, my rainforest adventure, my pilgrimage through storms of hot desert sand. And despite the effervescent spasm of physical strain, there would rise up from the cool depths important moments of clarity, moments when my muscles let go and I was swift and elastic—moments I knew I was exactly where I was supposed to be. And I believed it, which was the important thing.

Bundled inside my moth-eaten sleeping bag, I wake up from a lousy sleep; early morning light seeps through the canvas. I push open a tent flap to peer outside and gaze over the ridge. Swimmers are doing lengths along the shore, acclimatizing to the cold, the salt, the rolling swells. From up here they look like a pod of harbour seals. Coaches are shouting, waving, and signalling to their swimmers from the beach.

Behind my tent, at one of the other camps, some swimmers are gathered beside a driftwood fire having breakfast and coffee. I move back into the tent, slip into a pair of country tweeds, button the knee cuffs, stow money into a pocket, pull up my plaid golfing socks, and adjust my sweaters. I locate a canister of water and rifle through a pack for my toilet-kit and tooth powder.

After cleaning my teeth and closing up my tent, I set off, downward, along the path. The smell of bacon fat sends a stab of hunger through my insides. It appears that a group having breakfast near my camp have been ambushed by a travelling saleswolf who is promoting special oil that he claims will numb a swimmer from feeling any pain. "No cramp, no shoulder ache, no more soreness!" he shouts. The assembled contestants listen dubiously to his pitch; he seems strikingly undaunted by their collective squint.

"No pain?" A big man wearing a checked shirt with the sleeves cut off suddenly steps forward and puts the screws to the saleswolf. "Say, gee," he says. "You know what that stuff sounds like to me? I'll tell you what it sounds like—it sounds like a great smattering of snake oil bull*shit*. Now if you'll excuse us, you can take your peddling party somewhere else. I don't know—maybe off that cliff over there."

A boil of laughter rolls over the breakfast entourage, and the saleswolf scuttles away in a cloud of lifted sand. Looking closer, the big man without the sleeves looks familiar, but I'm not sure from where. He is throwing a towel over his shoulder and sauntering down toward the beach. Contestants disband to separate camps, and, as I turn, someone bumps into me and wheels around. A woman; she is accompanied by two men.

"Excuse me," she says. She has a large, flat face and pale hair; she peeks out from a winter cloche, woolly bobbles attached to the top. There is a delicate suggestion of age around her mouth, while the two men are young—quite possibly an entire decade younger than the woman.

We continue briefly in opposite directions before I hear the sudden halt of their footsteps on the path behind me. "Hey," she says, "wait."

I turn around to face her, and the two young men stand there, lurking, giving me a silent, united once-over. One of them has enormous eyes set well into his head.

She rakes over me with her albino eyes, looks closer, and speaks in a short rapid burst: "You look familiar."

Considering that I had travelled three thousand miles to get here, I hadn't expected anyone to recognize me, and I shrug my shoulders. "Couldn't say."

She is examining my face, which is making it difficult to slip away. "Where are you from?" she asks.

"New York."

"Hm," she says, searching my face from under her woollen lid. "Swell shopping there."

My reluctance to respond sets the stage for an immediate awkwardness, and I begin to dissociate from my body. This dissociation seems to be occurring with more frequency over recent weeks, despite efforts to stay fastened to the goings-on around me.

"I'm Bea," she nods, and the pom-poms attached to her lid bob. The two young men follow her lead by dipping their heads; one of them draws in a breath to speak—but he is quickly cut off by Bea, who is entirely focused on who I am and what my story is. "Here alone?" she asks.

"Yes," I say, glancing quickly at the men, and attempt to carry on.

"Wait," she says. Blue veins are visible under her translucent skin. She motions with a hand to the young man with the deeply set eyes. "I didn't introduce you to the Canadians. They're from Toronto."

I look at them, flat. "Hi."

Bea raises her nearly invisible blonde eyebrows. "Are you all right?" she asks me. "You look pale."

"On my way to eat something," I tell her. "Haven't had anything since yesterday lunch."

"Well," she nods, "before you go, this is George Young—he's the swimmer," she says, presenting the man with the large eye sockets. She motions to the second man. "And this is his buddy, Billy. Billy's a Canadian high-diving champion. They hitchhiked all the way here, nearly three thousand miles!"

"That's far," I say, numbly concentrated on my escape from this horridly stilted exchange of pleasantries.

I nod and try again to continue down the path.

George opens his mouth to speak but is cut off a second time by Bea.

She takes a step closer to me, blocking my progress. "*Your name?*"

We stand for a moment, estimating each other like two ends of a balancing scale.

"Savi," I say, thinking she likely wouldn't recognize the abbreviation.

"Hm," she says again, squinting at me. "Is that short for something?"

"No."

My name is Savanna, which means treeless. I am an empty, dry, treeless plain, and my stomach lining is about to start eating itself.

"I'm sure I'll see you all later," I say, sidling away from them.

"You will so," she says, suspicious, and I skirt off down the sandy path, dry grass poking up from the ground, through a family of cacti and a pasture of tall meadow plants.

Behind the main street of Avalon, there is a villa of small bungalows with canvas roofs. People on bicycles wheel down the narrow streets and chime little bells attached to their handlebars; they adjust bundled accumulations of food in the front baskets of their bikes. Alongside the produce sellers, artistic types have set up booths of pottery and silver jewellery, some are selling Pimugnan ceremonial objects made of soapstone and glassy obsidian.

I buy a loaf of bread, a block of white cheese, and a bunch of oranges from a table tended by a youngish man with shrewd grey eyes. There is a humidity to his eyes and a burnished look to his skin—Latin blood, or perhaps years of sun on his face. He is placing my oranges and bread into a paper bag.

"Swimmer?" he asks.

I nod, divert my gaze to the hill dotted with tents.

"Swimmers staking it out all over the hill," he says. "Never seen anything like it." He stands, holding the bag, looking at the hill, and then turns back to me. His dusky face is half-hidden underneath a round felt hat. I don't know why he doesn't just give me the bag. Is it some kind of island rule that you have to talk to everybody around here?

"You should tie any food you have at your camp to a tree," he says. "Wild goats. They come down the hill to lick salt off the rocks at the beach. They're not afraid of people."

"Can I have my bag, please?" I say, and he pushes it toward me.

Walking along the boardwalk I start to feel faint. I sit down on the edge of the wooden planking with my paper bag on my lap; wind lifts sand into airborne eddies and I have to shield my eyes against the flying grains. I reach for the loaf of bread inside the bag and tear off a large piece to eat. The bread is crumbly and doesn't taste like much, and if anyone knows good bread, it's me. My life has revolved around the making of bread since I turned fourteen. I know always to have the thermometer in view during the baking process to be certain that the dough rises under all the right particulars. There are many particulars in the business of baking, like remembering to make incisions on the tops of unbaked loaves to release steam and prevent breakage. Or in the case of fruit bread, raisins, dates, and apricots should be soaked for twenty-four hours in brandy to ensure richness and moisture of the final product.

My role in my father's bake house was to arrange interesting window displays with little cards advertising specials, to peel apples without wasting any fruit, to knead slabs of sourdough with the heels of my hands, and to avoid burning myself on the many hot trays and oven racks. My brother, Michael, was completing his first year of college when I was pulled from school, and while he sometimes helped at the bake house, he was never given quite the same opportunity to negotiate hot biscuit trays or pots of molten rhubarb because he was busy with studies and reading after lights. He was a vast and industrious reader; his teachers had always stamped him as brainy, with much scholarly promise, and so he was allowed to finish school and pursue college and university on scholarship. His blasé manner toward it all made me want to flip a table.

He used words like *regress* and *alter ego*. He planned to become a writer, he told me one night while I was mopping the checkered floor of the bake house. He was stationed at the long wooden table in the centre of the kitchen making himself a sandwich, his English driving cap on backwards. His shoulder bag rested on the table, laden with books. I knew he had been reading a lot of the modern stuff because I spied in his bag when he left it lying around. "Savski," he said. "You don't need school."

My ears started to burn.

"You've got swimming, at least for another few years, and everything important you can find through reading," he said. "Just read everything you can get your mitts on. 'Specially the new stuff. Sherwood Anderson had to leave school at fourteen to help his family and he's a goddamned *genius.* "

"Easy for you to say." I flung the mop into its bucket, launching dirty water onto my kitchen boots and apron.

"Sorry," he said, looking up from his assemblage. "Listen, I'm sorry how that sounds. Don't say anything yet, Savinski—but I've decided to drop the institution, beat it overseas."

"What?" I braced myself against the mop and planted a hand on my hip. "You're supposed to follow your genius fancy and get a degree."

He laughed.

I stared at him. "You're leaving me here?"

He considered the bread and cheese and condiment jars before him.

"Always better to write about your subject from a distance, Savski—not from right inside it," he said. "This country can't tell shit from Shinola. The bohos are leaving in *droves*. Any case, I'm blowing." And so he took off to Europe, leaving behind the freshly risen expectation that I would stay, a permanent compensation for his absence, and pick dried sourdough off my arm hairs for the rest of my life.

I've been in the throes of one big hangover for several months. My nerves are dulled even when I haven't had anything to drink; sometimes I break out into cold sweats for no good reason. My training may have conditioned me for the twenty-two mile stretch to Los Angeles, but in truth I haven't actually been training for four months, my eyes are hypersensitive, and my muscles have probably atrophied. I know dangerously little about the unpredictability of cold water and the drag force of tides.

When that wave of dissociation flows over me, I stare at my hands, opening and closing my fists. The action, the opening and closing, reminds me that I exist. Open, close, I exist. I feel my skin. I exist. I know this is not a normal question to be turning over—*of course I exist*, I tell myself one minute, and then I find myself drifting again, feeling blank.

The bake house occupies the lower floor of an old brownstone on New York's West Side. It is a cozy hardwood place, with brick walls, rustic decor, and a cobblestone fireplace. It always smells of newly roasted coffee beans and rising biscuits. I live in the small flat on the top floor. It used to be Michael's flat, but after he blew—and after much domestic debate—I was allowed to take it over. He had left a bunch of books for me to read: Twain, Wilde, Freud, Lewis, his beloved Sherwood Anderson, a phrasebook of common Latin, some issues of the *Mercury*, and a somewhat surprising naval account of the U-boat.

Amidst his piles of books and essays I found a dictionary, but it wasn't a real dictionary—it was a collection of invented words called the *Unabridged* by Gelett Burgess. There was a book of non-sense poetry, also by him, but I was more stuck on the dictionary. A *quoob* was defined as a misfit, a person or thing obviously out of place. *Moosoo* meant sulky. And as I flipped through the small book, I came upon spuzz.

Spuzz, *n.* 1. Mental energy, an aggressive intellect. 2. Stamina, force, spice. *Spuzz is that getaheadative zip, tang, and racehorse enthusiasm that has for its motto, "Do it now."* Spuz'zard, *n.* 1. An active, forceful thinker. 2. A cocktail with a "kick" in it (such as a dry martini [See *Looblum*]). *You can't down the spuzzard; he is elastic, and bounces up after every failure.* Spuz'zy, 1. Charged with brain-electricity.

Before leaving for the island, however, over the course of recent weeks, I was profoundly without spuzz. My eyes stung with infection. I abandoned all things productive and took to spending a phenomenal amount of time lying on my back in the middle of my hardwood floor. I put ice-soaked cloths over my face, positioned myself on the floor, and folded my hands over my rib cage.

"What are you doing?" A wary-looking parent would ask me,

or Michael, who had suddenly reappeared to announce his engagement to a lounge singer—the delightful and perfectly manicured Ida.

"Go away. I'm busy."

"Doctor said the infection has cleared. Perhaps you might get off the floor today."

"I'm occupied, thank you."

"And *what* might you be accomplishing by lying in the middle of the floor this way?"

Sometimes I took the cool compress from my face and stared at the ceiling. "I'm staring up at rock bottom. This is what it looks like." And I would make a feeble gesture with my hand toward the door, "If you please."

They would turn away, sighing, leaving me in my idle state to consider things I may have done differently, which were numerous. By this point, it had occurred to me, vaguely, that the problem might not have been Trudy Ederle herself. Sometimes I forgot about her damaged hearing. Hell. The girl is damn near deaf now.

"What are you doing?" The question has interrupted my fist exercise, and I have to squint upward from the boardwalk at a somewhat athletic, masculine silhouette backlit by the retina-burning sun. "Are you all right?"

"I'm fine," I say, resting my hands on the bag. There are crumbs of bread all over my sweater. "Why?"

It is the man who had sold me the oranges. "Your hand," he says. "You were looking at it as though it was going to fall off." The boardwalk faces a flat, mercury-coloured bay, and he stands in a weathered sheepskin jacket, looking at the ocean and lighting a cigarette.

"A swimmer," he says to himself or me, I am not sure, giving me a sidelong eyeball before gazing back at the water. Smoke trails from the burning tobacco between his fingers. "Tell me. Why would anybody want to put themselves through something so masochistic?"

"Masochistic?"

He looks at me with raised eyebrows. "Mad, if you prefer." He's watching me with those shrewd grey eyes again, and I decide I don't like him at all. His chin is slightly thrusted; he is waiting for a response.

"Your bread is lousy," I tell him, steely.

"It's not my bread, and I'm not sure you would know, since most of it is on your sweater."

"Sure it's your bread. You sold it to me."

"Nope, I was just minding the booth for a local. Not my bread," he says, exhaling smoke.

Was he not a local? I don't care enough to clarify this—he looks enough like a local from where I'm sitting. I don't know how to talk to him, so I say nothing, and without intending to, I stare back at my hand, a closed fist on my leg. The sign of the fig. A closed fist— with thumb between index and middle fingers—was a way to protect oneself from bad luck.

"You don't look like a swimmer," he says.

I knew it. I've shrunken. I've shrunken into an anemic piece of soft, useless tissue. Treeless, my name was a prophecy—a dry wind toward lifelessness.

"Oh, Jeez," he's saying now, and I know it must be my forehead. The furrows always give me away. "Listen, I'm sorry."

I manage to look him in the eye, and he's searching my face. Whatever he's searching for, he isn't going to find.

"Bye," I say, standing to brush away the crumbs.

I carry the bag of food against my chest, up the hill, and through the nomadic campsites. I stop to examine a cluster of those white flowers that grow from the tips of shrubby evergreen branches. Each flower looks like a small urn.

THREE

THERE ARE no borders here, no concrete walls, no cork lane ropes or black lines painted on the bottom of the tank. All the hours spent practising how to quickly turn at the wall will not help me here—the rehearsed underwater approach, the clean twist of my body, the shove off the tile. I can almost hear Higgins, his voice echoing around the yellow-lit, crumbling old tank: "A plague on your walls!"

I would bob up from underwater, water running from my ears and nose. "What?"

"Your walls! A PLAGUE on them!"

He would stand above me, a dark silhouette, his split-second pocket watch held inside his tight fist. He would shake his head, hand thrown in the air, and then move away to shout at somebody else. Back then, I was merely one amongst a team of many.

Maizee would laugh, spit water through the space between her two front teeth. "A *plague*, Savi," she would say under her breath, knitting her brow and mocking our coach. "Haven't you been listening to a word I've been *saying*? Straight as an *arrow*, supple as an *eel*. Don't take so long to *breathe*, you lazy scruff!" She would laugh and sing the word *eel*, which had become our inside-joke ever since we heard that Freud started his career dissecting eels, trying to locate their testicles. The study was a flop and he decided to be a head doctor instead. We thought that was hilarious.

Maizee was frosted over by a milky way of freckles, and she always kept her shingled, auburn bob protected under a rubber cap while swimming. At the end of every practice, I would pull off my cap and let the cool water calm my burning scalp while she would keep hers on, and we would turn onto our backs like river otters and swim a few lengths of the tank that way. With our ears and mouths above the water, we could talk about where we would acquire our next illicit bottle of booze, or about where her latest beau had tried to put his hands.

Maizee was an only child who had lost her father to the war, and her mother, a dressmaker, had initially put her on the swimming team for the purpose of instilling discipline and mental poise and, ultimately, to keep her out of trouble. While I was shuffling restlessly around the hot little kitchen like a moon circumnavigating a small universe of delicate pastries and medieval-sized loaves of bread, she was working with her mother as a seamstress. She enjoyed the construction of smooth fabrics into sheer, sultry, unfitted gowns and described the softness and rustle of the latest crêpe de Chine materials with concentrated reverence. She always grew attached to the frocks—to the silks and rayons, the various prints, fringes, piping, and soft inner linings—and she resented the day when her work was parceled out to shops or buyers. She said it was worse than giving puppies away.

Maizee had a large freckle in one of her eyes; it made her look as though her eyes were two different colours—one green, one brown. She was the sort of girl who would rip a stop sign right out of the grassy roadside and slam it onto the pavement if she lost her temper. But she was also gentle and protective—and I knew I could trust her, which was something I always found difficult.

The year going into the 1924 Olympics, we were seventeen. We worked every day, we trained every afternoon save Sundays, and at competitions we almost always placed in our respective events. I swam the overhand crawl—the fastest and sleekest of all the strokes—

and she swam breaststroke. We were both sprinters. On weekends when we weren't competing, we took a hiatus from our athletic selves and drank Gimlets in my flat above the bake house. Maizee brought the gin in a flask she kept on her hip. I supplied the lime and soda. We sat in two old armchairs opposite each other, and she got up every once in a while to perch on the windowsill and smoke her cigarettes.

"Ciggy?" she would always offer, extending her little package of smokes, and I would decline, sipping my gin from a large clay mug.

It was Maizee who discovered the bootlegging operation that existed in the very basement of the facility where we swam. There were some brazen adolescent boys who did the laundry down there and smuggled booze through the chutes. They acquired the booze legally through prescriptions filled by druggists, and then peddled it illicitly to regulars who worked in the area. Maizee had gleaned this knowledge through flirtation, an ability that came to her easily.

"*Bee*hive down there!" she announced with aplomb in the dressing room, grinning and elated. "They can get all sorts—French stuff—German stuff—*hell*—they've got *dope* down there. I got us a bargain—five bones for the quart this time."

We changed into our tank suits in cubicles with separate standing tubs side by each. She relayed to me what the laundry boys had told her about cocaine—did I know that Coca-Cola had actually contained traces of the real stuff twenty years ago? Or that there was a cough medicine called *Dr. Gray's*—still on the market—that was allegedly full of it? *Who knew*, I heard her breathe from behind her partition.

We had to rinse ourselves before swimming in the tank, and from over the partition I asked, "You don't have to go out with any of them now, do you?"

"I don't have to do *anything*," she said coolly, lifting her head above the divider and then disappearing below it. "He just said— whatever we needed, he could get it for us. Simple as that."

She read the English *Vogue* religiously. Her mother had design connections overseas, and issues of the magazine started to arrive with some of the special jabots brought in from London. She talked about wanting to go to Europe where drinking wasn't such an ordeal and the fashions were more sophisticated. "This mag is *so* avant-garde, Savi. Better than *Vanity Fair*. Look, they have articles entirely devoted to designing your own cocktail bar!" She would assume a British accent and read the title of an article out loud—"Planning a Gay Corner Devoted to the Shaker, the Cherry, and the Row of Happy Bottles?" And then she would laugh, toss it across the room, lean back into an armchair, and sigh, "God, I hate this town." But she didn't really hate New York. It was a starry Mecca brimming over with music and style, and she knew it.

We talked about Paris, about the fabled narrow, market-filled streets and small French villages surrounded by olive trees and vineyards. We *didn't* talk very much about Michael, who was over there, defying all expectations and drinking legally. But we adopted words like *meem* and *jip* from his abandoned *Unabridged*. *Meem* was a dusky half-light, and *jip* a faux pas or dangerous subject of conversation that was liable to lead to an explosion.

The subject of college was a near-jip, but we still talked about it with quiet curiosity—about the house parties and dorm life that we were missing out on. But we also dreamt of qualifying for the Olympics, of competing against the best in the world. It was a redeeming idea. We were first-rate, ace, killer, she'd say, "I mean—*look* at us." She would stand before the wardrobe mirror to admire herself. "How many girls swim as fast as we do? Tell me. How many girls really swim at *all*? Not *boocoop*. Don't you think our team has a strange, clandestine edge? Sometimes I feel like we're training for some top-secret operation. Operation Girls' Team—as though it's still taboo, all that stuff about the strain not being good for us. Nobody ever watches us. But the Olympics. Now *that* would be bang-up, *that* would make it all worthwhile. Sometimes I think it's nuts how much time we spend in that murky place."

She would spring quickly from one train of thought to another. "How do you think Higgy lost his arm?" she would ask out of nowhere. I recoiled a little every time I thought about how our coach may have lost his arm in the war.

"Infection," I would say, wincing, imagining that a lone surgeon had removed it with little more than a scalpel and a roll of gauze.

But Maizee didn't wince; she just sat there and exhaled blue smoke. We always got quiet when we passed rogues who lived on the street or in the Park—some of them missing arms or legs, some of them cracked up. I thought about how in battle they were praised as heroes and martyrs for their country, only to return beaten and limping, unable to work, reduced to selling matches from the sidewalks.

"He doesn't act like he's enfeebled. Sometimes I forget his arm is missing at all."

"Yeah," I would agree, and we would strain our ears to hear the live music coming from the radio in the bake house downstairs.

That spring it was humid and leafy, and Higgins took us to a championship meet hosted by the fancy New York Women's Swimming Association. We were in awe of the pristine facility. It had glass windows on all sides and sun streamed through in sharp slats of light. It was one of the only chlorinated tanks in the city; our home tank had to be emptied, scrubbed, and refilled every Sunday. White tile and metal railings gleamed. Nothing about the WSA setting was questionable, nothing about it reminded us of the crumbling concrete place that we had grown so accustomed to. We knew immediately that there wouldn't be a bootlegging operation in the basement.

Trudy Ederle belonged to the Women's Swimming Association. We saw her there, glowing in the sun, all gold and chestnut hair shining in the light. Trudy Ederle was my borough-rival for as long as I had been swimming. Maizee glared at the WSA girls from across the tank. "Spoiled little truant daughters," she hissed.

"*Victoriannas*," I said, thinking that Higgins wasn't joking when he called us his bunch of scruff. Scruff. Desperadoes, that's what we were—the whole pack of us. He had taken a good twenty minutes away from training time to rail on us before the meet, warning us against the deplorable epidemic of *flapperitis* that was sweeping the nation. Chief symptoms included a reduced ability to focus, profanity, back-talk, a lost sense of modesty, materialism, sneaking smokes, morbid discontentment, and, above all—laziness.

"Unacceptable!" he shouted. "You think it's *modern* and *sophisticated* to go around putting on your *rouge* in public, exposing your ears and knees to the whole world! This is a qualifying meet for the Olympic Trials. You show up with your boot strings tied up tight—there will be no floozies on that deck. Monkey sees, monkey says no. You follow? No eye rolls, no tobacco smoke. You show up with reeking hair and you're off the team. No bones about it. Vamoose. Gonzo."

We were in a haze of wonder that weekend, amazed by the custom nickel fixtures in the dressing room, the hot showers, the large changing booths, and steam room. We were electrified by the intricately tiled hot pool where we were allowed to soak our legs. We went to the hot pool after our races, sat on the edge, and pulled the shoulder straps of our suits off our shoulders to relieve the pressure. We watched other girls from other teams comb out their wet hair.

The clean light that sliced through the crystal water thrilled us, and in a tumble of jealous rage, we got ourselves qualified for the Olympic Trials.

FOUR

MAIZEE AND I made an agreement after qualifying: there would be no more drinking gin in my little flat, and she wouldn't perch herself on the windowsill and smoke her cigarettes. We wouldn't get tangled up into any affairs—which wasn't an issue for me.

The Trials were at another deluxe facility in New York that was only used in the summer months because half the tank was exposed to the outdoors. The other half was enclosed by an atrium of rafters and electric lights. Slabs of smooth stone surrounded the tank, giving it a Renaissance appeal; marble lips curled over the edge, and brass bars gleamed. There were high bleacher-seats on both sides of the tank where hundreds of people were gathering.

I stood on deck and listened to airhorns spurt raw noise that bounced off the water, off the walls. Iron scaffolding glinted in the bright light. Gutters dribbled. State flags hung from the rafters of the atrium. Standing in the humidity, I felt sick and fragile—like anything would bruise me or give me a headache. Water caught the light, reflecting a violent blaze, and shrill whistle-bursts split through the noise around the tank. The tank was metric—metres instead of yards—because that's how it would be at the Olympics. We always swam yards in training, and I had never swum in an Olympic-size tank before.

It was the preliminary qualifying opportunity for all the

women's one-hundred-metre events, and the hundred-metre crawl was my best shot at making the cut to the Paris Games. Warm-up was underway, and there was the impatient loiter of both male and female swimmers—a rare chance for the chaps and girls to compete at the same time and place but in separate heats and divisions. Contestants immersed in crossword puzzle books or flimsy novels found silent corners in which to wait for their events. I sat for some time in the women's dressing room with a towel draped over my head, just breathing. The smell of tile-bleach, shampoo, and rose powder all seemed to converge right where I was sitting. I removed the hood of terry cloth from my head; girls floated in and out of cubicles, in and out of chatter. I fixated on a long row of porcelain sinks with polished faucets where a WSA girl was adjusting her tank suit in front of a steamed-up mirror. Beads of mist ran down her reflection, and when she moved away, toward a wall of locked cubbies, she gave me a rotten eye. The floor tiles were cool under the balls of my feet as I took slow, careful steps out of the shower stalls to the bright and noisy tank.

It was June and getting hotter every minute; the mugginess blanketed my skin. Higgins was standing in the bleachers, in the coaches' observation section with his pocket watch. He waved me over and stepped down to tank level.

"Savanna Mason. You've got to breathe. Open up those shoulders. You follow me?" He pushed back my shoulders to open up my chest. I took a deep breath and stood deathly still. "That's the stuff," he said, inspecting my blank stare, "now breathe from your guts."

He stood with his hand on his stomach, reminding me where my guts were, the ones I was supposed to breathe from. "Mason. I want you to take a good look around. Go circle the tank and open your eyes. Nobody's got anything on you. What did we talk about yesterday? What did I tell you? Less thought, less trouble. You follow me? You're a shark. You didn't get here on a banana heat—earned your stripes fair and square. You qualified, understand?"

26

"They put me in a gutter lane. I'm the slowest going in."

"Don't worry about that. This is your race, Gutterball. Go walk around and loosen up. Then I want you over in seeding—breathing from *here*," and he clapped his stomach.

I walked around, scowling. I walked past other New York divisions, girls I recognized, girls I'd raced, lost to, and beaten. All A-1 calibre. I turned over their record times in my head. I saw Trudy Ederle right away. She was the WSA sweetheart, and she would make the final in the hundred, I knew she would. We both always did. She was adjusting the straps of her tank suit with her thumbs, revelling in the attention she was getting from her teammates and coach; they were all milling around her like iridescent insects. I could put a name to one of her teammates—Aileen Riggin—but she wasn't swimming the hundred AC, the "American crawl." Their female coach, Charlotte "Eppy" Epstein—less iridescent in a dark suit, the queen bee of the horde—was softly explaining some fine point with precise hand movements.

As I passed, our eyes clicked so quickly that we barely registered each other. I kept walking. I passed many girls, all with hovering, coddling coaches funnelling advice into them. One girl, very smooth and brown from the sun, was representing Hawaii. She sat like a stone on a bench, massaging her temples with her index fingers. I watched the timekeepers and referees for a while. So deadpan, this set. Always talking to the contestants in flat, curt tones as if we didn't know how it goes. As though we hadn't rehearsed our races or memorized all the rules; as though we didn't know our onions. I watched them fasten the cork lane dividers and check things off on clipboards.

I stopped walking when I recognized an assembled bunch of swimmers fussing over Weissmuller—this extra-slick contestant from Chicago they'd christened the *human hydroplane*. The day before, he had cleaned house in both the one-hundred and four-hundred-metre crawl. So now he could afford the time to loaf around with his chums and watch the girls' races. He was standing with another sun-browned Hawaiian, Duke Kahanamoku. Higgins told me that Duke had been the hundred-metre gold medallist in Antwerp four years before. There was a lot of fussing going on around these two.

I lurked where I was, near the marshalling area where the referees would be expecting me, and stretched. I swung out my arms, reached up until my elbows clicked, and stared at the water.

Maizee spied me in the corner. She limped over wearing a monogrammed towel wrapped around her solid middle. She had her knee bandaged.

"Hey, Sexless," she smiled, revealing the small space between her two front teeth. She had stuck to the pact too—but whined about it constantly. She stood beside me, staring at Weissmuller, and her unpainted face was looking confident despite her loss in the hundred breaststroke that morning when she swore up and down that her knee had popped out of its socket, fiercely adamant in spite of our coach's skepticisms.

"Hey." I snapped my fingers in front of her face. "How you handling the knee?"

"Between pills," she said, turning her attention back to me. "I don't think Higgy believes me, but he told me to wrap it up until finals tonight. I made the fifty in prelims yesterday, but they moved the fifty finals to tonight, 'member?"

"Oh yeah. I forgot. Blew my fifty yesterday. You can still race?"

She fidgeted with her towel. "Old hoss says so."

The spectators had resumed the infuriating scream of airhorn-blowing. They were waving American flags and eating hot dogs in the stands. I saw Maizee peering at my chipped paint. My fingernails were longer and scrubbier than I usually kept them.

"You need a manicure," she said.

"Bad luck to cut your nails on a Friday. You're the one who taught me that, remember?"

"Sure, but there are *six* other days in the week, you know. After Trials I'm giving you a manicure. I'll polish them up with silver so they look like ten tiny mirrors," and she held up her hands to demonstrate the job she had done on her own nails. They were silver, and they really did look like ten tiny mirrors. But I didn't want silver. I wanted gold.

"What lane?" she asked.

"Rolling a gutter," I said. "Lane six."

A cold wash of fear suddenly moved through my body.

"I can't wait until this is over," I muttered. "And you can paint my nails gold if you're going to paint them. Not silver."

"Damn it, Savi," she said. "Where's your lid?"

"What?"

"Your cap, Lulu!" She reached for the rubber cap in my hands and assumed charge of my pre-race groundwork. "I don't know *what* just happened—but you're awfully slow to the mark all of a sudden."

I did more arm swings and rotated my shoulders before dropping my hands against my sides, petrified.

"Now get that white off your face and key up," she instructed me severely and tucked my loose hair snugly under the rubber cap. "You've done everything right. This is not the time to be pepless. This is your time to show 'em, sister."

I took another grave breath.

The announcer's voice boomed through the funnel of a bullhorn. "THIS IS HEAT FOUR OF THE WOMEN'S HUNDRED-METRE AMERICAN CRAWL. ALL SWIMMERS IN THE PRELIMINARY ONE-HUNDRED-METRE AMERICAN CRAWL TO POSITION IMMEDIATELY."

It was time to take our marks. Maizee rubbed a hand on my back. "You know it's in the bag."

That cold sweep washed over me again. The clamour of people, coaches, airhorns, and whistle blasts were making me feel ill. I looked to the stands, searching quickly for faces I knew were not there, but brought my eyes back to the tank, fleetingly irked with myself for even looking.

A whistle sounded. Heat four, six girls. We were all supposed to stand directly in front of our lanes now, but I was frozen. Maizee was pushing me toward my lane. "Go on, Savi. Off to the start, now. *Toot sweet*—go on."

The whistle sounded again and so did the announcer. "LANE SIX, YOU ARE TO BE POSITIONED AT YOUR MARK IMMEDIATELY. THIS IS YOUR FINAL WARNING."

Higgins shouted at me from the coaches' observation area. "Savanna! To your mark!" It was as though I had entered a dream, or a nightmare, and my muscles weren't responding. Maizee shoved me, and I lurched forward. I positioned myself at the edge of lane six, in line with my fellow contestants.

"READY," said the announcer through his bullhorn.

Just as the gun should have sounded, one of the contestants fell into the tank. It was an Amateur Athletic Union rule that no swimmer could be moving at the start, and she must have lost her balance. "STEP BACK, SWIMMERS." We all stepped back, taking a collective deep breath and shaking out our hands.

"LANE ONE, THIS IS YOUR FINAL WARNING," the referee said to the contestant who had fallen in and waited for the overanxious girl to climb out and reposition herself at her mark. Adrenaline singed the air. We collected ourselves, stepped forward, and the officials started again.

"SWIMMERS, READY."

It was all one blur from that moment to the moment I caught the air. At the gunshot I felt a burst in my centre, a burst like the magnesium flare of flash powder. I carved into the water and ploughed into the tumble and chaos of a one-hundred-metre sprint. I had no idea where I was in relation to my rivals, and I was not thinking of them during the race. I was thinking about knifing as swiftly as possible through water, velocity, the incisions of my hands, and I did not breathe until I was nearly at the turn. My turn was an ideal pivot, spot-on, and in hot pursuit of a world-class finish, I shoved off the wall, sharp as a blade, and thrashed my arms with every last flicker of muscle I had in me. There was the swell of refracted light, white froth and blue tile. There were pieces of sound like breaking glass when my ear was exposed. A nauseating burn began to hive in my body; it started in my rib cage and swarmed into my arms and legs.

Out of both corners of my eyes there were blotches and comets, they snapped in a dreamy effervescence. I hit the wall and the spectators were roaring—an underwater roar of appraisal and excitement. I gained control of my breathing with no idea where I had come in; I could not see who had touched the wall first. The announcers did not call out the names and times of the top three finishers because it was prelims.

I was trying to blink away the dark blotches obstructing my vision, and everything was happening very quickly. We were instructed to get out of the water. I slipped out of the tank, slung my bathrobe over my back, slipped my sandals on, and in spite of my exhausted and quaking leg muscles, I hurried over to Higgins for my conference. He was looking at me, his owlish face beaming, his large eyes wide and glossy.

"Mason, that was one hell of a hot gutter swim! 1:12.5. Your second fifty was a faster pace than you've ever gone before. You have the fastest prelim time—you'll go into finals first, in lane three. Outside smoke!"

Maizee rushed me with a hug. "I told you it was in the bag! That's one helluva new best time. And you beat Trudles by a body length!"

I began to feel a sort of euphoria move through me, a sort of conviction. I was going into finals first. I had the fastest qualifying time going into the night session—faster than Ederle, faster than any of them.

Between preliminary heats and finals there was always what Higgins called a siesta, when everybody rested before returning to the tank at night for warm-up again—and finals—where the ultimate cut would be made. This was my ticket.

I had warmed up and was feeling excellent, very alert. I stood with Maizee on the deck that surrounded the tank. The sky was a deepening purple and although it was still warm, the humidity had waned to a perfect summer evening. The water reflected a harsher, artificial light and the interior atrium glowed. Cameramen took pictures; noisy bursts and flashes exploded around us. Timekeepers assumed their posts behind designated lanes, and spectators returned to their perches in the stands.

Maizee leaned toward me. "*Lissen*. I was in the steam room after having my knee wrapped, and I overheard some dirt about the women's hundred AC." My race. The final heat.

"What say?"

"Well, Clarke—California swimmer—she's swimming on two hours' sleep. Word is she went out for a night on the neck—can you believe? Coach put her on the rack, nearly pulled her from Trials completely. Doubt she'll be a worry. Word is she was complaining about her chaperones. And last night—his name was *Raoul*—isn't that hysterical? Some chap on campus who was selling these little clay whistles and flutes in the shapes of birds! A whistle-maker!" She laughed, covering her mouth with one hand. "And this other one—Wiley something or other—she's having nervous break- downs. Wiley dominates the backstroke events, so I doubt she'll be a worry either."

Maizee pulled a bottle of water from her satchel and reached out to offer me some. "Wet your whistle?"

While I took sips, she cleared her throat. "We all know Lackie goes out like a maniac. She'll lose it on the home stretch. I saw her in the dressing box with those Epsom salts of hers, rubbing the stuff all over herself." She stopped talking and gazed curiously around the expanse of mosaic tile.

"Weissmuller's not here if that's who you're looking for," I said.

She rolled her eyes at me this time but grew quietly subdued as a cluster of girls passed by us, and I thought that they must have been breaststrokers by the rotten eye she gave them. She turned back to me, "As I was saying, Lackie-Lackers thinks smearing that salt gets a free flow of blood to the muscles. What a Lulu."

She helped me with my rubber cap, number three printed on the side. It was almost time to walk out into the light, into the roar of people in the stands. I hopped up and down, swung my arms and shook out each leg. I would win the final. I would go to the Olympics. I would feel the sun on my arms in Paris and set a world record. Maizee kissed me on the cheek. "Off you go," she chimed. "Hit on all sixes!"

A referee signalled for my final heat to assume our positions, and in a tidy row we walked out into the bright light to our designated lanes. In the lane next to me, Trudy waved to the crowd and blew them kisses. We methodically removed our bathrobes and placed them on the chairs next to our unflappable timekeepers.

I adjusted the straps of my tank suit, and there was an announcement.

"ALL SWIMMERS TO THE START. THIS IS THE WOMEN'S ONE-HUNDRED-METRE AMERICAN CRAWL CHAMPIONSHIP FINAL. ALL WOMEN SWIMMING THE ONE-HUNDRED-METRE AMERICAN CRAWL FINAL TO THEIR MARKS IMMEDIATELY."

I slipped off my sandals.

We were poised and holding, waiting for the introductions, then the gun. "SWIMMERS, THIS IS THE ONE-HUNDRED-METRE AMER-ICAN CRAWL CHAMPIONSHIP FINAL. IN LANE ONE, ETHEL LACKIE OF THE ILLINOIS ATHELETIC CLUB, CHICAGO." Chicagoans went wild in the stands. Lackie, with her skin red and raw from the Epsom salts, took a bow. Airhorns blasted over the water and noisemakers were twirled. "IN LANE TWO, ALL THE WAY FROM THE PACIFIC ISLANDS—MARIECHEN WEHSELAU, HOLDER OF THE WORLD'S RECORD AND REPRESENTING HONOLULU, HAWAII." She waved wearily to the people in the stands who hollered and tossed colourful flowers on to the deck. "LANE THREE, SAVANNA MASON, WINNER OF THIS MORNING'S

PRELIMINARY HEATS, NEW YORK CITY." Sound began to distort; the roar and echo of approval became a kind of buzzing noise. I closed my eyes and shook my hands. "LANE FOUR, GERTRUDE 'TRUDY' EDERLE, NEW YORK CITY." Trudy leaned over the tank and splashed water over each shoulder, nodded once to the bleachers, and shook a fist of victory. There was a great detonation of applause.

I gazed out at the fifty-metre span of pale blue, blinked, and went over the plan—Higgins's strategy shouted at me in my mind: *Get out front and hold it, Gutterball. Start your sprint immediately off the mark. Hot pepper swimming, Tabasco burn. Don't hold back now. This is it.* Standing at the edge of the centre lane, pinpricks spread over my body, a thrilling bloom of exhilaration.

"LANE FIVE, EMELLIA 'MILLS' WILEY MCVAY OF SEATTLE, WASHINGTON." American flags were held up and shaken in the stands. "AND FINALLY, LANE SIX, ANASTASIA 'STASH' CLARKE OF SACRAMENTO, CALIFORNIA." After a moment of final commendation, there was a kind of hush. "NOW SWIMMERS—"

Feet parallel, we curled our toes around the edge of the tank.

"READY."

We crouched to our starting coils, muscles flexed and ready to spring forward.

The gun cracked through twilit air.

I hit the water slow off the mark, and it was Lackie in lane one who came up first. Over the first twenty-five metres I could see Trudy's hand enter the water marginally in front of my own—a blur of flesh in the corner of my eye when I turned my head to suck in air. I stayed with her, and although lanes one and two seemed to be on par with Trudy and me in the centre lanes, I knew we were ahead of lanes five and six. Arm to arm Trudy and I stroked in unison, pacing at a nearly identical velocity. In between breathing, a swell of refracted light and blue water passed underneath us. We reached into the fifty-metre turn and she pulled ahead by half a stroke. I was too aware of my position. Fragments of the shouting crowd bounced off the surface water and rang in my ears; I went faster, gaining ground, caught her again, and again our arms stroked in unison.

The second leg of the race, the pain came, the closing agony. Lanes one and two were visibly leading, and it was a battle for third between Ederle and me. I reached, pulled, whipped my feet, dug into the finish with everything I had left, heart beating so fast. Could see the end. I thrust forward, slammed against the wall.

We all hung on to the edge of the tank gasping, lungs and arms throbbing. In that final thrust into the wall, I was sure that Ederle and I had touched at the same time. We looked at each other, breathless, confused about our placing, hyper-aware of how much was riding on it.

The timekeepers above our lanes had quickly gathered into a huddle. They were waving their hands and pointing to their watches. A few moments later two place judges and some referees threw themselves into the scrimmage.

Place judges sit on the sideline and are required to closely watch the races. They are only called upon to resolve placement disputes, which is not often. In all my years of swimming, I had never experienced a dispute before.

With our muscles twitching, the six of us clung to the side of the tank, waiting, blinking, water dripping down our hot faces.

I peered over the edge of the tank, searching the coaches' section for Higgins, and saw that he was moving briskly from his post, jogging down the stairs to the deck where all the officials and judges were congregated. Eppy Epstein was right behind him. They paced over to the cluster above our lanes. I lowered my head and looked intently into the gutter.

Everything was painfully halted while the coaches, officials, and judges debated, and the swimmers had to stay in the water until the results were announced. My body was beginning to feel cold. People in the stands shifted in their seats, trying to read into what was being decided in that conference. It seemed like an eternity before the scrum broke apart, and within moments the announcer's voice stormed over the water, bouncing into the stands. Both Higgins and Eppy stood without expression beside the place judges. Or perhaps there was an expression, but I couldn't bring myself to look at his face for long enough to know.

"ETHEL LACKIE OF CHICAGO, FIRST PLACE IN A TIME OF 1:12.4." The stands roared, layer upon layer of noise pealed and bounced off the water. After our eyes had been roving anxiously from our coaches to each other, Trudy and I both turned away and rested our foreheads on the edge of the gutter.

"IN SECOND PLACE, ALL THE WAY FROM HONOLULU, HAWAII, IN A TIME OF 1:12.8—MARIECHEN WEHSELAU." The spectator applause rose in praise with each announcement, airhorns pealed, and coaches stomped. I glanced at Wehselau in lane two, she had just closed her eyes and looked as though she was about to cry. "AND IN THIRD PLACE, FINAL QUALIFIER FOR THE WOMEN'S AMERICAN CRAWL EVENTS IN PARIS—IN A TIME OF 1:14.2—GERTRUDE EDERLE OF NEW YORK CITY! CONGRATULATIONS, FINALISTS."

Relief and pride spread across Trudy's face. Hats were thrown from the bleachers. Officials hustled us out of the tank.

I quickly grew cold and deflated. Higgins was waiting for me with a towel, and Maizee shot at me from the left, wrapping me with her arms. I could feel the burn of salt behind my eyes, but I managed to ask Higgins what happened. Maybe I didn't ask—it could have been that the questions were all over my face. The three of us moved to an empty bench where swimmers and coaches conducted the post-mortem. He explained that Trudy and I had both clocked in at 1:14.2. The timers called in the place judges, and the place judges discussed our finishes into the wall. "It's called a Judges' Decision—a 'JD.' The judges placed Trudy ahead of you because her head was closer to the wall when she reached in for the touch."

I looked down at my arms. "But my arms are longer," I said. "How is that supposed to be fair?"

"Her head was closer to the wall."

"We had the same final time. I don't get it!" I attempted to hide my devastation under the towel Higgins had given me. Maizee was muttering reassurances and hissing insults about those vile judges, about WSA conspiracies, and about that sneaky ferret, Trudles.

"Well, I'll be damned," Higgins said, revealing his disbelief. "There's one for the books. *Un*-bloody believable." He rested his only hand on my shoulder. "Hell, kid. I never would have forseen something like this. When there's a tie on the clock, the JD trumps."

I stared at his hand. He was still holding his pocket watch. I fixated on it. The second hand was moving around the watch face with excruciating precision. The time didn't lie. Our time had been exactly the same.

The disappointment crushed in.

"But this is *finals*—they can't do this in a final heat!"

Maizee hovered there, close to my side, guiding me into the women's dressing room so I didn't have to lift my red face from the towel.

That night, I came down with an ear infection, and I couldn't sleep at all. I sat in my dorm room on the side of my cot, holding a warm, iodine-soaked cotton ball inside my ear. It sounded as though, inside my own head, I was underwater, post-implosion—liquid pressure surged in a tidal rhythm, holding me in the uncomfortable anticipation of the next surge of ache. With my good ear I heard the crackle and blast of fireworks that were exploding in volleys over the track.

I held the cotton to my ear as it stained the side of my face with the colour of rust, and I watched the drops of iodine fall to the floor.

FIVE

THERE ARE contestants on the island that I think I recognize from the Olympic Trials, but that was more than two years ago now, and it could be my imagination.

Down at the beach, I peel and eat one of my oranges. I run my fingers through smooth pebbles and watch swimmers coast up and down the length of the beach to size up their form, might as well assess the opposition. Many of them have excellent leverage and a loose recovery of the arm. I watch No Sleeves from a distance, and I can see he has a bad habit—a crossover. He reaches too far to the left instead of straight out from his shoulder. If Higgins wasn't screaming about our turns at the wall, he was screaming about crossovers.

I see that Canadian, Billy. He is watching a swimmer move through the water—he must be watching the other Canadian with the deep eye sockets. There's an older, slender, and drippy-looking man in a sports jacket who is also watching the Canadian swimmer. He's got a pocket watch attached to a cord in his palm; the tethers hang down to his knees.

The upper rim of the beach is occupied by a series of vending booths selling all sorts of stuff: vile oysters, gingerbread, flint, fishing gear, swimming grease, rubber caps, and cigarettes. The smell of gingerbread and tobacco comes in sweet waves. Swimmers are either returning from the water, having accomplished their morning swim, or they are preparing to get in. Out past the shoreline are several orange markers bobbing in the surf; strong wind sweeps over the water and a lifeguard resumes his post in an elevated chair on the beach. At the base of his chair a sign reads: *Swimmers must remain inside markers at all times.*

I decide it's time to take to the water, put my orange peel in a twill pocket, get up, and walk toward a mess of greasy swimmers milling around a driftwood fire. Lanolin and petroleum jelly have been smeared all over their arms and legs by Wrigley's solicited men. Allegedly the pre-swim greasing has become mandatory because a contestant was air-lifted to the mainland with frostbite and congestion of the lungs. The Wrigley men are all wearing olive-coloured sweaters and rubber gloves.

I locate a boulder near a rocky pier to peel off my clothes and stow my towel. If Maizee were here she would snap the back straps of my tank suit and tell me I was a lunatic, but she is somewhere in Spain exchanging more than just her vows. I stand in my itchy woollen suit and watch the Wrigley men coat the swimmers: behind their necks, under their arms and all over their legs—especially their inner thighs. The idea of letting someone grease the inside of my thighs makes the nerves in my hands and feet tingle. The lifeguard is eyeballing me. "All swimmers must be oiled before going in!" he shouts from his elevated chair. I look out at the waves, arms folded across my chest. I am *not* about to get oiled—that's for damn sure—and if I have to wait for him to get distracted and look away, I will wait.

I see the man who sold me the lousy bread; he is walking across the beach with rubber gloves dripping oil onto the sand. He's wearing these pants, these absolute frights—acres of baggy flannel hang from his hips.

The Canadian with the deep eye sockets is walking out of the water now; his face is bony but his body is thick. He is joined quickly by his buddy, and the older man who appears to be his trainer throws a blanket over his back—the three of them walk together toward the driftwood fire where there is a large cauldron sitting on a grate over brilliant flames. I thought the Canadians hitchhiked all the way here—so I wonder where the coach came from. No Sleeves is leaving the water as well, looking sort of inflated. Another Wrigley man is pouring hot liquid into mugs with an enormous ladle. It's probably got some sort of rum in it—I've noticed that rules about liquor are pretty loose around here. Maybe the island is part of the rum-running track—it had, after all, been a pirate station for years.

I see that the lifeguard in his elevated chair has started talking to another Wrigley man on the sands, and neither one of them is paying attention to the swimmers at the moment. I begin to move toward the water.

I stand where the breakers wash in, and a cold film of bubbles attaches to my calves. It feels as though the beach is being pulled out from underneath my feet as the tide reels in, drawing back sand. Fog has been looming over the water today, and along both sides of the beach there are boulders encrusted with sharp clams and barnacles. I wade farther into the water and can feel my bone marrow freezing. My nipples could cut glass.

Wavelets give my thighs icy little slaps. Waist deep, I plunge into a swell. The shock and physical smart of the first plunge takes my breath away, and the cold water stings the skin around my eyes. Lungs shrink, arms have to remember how to swim, how to pull and recover: stroke, breathe, stroke, breathe, stroke, breathe. It's too cold to breathe every three strokes, at least for now. That's it—catch, pull, push, recovery, catch, pull, push, recovery; rigid and unnatural for the first while. Cold, cold, cold, gasp to the left, an erratic series of strokes and gulp air to the right. Not amphibious yet. Blackness, the sound of bubbles underwater, vibrating rumbles from the harbour, green and grey waves—ice-cold numbness creeping through skin.

The waves are making it very jerky, and when I try to breathe,

I gulp water. I stop to cough before resuming my course alongside the beach, far enough away from the undercurrent that is pushing people toward the shallows. I continue for some time, trying to nail a rhythm, and it occurs to me that I don't have to thrash my legs very much. Of course—the salt! The buoyancy will keep my body high; so different from swimming in fresh water. For two summers in a row I competed in one of the annual Hudson River swims, and the water didn't feel anything like *this*. The Pacific seems saltier to me than the Atlantic did, but maybe I've just forgotten what salt water tastes like. Maizee said that the salt concentration of seawater is supposed to be the same as human tears, but I don't believe it—it's smarting bad already, biting into and swelling my eyelids. Swelling my lips. Will have to get adjusted—keep swimming.

I try, as I have been coached, to let go of my muscles and turn myself over to the water: stroke, stroke, stroke, *breathe*. Turn around in the other direction, continue; the cold has become bearable. I am rubbery, can't feel my feet. Hands—control the hands—cup them; splayed fingers spill water and ruin your catch. My thumbs are sticking out. Higgins taped my thumbs to the side of my palms once to keep them from sticking out like this, and I imagine my hands are taped, fingers together, *there*. Count strokes to know how many it takes to swim one length alongside the beach between the orange markers: sixty-four. Okay. Try to swim the same distance taking fewer strokes this time—stretch out, stay long, finish each stroke all the way back. Straight and supple; cut the water like an *eel*. Eel's hips. No, let's *not* think about eels. Set strokes to music beats. *No!* We have no bananas! We have no bananas for *me!* BANANAS! BANANAS! BANANAS! Stop. New song. Need a new song.

Treading water in the Hudson, my heart pounded against my ribs. The gun cracked and seventy swimmers surged forward in a cloud of silty white froth. I lowered my head into the green murk and held my breath. I imagine, now, that it is that race all over again. It was windy both times I swam that race, and rolls of river water lifted me up and down; I shuddered at the thought of deep currents welling up bones and human remains. I tried not to think about the dark water, or what lurked in the space between myself and the riverbed. Stroke, stroke, stroke, *breathe*.

Higgins had taught me a competitive strategy, and I decide to practise it. I alternate my pace, swim fast and easy to the rhythm of a song about whisky in jars. I imagine I am racing, coasting along at a manageable pace, when, all at once, I've got ankle biters on my tail. I pick up the pace into a sprint, bolt off and leave 'em hanging, then hold the original pace again. When the rival is scrambling at my heels again, I blow 'em off with another burst of speed. Shift gears, fast, easy, fast, easy, fast, easy—one potato two potato three potato four— five potato six potato seven potato MORE!

I was exhilarated by the river swims, the chase. I swam, hustling, trying to keep my lips sealed, and I didn't even notice that I had over-taken an entire pod of swimmers until I could glance back and see them behind me. It was amazing. There was nothing ahead of me but open water, wonder, and the possibilities seemed endless. I felt wild in the river, as though I had regressed to a primal state of simplicity, where humans lived in the ocean, travelled by sea, and could breathe underwater. When I turned my head to the left, I saw New Jersey. Now, when I breathe to the left, I can hardly see anything because of the burning salt.

Trudy Ederle had participated in some of the river swims too— but she had stopped participating and cleaning house by the time I put my mind to them. Race officials hose you down as soon as you come out of the river, which is enough to put most intelligent moderns off the idea. In any case, I read in the local island rag yesterday that Trudy—virtuoso that she is—has been giving tips to the Catalina contestants via reporters. She prescribes a steady tempo the whole way, to forget about rivals, to use chicken broth as fuel, and warns not to look ahead of you while crossing the channel. She remarked that she might sometime later make the Catalina swim but doubts it, as somebody will surely make it before long and then it wouldn't be necessary for her to try it. It's all about being the first and the fastest.

Stroke, stroke, stroke, *breathe*. Turn around, other way.

With my eyes burning, I don't know what is happening. An enormous wave crashes down on top of me and I am whirling in a cold spiral of light and water. Can't breathe. Lungs hurting—stuck—not—breathing—breathi—brea—

What the? I am being hoisted up and out of the water—into a boat? A boat—yes. Anger—WHAT!? What are you—Hey! I must be shouting because I hear it but can't feel anything. I can't *see*. "I CAN'T SEE!" The salt—that bloody salt has blurred my vision—I squint through swollen lids. I'm kicking at somebody—"Hey, YOU—Get *Off*! SCREWWW!" And I can hear an unfamiliar voice.

"*Lady*—" the voice is saying. "Look. *Lady*—just calm DOWN!" My eyesight is restoring as the boat grinds against sand and beaches onto shore.

"Don't TOUCH me!" I am pushing away a man who is trying to help me out of the boat.

"LADY! Jee-ʒuss! Would you, for the love of Christ—just RELAX—" All I perceive is profound, undeniable cold. I am still in the boat. Why am I still in the boat? Because this IDIOT is making me sit down. He is telling me that a riptide pulled me too close to the breakwater, and a breaker caught me under—blaah blaah blaah—I was perfectly fine—singing and stroking until—

The bread-and-orange-selling grease man is jogging over, and I look away. The man in the boat, oh, now I see. He is the lifeguard I snuck past, the one that had been eyeballing me from his elevated chair, and he picks me up and transfers me—like some kind of invalid—to the man whose name I have not gleaned. *Why*, for the love of *God*, is this *hombre* everywhere?

"Here," the lifeguard is saying to the bread man. "*You* can deal with this one. She's out of her tree." They help me to stand, and the impact of my feet hitting the ground sends shooting pain through my ankles. Through a salty unfocused haze, I can see a group of eager bystanders watching the drama unfold, and amidst them are the Canadians with their drippy coach, or whatever he is.

"Damn!" I spit. "Whutthu*HELL*izzwrungwithyu?"

The man has caught me and I shoot a nasty look at the lifeguard, who is off again, in the boat, to yank out somebody else. I steady myself on a rock.

"Easy," the man is saying. "Easy does it." He covers me in a wool blanket and rubs my back. I can only marginally feel his hands through a frosted layer of skin and shrug him away. He is ignoring my shrugs, which is making me rage. "That's enough for your first crack at it—three-quarters of an hour."

My jaw shakes uncontrollably. I gnash my teeth and stare at the ocean. Only a pathetic few are getting pulled out with the riptide, not many. He is talking to me: "You need to adapt to this water gradually—you can't knock it off all at once, and you were supposed to put some grease on. No coach here, I gather." He covers me with a second wool blanket and I can feel his hands on my shoulders.

"Stopit," I say, and he doesn't.

"Almost fifty contenders pulled themselves out of the race after they tested the water—they've already packed up their camps and gone home."

"I SAID—*GIT-YURRR-MITZZ-OFFFF-UVV-MEEE.*"

"I beg your pardon?" He turns and faces me sternly. This time I get a vivid look at his face. He is quite intense, and I look the other way, at rocks. "You want a nice advanced case of pneumonia? They just airlifted someone off the island with frostbite and congestion of the lungs." As though I haven't heard about that. "And don't move around."

"Whhhyyynoottt?"

"The blood in your arms and legs is much colder than the blood in your middle. If you move around, the cold will move into the middle, into your core, and that's not good for your heart. Stay still."

I decide to stay still. I didn't come here to have a heart attack. And I didn't come here to be saved, besides. I will have to be careful, so as to ensure that this does not happen again. I had been the first woman finisher in the Hudson races—fourth overall the first time—and now look at me. As I thaw out in a quiet wrath, I watch my arms turn from grey to blue to skin colour. That bloody salt—my eyes are stinging; I press my eyelids shut with my fingers to stop the tearing and dull the burn. And I worry about this for the race—my eyes are going to crystallize over with salt unless I wear those stupid, enormous motor goggles I brought with me.

"Solomon," says the dusky-eyed, bread-selling grease man, who is now lighting up a cigarette, "but I go by Sol."

He extends his hand in a low, easy swoop, and I reject it. My fears of losing control and making an ass of myself have already been realized in the short time that I have been here. I watch large breakers corrupt the surf.

SIX

ACK BEER *Charlie Harry Johnnie Emma nuts pip queen uncle yorker.*
I'm sure the head-case palm reader with the empty bottles lives in the
brush near my tent. When I hear the approaching sound of his glass
bottles clinking against each other in the dark, I retreat into my tent
until I know he is gone. I hear him mumbling his *dits* and *dats*, sometimes interjecting a *Do you copy?* or a *Back to you.*

He loiters about the periphery of my camp, and I'm sure he
is looking for me. He passes by and chants, *Red or grey she does not
know—red for friend and grey for foe. Red or grey she does not know, red
for fortune, grey for woe.*

I have seen him at the market. He perches on the edge of the
boardwalk with his leaking sack of empties; he doesn't appear to
solicit coins in an inverted cap, he simply watches everyone, and
I watch him rock back and forth, talking to his invisible alliances
from a corner of the planking where there is no chance he will see
me watching him. I wonder how he wound up here, how he became
the island crazy man. I wonder if he woke up one day and had lost
his mind while he was sleeping—or if it was a slow, agonizing fall
into madness.

I overheard at the fish booth that it will be a full moon on the
night of the race. This is not good news. Having returned to my camp
after hearing this lunar forecast, I could barely finish my tuna. Full

moons are ill-omened, worse than starless nights. I sat beside my pathetic, smoking fire and ate my fish beginning at the tail and moving toward the head; eating it any other way would be bad luck.

Maizee started all this: how to eat your fish, what direction you should sleep, and which shoulder to look over when viewing a new moon. There was a specific shoulder for everything: moons, spilt salt, eyelashes, pennies. And whenever she felt ill or if something happened that was not to her liking, she would always say, "Something in the air tonight. It should be a full moon. Don't you think so, Savi? Don't you think it should be a full moon?"

She was the one who never stepped on the cracks in the sidewalk and always tossed pennies over her left shoulder. "Oh, shoot, Savi, look out," she would say, "Gisby Street." She considered certain streets unlucky, usually because of random experiences she had had there, and we would take a wide detour to avoid crossing paths with Gisby Street. She told me there were laburnum trees there. "You know—those ugly trees with the hanging bunches of poisonous yellow flowers. They can give you a rash just looking at them."

It wasn't until an otherwise uneventful weekend before we qualified for Trials that I adopted her superstition into my routine. We were loafing around my flat with our Gimlets, listening to music from the wireless radio. Later we would hear the Tin Pan jazz from the cabaret across the alley, but it was still too early. Maizee was rifling through the cheap jewellery that I kept in a wooden box on my dresser, and she found something that I had all but forgotten about. She removed a delicate scroll from the box and unrolled it gently with her fingers. "What's this?"

It took her a moment to find the veiny flake that had been pressed to paper.

"Oh. *That*," I cringed. "My bean helmet. I was born with a membrane that covered my entire head. My parents thought it was a birth defect, I don't even know why I still have it." I winced at it with disgust. "Put it away, will you?"

She held the piece of dried-up tissue with both sets of fingers, thrilling to my every word. "Oh, my God," she said, mesmerized, "you were born *in the caul?*"

She turned the flaking scrap over in her palm to examine it closer.

"Don't you know that a baby born with a caul is one of the rarest signs of good fortune?" She blinked at me in disbelief, amazed that I had not told her about this sooner. Had I known it was some sort of big deal, I would have mentioned it. "Freud was born with one," she went on, "*Freud*, Savi. And sailors in Europe used to buy them to use as talismans against shipwreck and drowning. I suppose you know this means that you are protected from drowning for your whole life—has nobody told you that? I can't *believe* nobody explained any of this to you."

I shrugged.

"Don't you know what they call someone born with a caul?" She was looking with fascination at the dried-up piece of skin. "A *caul* bearer."

I took it from her hands to put it back in the box.

She watched me. "Freud says that biology is destiny," she continued. "Interesting that you would become a swimmer. How *apropos*."

The sun is disappearing into the ocean, and it feels like there is a membrane separating me from the world. I look down at the groups of campers gathered around fires on the hill—laughter and ukuleles sound over the hill every night. Sea lions bark. I think about sleeping. It will be lousy if I can't sleep. After the Trials, Higgins had taken up quoting Weissmuller's coach at almost every practice—Bill Bachrach says *this*, Bill Bachrach says *that*. Bach, Bach, Bach. He put renewed emphasis on sleep and nerve-building. "Good things to eat, good times, good fellowship, and plenty of sleep!"

Sleep. The crash of wind kept me awake all last night—I

couldn't settle down. I jumped with every cracking tree branch and with the splintering of waves against bluffs. I imagined snakes creeping through the grasses, slithering into my tent.

Now, through the membrane I can see that someone is walking toward my camp, pale hair glows against the darkening sky. It's that Bea woman. She has a heavy wool blanket wrapped around her, and she is approaching me with disapproval smeared all over her round, flat face.

"I saw you get hauled out of the water yesterday. You went outside of the orange buoys—and I heard you didn't have grease on, besides."

"Hello, Bea," I say, a little shocked.

"It would be a bang-up shame if something tragic happened. It would really gum up a good time. The rules are clearly marked all over the sands down there." She motions toward the shore many feet below my bluff. The surf fills the ensuing silence with the sound of frothing ocean wash. "The water is too cold for you not to follow basic instructions."

She appears to be waiting for me to reassure her in some way. "I'm about to hit the tent," I say. "But thank you for the unsolicited advice."

She eyes me with a queer, patronizing look on her face.

Despite the humiliating experience of getting hauled out of my first training swim, or perhaps *because* of it, I find myself defensive. There was little that could infuse me with rage the way being spoken to like an idiot made the hair on my neck catch fire. "The water isn't that bad," I say haughtily. "It's warmer here than Long Beach. There's a warm current that comes in from Japan."

She sighs. "Sure. Swell—but it's *January*."

"Yes. It is January. In *California*."

I peer into the brush, trees shining in the moonlight, and try not to imagine spirits or rattlesnakes hiding in the meadow plants.

"Listen," she says. "I saw you yesterday. Beside your fire. All by yourself. You're making me uncomfortable—you can't be a day over twenty."

"That would make me an adult."

"A girl should not be batting around on her own."

"I see. But the Canadians can hitchhike all the way from Pigtown and no one bats an eyelash. Listen, *Bea.* Are you from the Temperance Union? I can appreciate your concern, but we're in California—there are girls all over Hollywood looking for a show to star in. Now, if you don't mind too terribly much, you're on my bluff, and I'm about to cork off."

She's still standing there with her pale moon-face, looking reluctant.

I look at her growing exhausted. "Was there something else?"

"You didn't tell me your full name," she says.

Surges of waves roar against rock.

"I have placed you," she says. "The other day you looked so familiar—but I couldn't quite place you."

I stare into the smoking embers of my useless fire and curl my fingers into a fist. She's waiting for a response. Fixed on the embers, I refuse to get into this. It isn't any of her business. Our moments of silence are filled with the faint laughter on the hill, the plucking of ukulele strings, and the crush of the surf. It baffles me that she could possibly recognize me. The story was never front page, and I was sure it never made it out of New York. Besides, the whole thing had blown over months ago.

She sighs again. "You're Savanna Mason." She has assumed a maternal authority that makes me want to flip a table. "Swimming is a small place if one chooses to follow it. Listen, I'm sorry you got the rug pulled out from under you like that." Her disapproval appears to be waning. "Don't be sore with me," she says. "I'm curious is all. And no—I'm not from the U. You don't have to have a Bible on your belt to care, you know."

Fixed on my embers, my lack of response isn't discouraging her from talking. She continues, "A bunch of us get together by that big fire over there." She points to a large blaze not far from my camp. I don't have to look at her to know where she is pointing. "At mealtimes and what have you. You are welcome to join us if you get bored of being by yourself."

She turns to shuffle back down the sandy path into the hill speckled with camp fires but turns to me again. "The nickname for Toronto is Hogtown—not *Pig*town."

This time, she turns and fades into the purple dark.

So much for my self-imposed isolation. Opening and closing my fist, I really want a drink, but I'm not sure where to find the liquor that appears to be so ample at hand. I poke at my smoking embers with a stick. I wonder if everyone who came here for this race feels like a loser. I wonder if this whole event is fuelled by failures wanting to redeem themselves.

Well after the Trials, when it wasn't against regulation, Maizee filed and painted my fingernails. The radio in my flat reported on the slew of medals that Trudy Ederle was winning in Paris, and I looked miserably down at my manicure. Maizee rested her different-coloured eyes on me.

"There," she said, fed up with my lethargic indifference toward everything since blowing my chance, "ten tiny little mirrors. Now snap out of it, would you? Your sulks are rasping my nerves."

I shut off the radio with a swat. "She cleaned house in the AC events, Maizee. I didn't think she would do *that* well."

Maizee propped herself against the wall at the head of my bed and sipped the brandy I had snitched from the winter fruitcake ingredients downstairs. "Sip your drink, moosoo, it's got a nice burn," she said, sliding a cigarette behind one of her ears. "And I would hardly call two bronzes cleaning *house*. She scored her gold on the relay—that doesn't really count. Trudles is a spoiled little ferret. Her parents probably bribe her to swim. She's a Scorpio and Scorpios need material incentive. No, it's not fair, life's not fair—c'est la vie, Sexless. Look on the bright side—we can drink and smoke again. You get so fixated on the swimming and I just don't know what to do with you, Sexless."

"I wish you wouldn't call me that."

"Well, then." She leaned in. "Get over your sex complex. Play that Timmy Smith chap who's always leering at you. Then I'll stop calling you that. He's a choice piece, and we can do whatever the hell we want."

And we did do whatever the hell we wanted.

We rolled our stockings and powdered our knees. We drank. We swore. We danced. Bored, curious, and smashed, I let Smitty feel up my sweater. We kissed with our eyes open and he felt up my skirt, fumbling, pawing, and grabbing. The whirl was nothing short of deflating—a flattening negative, and I was quickly de-*Smitten*, if you know what I mean. I was curled inward, not really there, and from a perspective outside myself, I saw us on the divan—him holding me way too tight, smothering, and I thought, *blaah*. I didn't understand the fuss; I thought it was a colossal waste of time. He looked up at me, denied. "Bank's closed?"

But of course—I had not yet been introduced to Mr. Theodore Laswell.

I quit Smitty. Maizee quit calling me Sexless. But to everyone's astonishment, neither one of us quit the tank.

January brought a total eclipse of the sun, and I climbed the fire escape to watch it from the roof of the higher building next to the bake house. The city was at an extraordinary standstill, eerily serene in anticipation of the blackout; thousands of people had sought after hilltops, bridges, and skyscrapers to see it. I stood shivering on the cold roof in my whites as the sun moved sleepily over the moon and, for two minutes, it was like midnight; the apocalyptic darkness gave me chills. Then, as soon as the moon had slid aside and daylight crept back into a flood of morning amber, the city resumed its horn blasting, siren-shrieking, and general scream, and it was as though nothing at all had just happened.

The steady drift of a year elapsed, and as though her medals weren't enough, Trudy Ederle attempted to become the first woman to swim across the English Channel. It was all over the headlines. She didn't make it, and rumour circulated that she was quitting the tank for good.

My parents rejoiced each time a letter came from Michael. He had been gone for more than three years, and had confessed in his latest letters that he was working on a novel—a satire about American politics. The parental rejoicing would slowly deflate into sighing, and quiet discussions erupted about his ramblings, his abandoned scholarly potential, his *bohemianism*. Even in his absence I seemed to occupy a place in his shadow, but in spite of this, I missed his messy piles of books at the bake house after hours and his fiery rants against capitalism. On my seventeenth birthday he had surprised me with a letter about a certain fancy outdoor tank in the uppers that he and some former college chums had stolen into before he left New York. It was along 5th Avenue and very near the park. It was well worth the sneak, he said, and told me exactly how to crack the lock at the gates.

Meanwhile, as Maizee was cavorting with the laundry peddlers, rolling bottles of whisky into her towel, smoking in the dressing room, and showing up for practice with small blue marks all over her neck, her mother maintained that the swimming was protecting her from immoral temptations. My father, on the other hand, had me working overtime at the bake house, which may have allowed me to swim—but only in the afternoons. Swimming, he said, over and over like some sort of Greek chorus of negativity, was not the way I ought to be spending my time any longer. It was poor character and wasteful to hold on to futile ambitions.

I spent my nights puttering about the flat with a drink, and my days scaling, measuring, scraping dough out of the mixer, and managing the customers that would jam themselves against the front counter. At four o'clock most afternoons, with the smell of rising biscuits stuck to my skin, sourdough mix solidified on my forehead, and blueberry pie filling smeared all over my bake house whites, I showed up in the dressing room before practice looking pale. And in spite of my inability to compete, and my family's lack of enthusiasm, Higgins encouraged me to keep swimming. His definition of *wasteful* was not the same as my father's—he didn't want to see me waste what he still referred to as my physical intelligence.

Late one midnight frolic, Maizee and I sought after the fancy tank that Michael had written about. We could see the water, lamp-posts illuminating the four corners of a swimming pool, but our view was obscured by wrought-iron gates and leafy manicured trees. The tank was privately owned, situated on some sort of restricted green space. We were giddy and laughing, thrilled by the sneak. Maizee curled her fingers around the gate rods. "Come *on*!" she breathed, pawing the ground like a racehorse.

"Look out," I said. "I've got it!" I rattled and shook a steel contraption until it popped, untwined a ring of chain-link the way Michael had described, and closed the gate behind us without sound. The water was gloriously illuminated by underwater bulbs and the tank was surrounded by polished stone. The air was charged by dark-ness, and night bugs whirred in the trees. It was magnificent.

"Oh!" Maizee gasped. She ran toward the tank, silky dress flapping behind her, and leaped clear into the water, shattering the surface with froth.

I was both distracted and intrigued by Trudy's attempt to swim the English Channel. Swimming a channel was not something that I had truly put my mind to, but the idea began to capture my imagination. I began to feel the ocean breathe inside me, luring me to the challenge, to the wildness it represented. Trudy was the only woman I'd heard about who'd ever taken a crack, and articles about her attempt were tainted by allegations that women would forever remain the weaker sex. It made me bristle. It became increasingly clear that the only thing between an ordinary life and me was swimming. My goals may have been ambiguous, with three years until the next Olympic Trials—but quitting the tank would have been the ultimate doom. I believed that if I were to let that part of myself die—the part of me that was swift and elastic—that I would be irreversibly conformed, wake up to find myself in a vacant marriage, bored and irritated, up to my elbows in flour, with no way out. The thought of a traditional future made me perfectly sick to my stomach. Why would I want to belong to someone? Why would I go and give up my name, my rights, never mind my own *self* for something that could crash—right out of a clear sky—crash—and then there were babies to consider, besides. *Blaah.*

Sometimes Maizee and I drank so much on weekends we made ourselves sick. We stayed up all night, and when the stars paled, we would climb the fire escape of the building next to my flat to watch the sunrise from the dirty rooftop. We would sit up there with our flasks emptied and our legs hanging over the edge. Sometimes we could still see the moon before it was overtaken by the slow burst of dawn and the Hudson River threw back the advancing red light. It was a warm autumn, and the early mornings had been spectacular—deep crimson and acid-pink. For a few weekends in a row we sat on that rooftop and watched.

Maizee slouched forward holding a cigarette as it burnt its way down to her fingers. She spit onto the sidewalk below. "I feel like death warmed over," she said.

I watched the light on the river. "I heard there's going to be a swim race in the Hudson next weekend. From Battery to Aquatic Park—a mile or so," I told her.

She made a retching noise. "Disgusting," she said. "Vile."

The sky bled and covered our hair and faces with red and gold light. Pigeons warbled from the far edge of the rooftop.

"I've been thinking about doing something different, Maizee. Something that's never been done before."

She gagged. "Do you have any Aspirin?"

"I'm going to talk to Higgins about swimming the English Channel."

She looked at me as though someone we knew was dying. "That's the coldest shipping channel in the world." She looked repulsed and stared blankly at the cityscape. The sound of car horns multiplied. "Wait," she said. "This is about Trudles again, isn't it? Do you smell smoke? Because *someone* is raking it over the coals again. Damn it—you've got to let it go already."

She laid down on her back, on the concrete rooftop and moaned. The city windows reflected the burgeoning swell of red. "Do you have any Aspirin?"

Below us on the streets, trolleys were starting to bang and people were coming out of the woodwork.

"What's that saying about red skies?" I asked her.

She covered her eyes with the back of her hand. "Can't you hear me? I am asking you for a painkiller."

"You know—the one that sailors say? Something about red sky at night, sailor's delight, red sky by morning?"

Her voice was raspy and tired, "Sailor take warning."

She rolled onto her side to vomit.

SEVEN

A SOUTHERN front and temperate spell of warm wind has blown out any previous chill. The sun is hot and white. I am sunning myself on the sands after a much more successful training swim along the shore. I sit at the beach raking my fingers through pebbles and watch other contestants stroke through the water. During my swim, the conditions were windless and glassy, but I ran smack into a swarm of jellyfish—they slid down my body, slithered into my face with their translucent tentacles all over me. It was disgusting but didn't hurt.

Swimming alongside the island's rocky shore and wearing my enormous goggles, I can't stop my mind from peppering the sea with freakish creatures that probably do not even exist. I imagine scattered bones clattering up against one another in the tide like I did in the Hudson; hear watery howls and ocean groans; see pale lurkings draw up, out of the depths, jerk my head up, choke—then, pallid hands. With the goggles secured to my head, my eyes are not burning afterwards, but my tank suit has begun to chafe the skin just under my armpits, and I am not sure how the wool won't rub my skin into a bloody mess across the channel.

Any case. Now it's too hot, and I stroll to the water's edge to cool my legs where there is a lady at the shoreline—she is wearing a sporting outfit and holding a thermometer. She has the physical poise of an athlete; I assume she is another contestant, except she might be too old, it's hard to say. I stand there, calf-deep in the water, watching her. She is watching a swimmer who is stroking along-side the beach, but sensing me in her peripheral vision, she turns to me and smiles.

"Rhea James," she introduces herself. "I saw you get pulled out the other day."

"Oh." I squint at the glare off the water, shrinking. "Swell."

I tell her my name and ask if she is swimming too.

A touch of silver glints amidst the dark hair tucked under her lid set low on her brow. A sort of vehemence shines from her dark, nearly violet-coloured eyes.

"No. I'm coaching." She points to the girl executing a precise crawl in the water along the shore. "That is my swimmer over there—Ella." The water is clear and quiet on the ocean, obsidian-smooth, and the girl's feet leave a small trail of bubbles as she coasts past us.

My curiosity is piqued. A woman coach. I hadn't thought there were any woman coaches here. In New York the WSA girls were coached by Eppy Epstein, but this was *ocean* swimming. "She has a swell stroke," I say.

"So do you. I saw your form out there, the way you held your leverage in the waves and riptide."

She glances back and forth from her swimmer to me. "Are you the girl who came here alone from New York?"

A little jarred, I draw my shoulders from a slouch. "Rumours travel quickly around here."

"Most girls your age would have a chaperone with them."

"Hm," I say, thinking, A fire extinguisher? No thanks.

"The ladies are not viewed in the same vein as the gents, as I am sure you're well aware. A quick word of advice, should you chose to take it—if you are not going to let the Wrigley reps grease you up before swimming, you ought to protect the skin around the edges of your tank suit with Vaseline at the very least. Otherwise you'll rack your skin."

I bring my flattened hands to the chafes under my armpits and press.

"Getting excited about the race?" she asks me: a brighter tone. "One week to go."

"I wonder if I should feel more terrified."

"Well," she says. "I encourage my swimmers to avoid using the words *should* and *feel* in the same sentence—not a good mix, in my experience. We underestimate the effect of words. Especially the ones we say to ourselves."

"You sound like a head doctor."

"Oh," she waves off my remark as though it were a fly buzzing past her ear. "All I'm saying is that it's important to consider the implication of words, too many *shoulds* aren't good for anyone. A little like cocktails, if you will—one too many and you'll be under the house."

We exchange smiles.

Perhaps I hadn't expressed myself accurately just now—perhaps it is not that I wonder if I should feel more *terrified*, but that I should simply be feeling *more*: more drive, more life, more desire. I had felt it before, before it was taken away—and maybe that's what I'm doing here. I must exhaust the person I used to be—exhaust her out, moult out of that old skin, peel away the layers. Recover my spuzz: force, power, spice, and adaptability. This race was not about being the first and the fastest—not any more. A prickly line draws up from my navel—a queer motivation of no material consequence.

My having turned inward has halted our conversation, and when I catch her gaze she adjusts her lid. "I must get back to Ella. Good to meet you, Savanna. Do yourself a favour, will you, and nurse those chafes."

I watch her follow her swimmer along the beach, raising her arms and waving in a secret sign language that swimmers acquire with their coaches when they have worked together at length. It makes me think of Higgins; it makes me sad in the stomach.

I put my mind to the prize money. If the total jackpot is forty thousand dollars—and twenty-five thousand goes to the winner—and fifteen thousand goes to the first woman finisher—I wonder what happens if the winner *is* a woman? Would she collect forty bones? But Rhea James was right when she said that women are not yet viewed in the same league as men. Despite the seemingly obvious female capacity for athletics, there still seems to be an attitude among some of the male contestants, as though our presence in the race is a bit of a sideshow.

There's been island controversy over a contestant who doesn't want to wear her wool across the channel. Just grease. The scandal has sent the Los Angeles Temperance Union into a squawking flap and the male contingent think she's pulling a publicity stunt. Swimming nude, the union is bawling, would be an outrageous display of "brazen vulgarity."

All afternoon, seagulls swoop and scream in the mind-numbing blue sky; everyone lounges at the beach, basking in coconut oil and the above-seasonal heat. A few yards from my post, Bea is loafing comfortably in the shade of a wide-brimmed, round sun lid. It looks like a Japanese fan. Her tank suit is clearly off the expensive rack, a dazzling peacock-blue, and, as though her wrap and sun lid were not enough protection, she has also planted a sun umbrella in the sand beside her. I see the Canadians approaching my remote post on the beach, pull a towel over my face, and pretend to be sleeping.

"Excuse me. Savanna Mason?"

I don't know which Canadian is talking to me, but I gather they have gleaned my full name from Bea.

"Excuse me under there? Hello?" the voice repeats.

I drag the towel from my face and shield my eyes from the sun with a flat palm. They are both red as lobsters in their swim trunks, clearly having overexposed themselves to the sun. "What?" I say.

They're staring at me as though they've never seen a girl in a

Jantzen before, and perhaps they haven't—being from Canada and all. "What were your names again?"

"I'm George Young," says the one with the deeply set eyes, "and this is Billy Hastings. You met us with Bea a few days ago."

"I remember. You're the swimmer. He's the diver."

"Listen," says George. "Bea told us you've been to the Olympic Trials—and we heard you've been training for the English Channel too. Only five men have ever crossed it—when are you planning to swim the Channel? Is the Santa Catalina race a training swim for you? I hear it's the same distance across."

"Bea didn't tell us the whole story," says Hastings. "Said you were supposed to go to Europe last fall. Made it sound like you were kicked in the teeth or something."

Minute pinpricks begin to spread over my skin.

George blinks his gigantic eyes.

There is a quality about the two young men that is reminding me of everything I came here to forget. Maybe it's their close proximity to my age, maybe it's their questions. A cool mist of panic sweeps over me, accompanied by an eruption of images; pieces of memory pop and fizz in my mind—Tad and Bobo. The Laswell mansion, the reception hall, gleaming marble staircases, arches, and ornate thresholds. The velvety nightclub, the crush of silks against flannel, the garden house. Early morning light streaming onto Tad's smooth, exposed back.

"You're blocking my sun," I say, and they scuttle to the side.

After several drawn moments of silence, George fills the lull by launching into another patter of questions.

"Do you s'pose it's true that Wrigley booked this race for January because he figured no one could possibly do it?" he asks me. "Rumour is it's a come-on. You know, lure tourists to his island, drawn by the swim, make a profit off 'em—not have to pay out? We heard some washout tried crossing a few years back—in September, mildest time of the year. Fell down badly. Some tidal wave, and sharks."

"Oh," Hastings waves a hand, "I heard there are more rattle-snakes in the island grass than sharks in the channel."

George sees me cringe. "Don't you worry about it," he says. "They brought wild boars over from the mainland to depopulate them. You should come down to the big fire to eat sometime. Meet everyone. Have a drink."

The word *drink* tings like a chime.

"There aren't enough young people here," Hastings says, almost whining.

I look at George and his caveman bone structure and resist the urge to call him Sockets from now on. "Don't you think a failure would be bad publicity?" I ask.

"Yeah. I s'pose it could be. But judging by his doublemint empire, one would think he's got his finger on the pulse of publicity. To think, all those millions over chewing gum. Did you know he owns the Chicago Cubs? He's bringing them here for spring training."

"They always spit on their new bats for luck," says Hastings.

I gather they are both fans of baseball.

"Did you two really hitchhike all the way from Toronto?"

Small, proud smiles pass over their faces. "Sure did," George says. "At first we didn't know that we would have to hitch though. Billy and I decided the rattler from T.O. was too expensive, and then we saw a used motorcycle with a sidecar for sale at a local shop. So we pooled our money and bought it."

Hastings cuts in. "George's coach at the West End Y thought he was crazy. Said he would lose his form in the weeks that it would take to get here. We left at the end of November."

George swipes Billy on the arm. "Anyway. The cycle kept breaking down, and we had no cash to fix it."

Hastings: "Then, in Little Rock, Arkansas, we ran into this pair who were on their honeymoon, and they gave us a lift all the way to Los Angeles. We've been in California for three weeks or so now."

"Do you have a trainer or something?" I ask George. "I thought I saw someone timing you from the beach the other day."

"Oh," he says. "That was Doc B."

"Doc B?"

"Doc O'Byrne. He's my business agent."

"You have an *agent*?"

"He's like a coach—a manager and a trainer. When Billy and I got to L.A. we had no money left, and there were still three weeks until the race. We met him at one of the indoor tanks when it was too windy to train at the beach. He was an operator there, and he offered to cover our costs going into the race—and he'll be my spotter across the channel. Do you have a spotter yet?"

"Not yet," I say.

"Wrigley is soliciting a whole slew of boats and locals to help out," says Hastings.

"I've heard," I say, then turn back to George. "I don't understand your agent, I mean—if you don't have any money, what's in it for him?"

They both pause, and it's Hastings who answers the question. "If Geo here wins the race, Doc will take forty per cent of the money."

"Forty per cent?" I ask. "Isn't that more than ten *grand*?"

"Yeah. I s'pose." Geo shrugs. "We needed to eat."

They dip their heads. "See you at the fire."

I could almost be back in New York with a story like that. High stakes.

When the Canadians leave to continue their trek down the sunny beach, I see that Ella is back in the water, swimming that meticulous crawl of hers. Rhea James is barefoot on the hot sand at the shoreline, twill trousers rolled up to the knee.

Laswell never asked for a percentage—I guess that's why Higgins thought he would make a good backer.

EIGHT

I COULDN'T wait to tell Maizee about my meeting with Higgins, but we usually got split up for talking too much, and we were in separate lanes. We swam a breezy quarter-mile warm-up, and then, to my astonishment—having whistled the team to a stop—Higgins looked at me and pointed to Maizee's lane. "Today you are going to train with Workish in lane five."

Higgins had given Maizee the in-training alias "Workish" because she was growing shiftless and bored—she whined in a coy, babyish sort of way, moaning that she *wasn't feeling treʒ workish any more*. She had started to brood about swimming when we were hanging around my flat on the weekends. "I'm bored with the tank," she would say, flicking ashes out my open window. "I want to hit it up, Savi—*carpe diem*—you know what I mean? Besides, it's only a matter of time before I get the old heave-ho."

Higgins was still pointing to lane five, his pocket watch sealed in a newfangled waterproof case and secured in hand. "Specificity of training!" he yelled. "Today we're tearing down our reserve in order to build it back up stronger. I want you to swim your best short-distance event at racing speed seven times over. You'll get a breather between repeats, not much—listen for the whistle." Usually when we did "specificity of training" we were instructed to get out of the tank between each repeat and start each sprint from a plunge. Today he wanted us to do them all from a shove.

I sank under the surface, glided underwater two lanes over, and bobbed up with Maizee. She snapped the back strap of my tank suit.

"He said he would do it!" I said, ecstatic.

"Who's doing what?" She gave me a sidelong glance.

"No talking—no griping!" Higgins yelled, projecting over the tank. There was a ripple of protest from the less keyed-up; then it became so hushed you could only hear the muttering from gutter level.

"The Channel swim," I said, hushed but intense. "He said he would change my program and coach me for long distance!"

"On the minute-mark. Ten seconds apart!" Higgins was shouting. "Put your backs into it! Hot pepper set, ladies—here we go!" The large pace clock with the big red hand marking the seconds rotated toward the sixty. As it smoothly hit the top of the clock, I shot off the wall. I would be swimming my hundred-yard crawl seven times through, and Maizee would be shooting off the wall ten seconds after me to swim fifty-yard repeats of breaststroke.

One week earlier I had repeated myself to Higgins, "I *said*, Ederle blew the Channel and I want to try."

His entire face had creased up. He glanced down at his blotter and took a deep breath, pressed his index finger to his temple. I met his eyes. "Ederle has been swimming over-distance since she was thirteen," he sighed. "Her bottom—that is to say her endurance—is much more developed than yours. Let's not forget her twenty-nine American and world records. Let's not forget her three Olympic medals."

The year of the Games she made it into *Vanity Fair*'s Hall of Fame, nominated by sports experts. She was ranked as the world's champion swimmer for distances up to 880 yards and pronounced the best woman swimmer of all time. "Let's not forget how many times I've beaten her in the hundred-yard," I said.

"Not when it counted most."

My ears burned.

"Well. She blew the Channel."

"I see. The shoemaker wants to go beyond his shoe," he said, holding a bunch of papers and tidying the pile. "You're supposed to be thinking about Amsterdam. You know, the *Games*."

Higgins was hot on the Games, but I pressed. He wanted time to consider. For a week I waited, and in the meantime I swam with a whole lot of snap and with banner precision. There was the brush of tile on the balls of my feet as I shoved off each wall. There was the contraction and relaxation, the push and the pull. "Good work," he said, several times over the course of the week, which sent hot tiers of hope down my body.

In the spirit of banner precision, I reappeared in his office exactly seven days after first accosting him; the smell of tank water oscillated into the room in damp surges. "I want to train for distance," I told him again. "And I want to start today."

Maizee and I hauled through our repeats, holding pace. "That's it, hot peppers!" Higgins barked in between the sprints. "Hold that pace!" I hit the walls breathing hard and feeling the throb of my heart and muscle. After the first two sprints, Maizee and I hit the groove where we could have a fragmented chat between repeats. She slammed into the wall, cheeks red.

"You'll be bored to suicide," she breathed. "That's Clydesdale stuff, dopeless, my God. How are you going to pay for the trip?" The whistle shrilled and I shoved off the wall, cleaving into the lane. Stroke, stroke, stroke, *breathe*. Flicked thumb past thigh before each new recovery. Tabasco burn. Refracted blue passed underneath us. One hundred yards and we were at the wall again. She was breathing fast and held on to the wall.

"Higgins says he might know a backer to fund it," I said. "Some rich patron. Investment banker, I think—bond business type."

"Higgins? Since when does he know any Greenbacks?"

There wasn't much time between repeats; the whistle shrilled and I had no time to respond. We shoved off the wall again.

I flutter-kicked the legs, snapping my feet up and down like little whips. "You think it's twenty-odd miles straight across," Higgins had said in our meeting before practice. "Well, you're wrong. The English Channel is much longer with the current—and for every yard you progress, you may be pushed back half the distance. Throw in some wind, waves, fog, and jellyfish. And there is no resting, you follow me? Stopping brings your temperature down. It slows your heart. The cold could kill you—that's right, you heard me—stop your pump. You might imagine how I bloody well feel about that."

He paced the side of the tank as we swam, back and forth, and halfway through the series of sprints I heard him shouting my name through the spray and slosh of the water. I bobbed up, blinking.

"What are you thinking about?" he shouted, hoarse but clear. I didn't answer him quickly enough. "Your pull is looking rotten today—stinks." He held his arm in the air. "I can smell it from here." His criticism startled me; he had said nothing but "good work" the whole week before. I paddled to the edge of the tank where he was waving me over. "You're not catching the water," he said.

"I'm trying to keep my shoulders flat. Bend my elbows."

"Lousy position for distance swimming. You're banking too much on your legs. Your arms give you at least seventy-five per cent of your propelling force. Take it down a peg and think about your pull. Your pull is *paramount*. Think about it. Go again." He waved me away. Maizee was swimming her breaststroke repeats looking apathetic. "Breaststroke!" he yelled at her. "Not *rest* stroke!"

I plunged back into the tank, thinking about my pull. It was not long at all before he flagged me down again, shaking his fist. "What are you thinking about?"

I stopped at the edge again. "My pull."

"Look, Savi," he said. "Get out." I clambered out of the tank, dripping and flushed. "First, you're slouching. Lousy posture." He pushed my shoulders back with his hand to open up my chest. "Look at me," he said. I was distracted by the other swimmers who were stroking through their routines, splashing when they hit the walls to turn. I was missing my repeat.

"Look at me," he said again. I looked at him. "Start the catch slowly," he said and demonstrated the crawl to break down the different parts of the stroke. He could do this very well, even with one arm. "After the entry of your fingers, you've got to catch the water with your hand—you're rushing your leverage and forgetting to catch. You follow? Look—" He moved his arm in the correct form. "Feel the water against your hand and build power through your pull, then push all the way *back*," he said. "Finish the stroke at your hips. Do you see that? It's a pull *and* a push. Now show me." I wiped my nose with my arm. He waited.

I hung my torso forward, awkwardly performing the motions while he shouted. "Pull straight down. Then change to a push. There, better. That's the stuff. Now, do it again, slowly."

"I thought I was supposed to do this racing speed."

"Right," he said. "Change of plan. Forget the hot pepper sprints today. I want you to swim the rest of your repeats thinking about your pull and nail what I'm saying."

I caught a glimpse of Maizee turning slothfully at the far wall, and Higgins wasn't getting on her tail about her lousy walls; he just stood there and shook his head.

She took long, slow glides—the picture of leisure. When she got to the wall where I was standing on the edge she stared unhappily into the gutter. "Not another 'peat," she muttered. "These *peats* are killing me."

The whistle shrilled and I plunged back in, rose to the surface, and started to swim—catch, pull, push, recovery. I swam, following the black line painted on the bottom of the tank. Face down, exhaled through the nose, snapped face to the side for a breath. I thought about my entry, my fingers—catch, pull, push, recovery. Just as I was about to fall sweetly back into my groove, I heard him again as I was turning at the wall, ears exposed to the air: "What are you thinking about?"

I slapped the water. Despite my newly charged drive to train for distance, it was only the first day, and I was unaccustomed to this much coaching, it was interfering with my repeats. "Over here," he said, pointing to the deck beside him. "Pronto!"

I breaststroked toward him, face slack under the water, and bobbed up at the edge of the tank. He was looming over me from above. "I told you to take it down a peg," he said. He put his hand on a hip. "Out."

I climbed out again. "Do you know what Bachrach asks Johnny every workout?"

"What?"

"He asks Johnny, *What are you thinking about?*"

I stared at him.

"Do you know *why?*" he asked me.

"Why?"

"Because it is *essential* that you relax in the water."

"I am relaxed in the water."

"Not relaxed enough. Form, not fight. Johnny is always relaxed, he's a snake in the water, an *eel*—even and especially while swimming all out. That's what makes him the best. You? You're always on the crank to race. I know this must sound outrageous to you, but your effort is making your stroke less effective."

I slumped a little in my sagging wool.

"Listen," he softened. "You're a champion sprinter, really, we know this already. I give you a hot pepper set and you go bananas. But you simply can't swim twenty miles yet, never mind sprint that kind of distance. Now, I want you to let go of your muscles, stretch out and relax. Breathe, you follow me?"

I glanced at the other swimmers, the breaking water, the big clock on the wall.

"Lean forward," he said. Carefully, he held one of my arms in his big hand and physically manipulated the arm action of the crawl stroke. "You see," he said and bent my elbow all the way through the consecutive revolution. "Follow it through with a *push*. You follow? Just so. Keep the elbow up, higher. Let your forearm and wrist hang down as you clear the water. There, think about it, try again."

I started for the tank. "And Savi," he said. "Get those thumbs of yours glued to the rest of your fingers or I'll have to tape them to your hands." I looked at my hands and placed my thumbs against the edges of my palms. I started for the tank again. "And Savi," he said, "if we're going to do this, you're going to have to stop staying up all night doing God knows what it is you girls do these days." He blew his whistle for the rest of the team and thrust his chin at Maizee who was floating on her back, completely missing the repeat. "You understand what I'm saying."

I dropped into the water and shoved off the wall. Stroke, stroke, stroke, *breathe. If we're going to do this,* I repeated his words in my mind: *we.* I slowed down the parts and tried to remember my feel for the water. Catch, pull, push, recovery.

Higgins attempted to light a fire under Maizee, who wasn't responding to the challenge. "Hustle!" he yelled at her. "Shake a leg!" The clock ticked steadily. Higgins's shouts and whistle blasts ricocheted around the tank, and the water obscured the noise. Nearing the end of practice, I hit the wall and he held up one finger for the rest of the team, "Last one—fast one!"

I shoved off the wall and felt the water; stroke, stroke, stroke, snap the head for a breath. Head down and facing the refracted light underwater, I wanted to blast through my last hundred yards without thinking, but instead I tried to give myself over to the water and merge my speed with his coaching lesson—catch, pull, push, recovery. I felt the water resistance against forearms, closed my eyes, and focused in on the catch and pull of my longer stroke, the beat of it, tinkling of water spilling in and out of ears. Pulled long and forward, arms all the way over. Four lengths of the tank, three shoves, and we were back on the wall.

Maizee spat at me through the space between her teeth. "You'll sink to the third hell of depression swimming distance—think how many dirty *peats* he'll make you do. I bet he'll make you do physical jerks in the morning and take long stupid walks."

I pulled off my cap and let the water run over my scalp. We turned onto our backs and floated. "But on the upside," she said, "how rich are these swanky Greenbacks?"

NINE

WARM AIR. Orchestra music travels over the water from the St. Catherine Hotel; a breeze moves through the tops of high palm trees. Ship lights glint far off in the channel, and a driftwood fire glows at the heart of the beach. The air smells like those urn-shaped evergreen flowers, burning sage and coastline. I slide down a cliff toward the beach and brush sand from my plaid skirt. As I draw up to the congregation of people gathered around the main fire, I overhear talk about the swimmer who was airlifted to Los Angeles with congestion of the lungs. He was a strong contender—odds-on calibre, they say—and he had swum the English Channel in less than eighteen hours doing breaststroke.

Bea is sitting beside a man, presumably her husband. She sees me. In an effort to sharpen up and define that round, albino face of hers, she has pencilled in slender eyebrows, coated her eyelashes with mascara, and coloured her cheeks with rouge. She motions for me to come over, but, still agitated by her rumour-mongering, I stay where I am, sitting on a flat rock by the fire, and watch the last of daylight disappear into an obsidian sky. I can see that she has a bottle of real Bacardi—not swamp root—planted in the sand beside them. Sea lions are barking from the rocks.

There are the familiars: No Sleeves is here with his raucous, bellowing laughter. The Canadians lurk on the periphery of the group like strays, red and peeling, watching the social activity. Doc B, the *agent*, sticks out like a quoob from across the fire, hands stuffed into the twill pockets of his pants. For a moment I am certain he is giving me rotten eyes—as though I have offended him somehow. There is something about him, something scummy—I still haven't put my finger on it. But I am agitated, and Higgins used to say that it was easy to create troubles that didn't exist while agitated, so I disregard his drippy gaze.

There are a number of unfamiliars, fresh-looking and above average in dress, whom I understand to be intimates of the Wrigley family—the moneyed, mannered, chewing-gum-endorsing Wrigleys. A man with dark, shellacked hair plays the ukulele, and a couple of manicured women in chiffon dresses sing about aching hearts and broken vows: *you've had your day*, they warble to the twanging strings of the intsrument, *now you must pay*—

Now you must pay. Pay for tickets, trains, clothes you will never wear again—pay for being so stupid and naive. Encapsulated in that film that is muting out the surge of colour and music, muting the pull of that old connection, that spuzzy drive. A smear of images passes through me like a tall column of water thrown up and out of a hot spring: silks and dark velvet curtains reflected in the brass instruments at that club in Harlem—flesh moist from dancing, from new desire.

Every blood cell in my body expanded when Higgins told me that Mr. Peter Laswell, financier extraordinaire, was interested in backing my Channel swim. Higgins described him as a captain of industry, a little eccentric, but—bottom line, he was keen. I understood that he had responded to our proposal with gusto, saying that he had been waiting months for such a proposition, that he had grown sick to death of all the fund-seeking applications toward the slow exploration into the Antarctic—one failed expedition after another— not to mention the dull, microscopic advance of the sciences. Said he wanted something *human* that he could *see*. Said he wanted to watch me swim before he committed for certain. He would drop by the tank for a first meeting, Higgins told me, grinning, and the preceding excitement only persisted to build—wave upon radiant wave of phosphorescent thrill.

I hate the friends of the Wrigleys. I hate the way they smoke their cigarettes from long, thin holders made of metal and bone. The women have their blonde bobs set perfectly in identical cold waves, and it only strikes me as bizarre—as though I have inadvertently and abruptly been dropped onto a film set. I hate actors. The women in their designer dresses are still singing to the ukulele; throaty canaries, chortling. I can't stand singers—the way they move their manicured hands around, closing their heavily shimmered eyelids while they coo about moonlight and roses.

When Michael first brought Ida to New York to announce their engagement, he told us that she had been singing professionally from the time she had turned sixteen, that she had fantastic pipes and "really brought the house around." He told us that she had been on tour through Europe—and that they had met at a rattler station in Nice. I took inventory of Ida from across the supper table: the lustrous bob, nice silks, and a melted-down cymbal's worth of bracelets on her wrist that clanged whenever she rested her arm on the table. Her blue frock—and some sort of bust-reducing affair underneath it, I noted. Lip rouge, not too bright, not too dull. The requisite debutante deadpan. I hated her.

But Laswell came before Ida, and one day in the middle of training, Higgins blew his whistle and I stopped at the wall. Two shadows loomed above me—Higgins, and beside him, a man in an aviation suit with goggles strapped to his brow. I pulled myself from the tank, wool suit dripping water down my legs and onto the concrete. Mr. Peter Laswell was tall and very suntanned; he flashed a stock-taking smile and a row of flawless teeth.

"Delighted!" he said, and I smiled back, a little confused by his goggles. He drew them from his head and gazed down at his uniform before thrusting his face back to our meeting. "In case you're wondering about the get-up," he said, "I've taken the afternoon for a speed on the old cycle—first iron jaunt of the season."

"Oh," I said, grin frozen in place from one ear to the other. "Swell idea." I was uncertain what else to say; he already knew all about me through Higgins. I hoped I had adequately hung out my talents. I stood, waiting for him to say something.

"I won't take up too much of your time, Miss Mason. Clearly, you are in fine form," he said and gave Higgins a mock punch in the arm. "Young lady, you have got yourself a deal!" An eruption of pinpricks spread over my chest and legs, and the little hairs on my arms stood on end.

A fancy lunch had been arranged between Higgins and Laswell while I was swimming, and, after the brief and dreamlike first meeting, I spent a generous amount of time with Higgins in his small office beside the tank discussing the nature of the relationship I would have with my backer, and what to expect. While he approved of the preliminary arrangements, Higgins warned me not to go thinking that Laswell had the right brain to understand my endeavour the way *I* understood it. "Sure, he's on the level, but these people, the well-to-dos—they're press hounds. They're always on the lookout for reasons to hold society puppet shows. You follow? 'Croesus is king. . . . Not thinkers, but rich men rule the world.' Elmer Davis, the playwright."

He told me that we would go over all the etiquette and table customs that I ought to be familiarized with: fork-holding, faux cheek-kissing—fine manners, et ceteras. To my surprise, he seemed startlingly well versed on social graces. After he quoted Elmer Davis for a second time, I looked at him suspiciously. He carried on, ignoring my dubious stare and quoted from a vintage *Hints on Etiquette* manual. "Nothing exposes a man's breeding more," he said, "than his habits at the table." I could hardly believe that there were actually books about this—books about how to use your knife to cut food, one bite at a time, warning to *never*, under *any* circumstances, cut up all the food on your plate in one sweep.

"How do you know so much about this stuff?" I asked him.

He looked at me, paused. "What do you mean?"

"Just now, Elmer Davis, utensil etiquette, the spiel—you sound different."

He arranged some papers into neater piles on his blotter. "I'm not fresh off the bean cart, Savanna. You think I've never been to a fine luncheon before?"

"Never mind," I said. "You just sounded, I don't know—different."

He started to put his papers into cardboard folders, leaned back in his chair, and looked out the small window.

"How do you know Peter Laswell?" I asked.

He gazed intently out the window for what seemed like a long time. I waited.

"Sorry," I said finally. "I don't mean to jip you. Never mind."

He turned his attentions back to me, puzzled creases wrinkled his forehead. "I beg your pardon?"

"Oh," I said. "Basically, it means asking too many questions on a touchy subject. Sometimes *jip* means a *faux-pas*. A jip-Edison is to grill someone, you know—give them the third degree, and also—a jip-lish is the explosion that can sometimes result from any or all of the first."

"Oh," he stared at me. "Of *course* that's what it means."

"So," I kept on. "Is it a touchy subject?"

He leaned over his blotter and hesitated, curled his lips into an uncharacteristic sly smile. "Savanna," he said. "Truth is—I had a rather privileged youth."

"Oh?"

"Before I left home, long time ago now, I learned a thing or two about breaking bread into pieces before buttering it."

"You *did*?"

"Don't look so shocked." He grinned, almost defiantly. "Or I'll be insulted."

"I just—"

"Yes, I know." He cut me off, swept his arm in the air. "Any case, I'd be worth a bundle if I hadn't skedaddled."

"Skedaddled?"

"Cut out of the family kale."

He swung his arm behind his head, oddly self-righteous.

"What do you mean, *cut out?*"

"Oh." He exhaled through his nose and messed up his hair. "The *recap*," he said, "goes a little something like this. My father was not a very nice man, not a very open-minded sort. There was the *requisite* study of law and the *requisite* expectation of marriage—neither of which appealed. Hell, I mean—everyone to his taste and all that— but society's formulas made me rather sick to my guts. When I was twenty, I packed up my things and I blew."

I bugged my eyes at him. "You left? Just like that?"

"In another life, Savanna, I might have followed the map I was handed. But I didn't fit the cast. And I wanted to see what life was all about—outside of tea time and racquet sports and lectures from the old man."

I looked at his arm, or rather his lack of arm. "Where did you go?"

"Boston. Chicago. I spent almost a decade fixing boats and lifeguarding beaches in the Sunny. Then we got ourselves mixed up in the war. I was on the fence of being too old by then—but I had experience with saving lives. Well, now I have a pretty good sense for what life is about and I don't regret my choices for a second." He looked solemn for a moment and pushed some leaflets around his desk before brightening again. "I'm investing," he said, holding up a real estate leaflet with a palm tree on the front. "My very own slice of the Sunny." He smiled and looked dreamily passed my head.

My mind snapped to Michael.

"My brother, he threw over a scholarship to Yale," I said suddenly. "My parents flipped their lids. He's still over there—writing a book."

Higgins beamed. "A novel?"

"A satire."

"Is that so?" He paused. "And *you* want to swim the English Channel."

I didn't see the connection. But I still bristled when I thought of Michael's blasé manner over scholarships and school. He never had to fight for anything—not school, not freedom from the bake house— not even the flat he lived in before I took it for myself.

Higgins burst into laughter. But underneath his amusement there was irony; it coloured his delight in a way I didn't understand.

"Something funny?"

"Oh." He rubbed his face in his hand again, sighed. "Not really. I was just thinking about your parents, such practical creatures, and both kids turn out dreamers, desperadoes." He looked at me and winked. "I feel a little sorry for them."

I did not mind being on the outside of the *la-dee-da*, not yet having been acquainted with their world of frosted glasses—or Tad's hundred-million-thread-count sheets. I was removed and focused on the swim.

Soon after the fancy lunch, there would be a gala. "Gala with a capital G," said Higgins, repositioning himself in his chair and directing our talk back to the subject of Laswell. "And although you may not want to do this—pride and all—I suggest you talk to Maizee about having her mother make you a stylish gown for the occasion. An appropriate dress for a highbrow affair of this calibre is outside of your means."

"Corking sundown," Bea says, startling me out of my geyser of images by popping a stopper out of a champagne bottle.

Memory grinds to a halt. She sweeps a woven mat onto the sand beside me and sits on it. "Why so balled up?"

I look at her without saying anything.

She leans back against a drift log and strokes sand from her silky blouse and skirt outfit; while her recent disapproval appears to have passed, my annoyance with her has swelled.

"What's the idea?" I ask her.

"I'm sorry?"

"What are you telling everybody who I *am* for?" I hiss.

There is a large grate over part of the fire where hot dogs and potatoes are roasting; the smell of burning driftwood and wild sage fills the air. She waves an ivory hand, dismissing my question. "Tell me," she says, "what will you do if you win the money?"

"What?"

"The money. What would you do with it?"

Seeing her now in silky wraps and sandals, I would bet my celluloid tent she's a pocket-twister who would spend it all on shoes. I'm glaring at her.

"Stop changing the subject. What are you talking to everybody for?"

"Share a hot dog with me?"

"I don't want a hot dog. I want you to stop telling people who I am and where I'm from. There is no story."

"Relax." She rolls her kohl-shadowed eyes. "I only told the Canadians."

"Only the Canadians?"

"And my husband. Don't worry about it. Baked potato?"

"I don't want a potato. You told that woman coach, Rhea James."

"No, I didn't," she says. "The Wrigley reps must have told her. The Wrigley reps know everything about every contestant. You worry too much—look at yourself, always clenching your fists and looking pale. You've got dark circles under your eyes all the time, worry worry worry—it must be taxing. You said yourself there's no story, so don't get so balled up. Have a hot dog with me and tell me all the stuff you would buy if you won."

The question of what I would do if I won the money flits only sketchily through my thoughts. If I were not the first female finisher, I would have no choice but to return to the bake house, where the windows would be fogged over by winter body heat, cigarette smoke, and steam lifting from mugs of hot coffee. I would slip into my bake house whites, descend into the warm oven draft, and clap flour onto my hands. I would stand there, in the middle of the kitchen, warming a handful of pastry in my palms, and have a nervous breakdown.

"Don't be sore with me," she's saying. "I'm a reporter."

"Oh, *gee*—that makes me feel better."

We both turn in unison when we hear a loud, husky laugh emitted from No Sleeves. I turn back to Bea, slackening. "Since you know everything about everybody—who is that? The one without the sleeves. He's looked familiar to me since I got here."

She removes two baked potatoes from the grate over the fire and puts them on a tin plate to cool. "That's Norman Ross. He's got a raft of American and world records. Olympics. Whale of a trainer, came from the Illinois Athletic Club in Chicago. You probably recognize him from the last Trials. People call him 'Big Moose.' Swimming is a small place—you know what I mean? I follow this stuff. The reason I told the Canadians who you are is because in some ways George's story seemed so remarkably similar to yours."

"What could I possibly have in common with George?"

"I don't mean the English Channel." She straightens the woven mat she is perched on. "I mean—here is what I know about you. You work at the family bakery, and you swim for a weedy little team that's not even on the map. That's what it said in those articles." She glances sideways, a careful eye-flash. "You both quit school when you were about fourteen because you had to work. George works as a clerk in a retail meat market—or maybe he's a bellhop. Any rate, he swam out of one of the city's no-name tanks, never heard of his coach—Johnny Walker they tell me, I know, funny—like the whisky label. Yet he still seems to have pulled off a couple of Canadian Amateur titles—so you see, I s'pose I saw a parallel there—between the two of you. Big Eastern cities. You're about the same age, aren't you? Maybe you're a few years older, sure. Ballpark. But of course nobody's heard of him here, being Canadian and all. Oh, and I heard his mother's a widow *and* a cripple. Lost his father a long time ago." She winces, sympathetic, but also visibly proud to have gleaned such tragic information. "Any rate, I heard about all of this and I felt badly for him. So a few nights ago when you were squirrelled away at your camp, and Geo asked who you were, I told him that you had been to the Olympic Trials, and that you were training for the English Channel. I didn't say anything more. I swear."

"Why did he assume it would please me that Ederle isn't here?"

"Because *all* the women are happy she isn't here. Better chances for the female purse. Hell, I'm thrilled she turned down the offer—over the moon."

I look toward the Canadians and see that they have acquired beer. They're talking to Doc O'Byrne and smiling. "Well, he looks as though he's having a perfectly swell time to me," I say and glance back to where Bea and her husband have that bottle of rum planted in the sand. "They told me you would have drinks."

"Bit of a cellar smeller?" She lifts the freshly uncorked bottle of champagne from her side. "Left over from the New Year's festivities. There will be another New Year's party in a couple of weeks, after the race is all said and done. The Chinese New Year lunar festival at the second new moon after solstice. Should be a bang-up time."

"Where do you get your stuff?" I ask her.

"This was given to us by someone on the island, but we also brought some whisky from home. My doctor prescribed me a couple of gallons before we left. You know, *nerve tonic*." She grins. "That Bacardi isn't ours."

After downing our first round of champagne and soaking

up some of the alcohol in our stomachs by eating baked potatoes, she tugs on my sleeve, restless. "Come on," she says. "Let's walk around."

"I feel crispy from yesterday's beam-bath," she says as we meander, and she gazes at the sky, pulling me with her. We stroll along the beach in the direction of a smaller blaze. She points to No Sleeves. "That fella that you were asking about earlier," she then points to a small waif girl with dark bobbed hair and an impish face, "that's Vee. They were lovers once." She bats her painted lashes. "But now they're both shackled to other people."

"Why do you care about everybody's personal lives?"

"I told you. I'm a reporter. Did you know the divorce rate is one in six? *Fact*."

More fires are being ignited. People hold torches, pile rocks in circles around driftwood. She points to a bunch of people near the water. "That pack over there," she says and stumbles on a small log. "Big orgy. Got busted skinny dipping off the rocks last night." We drift along the sands and eventually she guides me to a fire where several girls are gathered around the burning wood. "I know them," she says. "Let's go over there for a little GT."

"Gin and tonics?"

She looks at me, amused, "No, Savi—*Girl Time*."

We approach and the girls raise their heads. They are wearing filmy gowns and kimonos, some of them smoke cigarettes. "Hi, Bea," one says. "Swell warm wind tonight—Santa Anas blowing through. Who's your chum?"

Bea introduces me, and half a dozen girls consider me coolly.

A homely redhead with a Southern drawl is suddenly excited. "Savanna? Savanna Mason? You're the girl who came from the Apple all by your lonesome. Swell shopping there. We heard you swam against Ederle at Trials—a JD—now there's a slam in the teeth!"

A ripple of *brutal, harsh* moves around the loop.

I narrow my eyes at Bea, and she shrinks a little. "Sorry."

A pretentious laugh comes forth from a girl sitting regally higher on a giant rock. She has a quality that reminds me of the caterpillar that lounges on the toadstool in Alice's Wonderland. Her loose, curly bob is held to one side by a pearl hair clip; a silky wrap is folded around her elbows. "Touchy subject?" she asks, raising a bottle in my direction. "Hear, hear." She tosses back a drink. "We *love* touchy subjects."

Bea and I sit down, cross-legged on a drift log. Clockwise around the fire loop the girls recite names that I forget instantaneously—except for one—the regal one—her name is Charlotte. Charlotte Moore Schoemmel.

She is also from New York, she informs me, and explains that she is *the one* who swam around Manhattan Island in September, and *the one* who swam the one hundred and sixty-five miles from Albany to New York City. "That was in October," she says, "to prepare myself for this race."

It seems almost impossible that I have not heard of those swims. But then I remember the autumn months—and *of course* I hadn't heard of her. I spent them lying on my hardwood floor staring up at the ceiling and sleeping.

"Pyjama party," she says, spying my eyes on their negligees. Her legs dangle over the rock. "Tell us, *Savanna*—what do you think about the prospect of swimming this race nude? Do you think it's a cheap run at publicity?"

The girls emit a euphony of synchronized giggles, blowing thin smoke and sipping their drinks.

"I haven't really thought about it," I say.

Charlotte smiles expansively from her royal seat and, although I am already aware of the anecdote, she explains that she has announced to the press and the race officials that she is going to cross the channel completely nude. The press has already stamped her the Manhattan Venus de Grease. "Quite the outrage," she says from her granite throne. "You can imagine the fuss, nothing but axle grease.

The union is calling me a *vulgarian*—you can hear the shrieks of horror all the way from overtown."

We all turn and gaze casually out at the dark water. "My name is being smeared all over the island bans," she says and takes up her drink. "Small wonder Freud and his gospel are causing such a racket. Sex and neurosis are all the bloody rage."

The excitable redhead passes a flask around the circle. "My husband would be beside himself, right up a tree, if I swam without a suit on," she says. "He was such a police dog before we married."

"Well," says Charlotte. "That was before you were married. And he's not here."

The redhead deflects from further talk of her husband and says, "Read what Ederle had to say about the suits?"

Everyone listens.

"Says—*personally*—she thinks there is room for modesty in swimming, as in everything else—and frowns upon any girl who would consider swimming unclad."

Charlotte yawns. "Quelle surprise."

"I heard she ripped her own suit in half to make it easier to swim long distance," says Bea. "I heard she's the inventor of the two-piece."

"Everyone is a bloody inventor these days," says Charlotte, ·blasé. "Any case, you know what I told the press? Sure, I gave them a statement to chew on, I said, 'I won't wear a bathing suit, but my suit of grease will be far more modest than any bathing suit. Modesty or immodesty is a state of mind. I deny emphatically the insinuation that I am disposing of the bathing suit merely for cheap publicity purposes.'" ·

"Hell!" says the Southern drawl suddenly. "You're right. My husband isn't here and it's my decision, now isn't it? What say we *all* do it in the buff?"

There is a stir amongst the girls as they divert their attentions from the Sheba to the redhead. Charlotte runs fingers through her short curls, temporarily out of the limelight while the group hashes out whether a suit of grease would, in fact, be more modest than a bathing suit. Axle grease being so thick and dark in colour, she says, it would actually cover more than a suit.

"Grease washes off," I say, "especially after ten hours."

They all turn and squint at me.

The redhead pulls a newspaper from a satchel, assumes a snooty demeanour, nose thrust in the air, and says, "Ladies, I give you testimonial courtesy of the Women's Christian Temperance Union." She begins to read. "'Be it resolved, that we, of the Los Angeles WCTU county executive committee, a body of Christian women toiling in every way possible to uplift humanity, protest against nudity in any contest, particularly in the Catalina race.'"

From the stone, Charlotte laughs and raises her slender eyebrows. "Well, they lost their inane little gripe, didn't they? Read the part about the city council's verdict!"

The redhead resumes but drops the tone. "As far as the council is concerned—the city council states that 'feminine swimmers might wear grease, regulation swimming suits, or the full-skirted and bloomered suits of the Gay Nineties.'"

The girls rouse in approving cheers and loll onto their sides; the flask continues to go around the fire, and I begin to feel quite light and happy.

Charlotte looks to me. "Only an imbecile would swim across this bloody stretch while her suit eats away at her ravaged skin."

"To hell with *that!*" says Bea. "Brazen vulgarity! Hear hear!"

"Hear hear!" The group raises their various cups and flasks.

Everyone is pleasantly high, and I forget that despite my increased drinking over the course of recent months in New York, my tolerance is not especially good. The redhead's name is Louise, everyone calls her Ousi. Ousi, I think to myself, Ousi Ousi Ouisi—until it makes no sense and sounds absolutely hilarious. I let the liquor course through my body like tropical currents under the ocean, warming me to the core.

"A nice burn," Maizee always said about the brandy I could scavenge from the bake house stash—but after I started training for long distance, I stopped getting smashed on the weekends. I only had a small drink with her now and then after a particularly tough week of training. We still lounged in my flat in oversized pyjamas on most weekends, leaned back in my two old armchairs, and gazed happily at the haphazard mess of clothes and cosmetics strewn about the floor. She smoked and talked, and I listened. My eyes were always cloudy and red around the edges after swimming. Muscle sinews convulsed and twitched like violin strings plucking all out of tune. We swayed to the jazzy music that floated up from the cheap cabaret across the street, and Maizee sipped her drinks. For a while I didn't tell her about the gala, and was avoiding the inquiry into whether her mother would make me a lavish dress.

"Did training rack you pretty bad?" she asked me one night, exhaling smoke.

"Pretty bad."

She reached for a bottle of scented talcum powder and brought the container to her face to smell it before putting it back on the small table between the armchairs. "I thought you might have bailed on this Channel business by now."

I took a sip from her brandy and let the heat run down my throat with a sear.

"There's going to be a big fancy soirée next month," I said. "Higgins told me that rich people become *backers* so they can pull a big party and upstage their neighbours."

She was quiet for a moment. "A party?"

"At a mansion on the East Side."

She visibly turned this over in her mind.

"I need to ask you a favour," I said. "A really big one."

She rose an eyebrow. "Oh yeah?"

"I was wondering if your mother could make me an evening gown for the party. I don't have anything to wear." I could hear the quickening thud of my heartbeat knocking against my ribs.

She lit a second cigarette, inhaled as she lit up, exhaled, and leaned back into the chair. "Do I get a *summons* to this swanky bash?"

I felt heat rush my face. I didn't know if I could bring someone to the affair, never mind a girlfriend with a mouth like hers—and Higgins had made such a fuss about my table manners not being up to spiff. I was already paranoid about my own lack of verbal and cutlery-holding dexterity.

"I have a lunch meeting this week," I said, "where I will see the backer again—and I can ask Higgins about the party, and get the idea, okay? I don't know what it's all about."

"Oh," she said, lifting her nose in the air, "you have a *lunch*."

She looked contemptuously out the window.

Many drinks later, I am with Bea and we are walking to a restaurant where she says they sell import from the cellar. We stumble, laughing and tripping over each other through sandy paths; there is another party in town, and African rhythms surge through the trees. Tall grass brushes our bare arms, and I wish the Canadians hadn't said anything about the rattlesnakes. Bea blows her cheeks out and laughs at nothing. She talks about a place on the island called Vinegar Hill. "Believe me," she says, "we don't want to have anything to do with that stuff. That stuff is rot-gut."

"What is it? A restaurant or something?"

"Are you kidding me? No." She's speaking slower than she usually does—a little slur here and there, while I become increasingly weightless and glad. "It's this really old barrel house up Marilla Street at Vieudelou where some island hoods cook up this nasty moonshine. I heard that a crew of *revenooers* came over from the mainland about a month back and smashed the stills to pieces. I heard they used all kinds of baseball bats and axes to break them up. Everything was poured down Marilla Street and after a day or two it positively reeked. It wasn't the first time they'd come over to trash the place, and it always stinks up the road, that's why it's called Vinegar Hill."

The story makes me laugh, ridiculously. Stinky Vinegar Hill.

Along the path we pass Hastings and Geo "Sockets" Young veering toward the beach. "Good evening, young Canadians!" Bea shouts, a high-pitched wail.

I double over in uncontrollable laughter. When I have gathered enough air to speak, I say, "I really wish you hadn't told me about the snakes."

Sockets points to his buddy. "It was Hastings!" He swipes Hastings on the arm.

Hastings grins. "I didn't say anything about the skinks."

Bea's eyes are loud. "What skinks? What's a *skink?*"

Skink, I think to myself, skink skink skink. I start laughing again and I can't stop. It's the most hilarious word I've ever heard in my life.

"Can *somebody* please tell me what the hell a skink is?" Bea is still asking.

"A lizard," says Hastings. "Lizards all over the place."

Bea pinches up her features. "Swell."

"If you lick a lizard all over," I announce, "your tongue will have healing properties." And I erupt into another boil of hysterics.

The hysteria fades when Geo asks, "Have you arranged for a spotter to plot your swim yet? I hear they're running short on boats."

"Nah," I say, waving my hand through the air. "Not yet." But through my inebriated haze, a small pang of anxiety bounces off my centre.

"To the bar!" Bea shouts, beaming—lifting up her arms to the sky.

"Before long," nod the Canadians, and we leave them, skitter out of the path and onto the main strip of Avalon, walking briskly to the restaurant. Bea laughs and stumbles on an uneven piece of boardwalk along the main street. She stops and lets the warm wind roll over her bare shoulders and flushed face.

"My tolerance is usually much better than this," she says. "How embarrassant." We stop on the boardwalk and face the ocean and the wind. I feel as though the boardwalk is oscillating just a little underneath me, but I also feel a fiery rush of energy coursing through my chest. Bea fans her red face with one hand. We resume our walk and pass the gambling casino; we arrive at our destination, blotto, and bust through a pair of swinging doors. Bea goes up to the attendant behind the counter, pulls a bill from her knee-high stocking, and tells him we're looking for liquor. He guides her into another room to take the money and I wait at the counter.

In the corner of the room is Solomon, leaning back in a supple, athletic slouch. He is sitting with some others eating a late supper, and I look away, except I know that he has seen me. I sit on a high stool waiting for Bea and watching the ceiling fan revolve in circles above me. She is taking some time, and a second restaurant man asks me if I would like to order something; I decline as soberly as possible, but he brings me a glass of water.

"I see you have warmed up since the last time I saw you," says Solomon, who is now standing beside me. He is not wearing his slouchy felt hat, and he extinguishes a cigarette in the glass ashtray in front of me.

"Oh. Yeah," I say. "Sure." I look past him, through an open window where small electric light bulbs glow along the wooden docks of the harbour.

"I should warn you," he says, "the island brew's got a nasty kick. I wouldn't touch it with a ten-foot pole."

"Thanks for the unsolicited advice," I say coolly. "People sure seem to dish it out around here."

"That's not the idea."

I look at the cigarette butt that he has just crushed into the ashtray. "Oh, no? Because those smokes will ruin your golf game."

"Fair enough," he says. "But do you think it's a good idea to be experimenting with your health so close to the race?"

"Oh!" I say. "Don't tell me I'm getting more unsolicited advice."

"Why do you open and close your fists like that?" he asks me. "Do you have numbness in your hands and feet?"

"What?"

A second pair of swinging doors bursts open and Bea reappears—tall, flushed, and proud—carrying a paper grocery bag. She glances quickly at Solomon, who is still standing beside me, and seems to look right through him.

"Off we go, Savi," she says, pushing me off the bar stool. I leave Solomon and our unfinished talk without looking back. Outside, Bea hooks her arm around the crook of my elbow. "Did that man say something that upset you? What happened to your nice buzz?"

"No. He didn't say anything."

"Nothing at all?"

"No."

"He didn't say anything about *me*, did he?"

"What? Why would he say anything about you?"

"You should watch your step around him," she says.

"Why?"

"The locals don't know why he came here. Came here a few months back but people don't know why. Heard he used to be a doctor in Boston—some sort of hot-shot surgeon type. Hasn't made clear to anybody why he came here, says it's because of the fishing. The *fishing*, Savi. Any rate—where there's smoke there's bound to be fire."

"Why has Wrigley solicited him to help with the swimmers? He wears the green sweater. I saw him wearing it."

"Wrigley didn't solicit him."

"How do you know that?"

"You keep forgetting I'm a reporter. I ask a lot of questions."

She leaps onto a stucco ledge near the path toward our camp, "Never you mind!" she howls, her night-wings inflated with a second wind of energy. She lifts the highly coveted booty—"Hallelujah, we are saved!" After a few swigs the booze slackens me again, and we run out into the night, the music weaving through palms, our bottle secure under Bea's thick white arm. The next thing I know I am swimming and there is phosphor in the water—brilliant glowing traces and it is so—very—very—lovely—Bright—shining waves—warm wind and a starry—starry—sky—

TEN

THE FANCY lunch fell on a perfectly brilliant summer day in early June. The trees were leafy and the city was alive, vibrating with freshly polished cars, perpetual construction, thousands of people, Broadway shows, and radios calling out stock exchange numbers that were reaching ever-increasing new highs. It was hot but not sweltering—the most flawless of summer temperatures. If the world was an oyster—as everyone was saying it was—the city of New York was the iridescent pearl at its centre. Peter Laswell owned one of the city's highest towers, and at the top there was, as he described, "a mighty little bistro." This was where he proposed we meet for lunch, and where the press would later join us for a photo shoot.

I had dug into my bake house earnings to buy a dress that was modelled after a Coco design; it was a delicate and simple satin crêpe with a lacy fringe that brushed just below my knees. I took a red-hot bath and slipped into my crêpe, powdered my face, and stroked mascara onto my lashes. The necessary assemblage of lid, clutch-purse, beads, and shoes was a small hurricane of nervous deliberation as I hurled random accessories out of my trunk. The flat was in chaos when a cabbie punched his horn outside my open window. Higgins had arrived.

I ran down the narrow staircase and saw my parents in the kitchen. They were flattening pastry with rolling pins, pinching it into circular pie crusts, folding the edges around pie plates. Pies were the best sellers and a great deal of care had to be taken with the crust—not too solid, not too flaky. It was a Friday, and I was leaving them to orbit around the bake house without me.

I stood for a moment beside the cherrywood table where teas were steeping in cauldrons and coffee streamed through a percolator into an aluminum pot. I gave the kitchen a once-over; the scullery beside the sink was already full of dirty dishes.

"I'll be back for clean up by three."

Their eyes passed over my new dress. My father sighed. "Where are you going?" he asked huffily. "It's not even noon."

"I have a lunch meeting," I said.

"A *lunch* meeting?"

He made a face as though the bottle of milk in front of his pie station had suddenly gone bad. "I don't understand what this is all about. Swimming is not a vocation, Savanna, it's a *diversion*."

"I'll be back," I said again, and they both returned to the pinching of crust.

Outside, I used my clutch-purse to shield my eyes from the high sun. Higgins stood beside the cab, smiling, and opened the door for me to step inside the car's belly. It was the first time I had ever seen Higgins in a dress suit. A silvery cuff button blinked from his arm-occupied sleeve.

"Morning, hoss," I said.

He straightened his pressed collar, smiled.

His empty sleeve was neatly pinned and he smelled crisp—like cologne or aftershave. He told the cabbie where we were going, and we were off, spring wind sweeping through the open windows of the car.

"My parents," I said. "They think I've gone crackers."

"Naturally."

I laughed. "My father should win a medal for the amount of sighing he achieves in a day—every time I see him, it's *why* this and *why* that—always trying to start a bun fight. But it's the look on his face that really smears." I glanced down at my dress. "He looked at me like I was wearing a bag."

"SDI," he said brightly.

"What?"

"Self-doubt incarnate. Heaven knows we all get the chance to negotiate a few of those in life."

I pulled a small mirror from my clutch-purse and repeated it to myself. "Self-doubt incarnate. That's a good one, hoss," I said and frosted my lips with colour.

We drove past a row of laburnum trees; Maizee hated those trees, with their venomous golden chains. She told me they were not native to America, that they came from the mountains in Europe and the Orient, but that a troop of city planters had found ways to cultivate them here. The car sputtered and our cabbie adjusted his mirror.

"Well," I said, "I guess it's not the end of the world that they think my Channel swim is ridiculous. Or that I'm crazy. *Non compos mentis.*"

Higgins jarred. "Since when do you toss Latin around?"

He looked at me with the same startled expression I must have had on my face when he confessed his privileged youth.

"Don't look so shocked," I grinned. "Or I'll be insulted."

We smiled at each other.

"I'm sure my self-doubt incarnates hate you," I said finally.

He laughed out the window.

An elevator carried us up the high tower very slowly. I fixed my lid and my lip colour, and when I realized my paint was chipped I scowled at my hands. "Remember the knife and fork," said Higgins, "fork in your left hand, knife in your right. Elbows tucked in. Hold your cocktail glass by the stem, not the bulb. You only hold glasses at the bulb for winter drinks—brandies and ports—which reminds me." He leaned closer and lowered his voice. "Don't be shocked if he orders a round of cocktails before lunch." Higgins had already alerted me to this likely scenario in one of our meetings, and that we would only report having tasted "unmixed tails."

The elevator clamoured and stopped. The lift man looked at Higgins, expectant, and my coach gave him a coin. We were at the top of the whole world, in an enclosed lounge area with high ceilings and large open windows; the floors and walls were mosaic tile. There were several round tables with chairs in this room and a sign that told us to wait. It was empty of guests.

Higgins continued, "Don't forget to break your bread into pieces before buttering it. Don't slurp your soup. Oh—and we won't be talking about the swim or any business until after the meal. Business-talk before eating is very gauche."

With a towel draped over one arm, a man dressed in white and black suddenly appeared out of nowhere. "Good day," he said, bowing a little. "Please. For the private party." He led us through the tiled room and through French doors onto a rooftop patio. The city view and blue sky opened up like an enormous flower as we were led through a maze of carefully set tables, each one protected from the sun by a giant umbrella. The host or waiter—I wasn't sure what he was—continued to guide us to a private section where three men in dress suits were sitting around a table.

"Miss Mason!" Peter Laswell stood and lifted his arms in welcome. "Clem!"

He startled me by taking both my hands into his and kissing the top of one of them. I squirmed and felt myself redden. He beamed. "You look lovely," he said, standing back to get a better slant. "Mighty outstanding." He was still holding my hands when Higgins clapped him on the back and I was released. They exchanged enthusiastic greetings and low swooping handshakes.

"Please," Laswell said, gesturing to the two other men at the table, "let me introduce my partner in business, Robert Bobrosky."

Bobrosky dipped forward; he was also fifty or so, much shorter than Laswell, with green eyes and a calm disposition. It appeared I would not have to go through the cheek kissing that Higgins had warned me about, and I was relieved that Bobrosky didn't go for my hands. Then Laswell waved toward a much younger man. "And my son, Theodore."

Theodore bowed, holding his cloth napkin to his navel, and when I met his eyes, I was struck by how extraordinarily large and brown they were. At the same time I looked at him coolly, entirely prepared to dismiss him for the high-hat spoiled son that I imagined he probably was. "Everyone calls me Tad," he said softly. I had expected a more brash and energetic voice like his father's. He did not share his father's more eccentric air, and from what I could gather, his suit hung off his body remarkably well.

"Please, take a seat," Laswell encouraged us, and we all took to comfortable, upholstered chairs. "Can I offer a round of bevies? Martini cocktail? Manhattan? Sweet gin, dry gin—what's your taste?"

I took a breath to answer.

"Wait!" he rose a flat palm. "Let me guess."

I glanced to his partner and son, who watched casually as Laswell held his palm to my face, furrowed his brow, and closed his eyes. He had an enormous palm—all five fingers splayed and obscuring my view of the table. His intense concentration almost made me laugh.

"Ward Eight!" he said finally, baring his porcelain smile. "A classic smoky bourbon sour—dash of grenadine and juice of the lemon."

"Hm," I said, never having tasted one. "Swell!"

His brow smoothed. "You know," he said. "I am very intuitive. I have a sixth sense when it comes to reading people."

I nodded.

"And my hunches tell me that you are quite the hidden gem. I am honoured to champion your swim."

He ran his hand over the tabletop. The drink order was quietly taken by a host, and some batting of gums ensued among the gents at the table. I took inventory of the place. It screamed white linen, crystal, and multiple courses. I reviewed with myself which plate and glasses were mine: the bread plate was on the left and the water glass on the right. Our host soon returned and delivered a tray of balloon glass cocktails and disappeared again. The drinks were adorned with a swirl of orange rind and a cherry. "Ah," Laswell grinned at everyone at the table, "to the wards."

"With great thanks," Higgins said, honouring our backer, and we all took to our drinks. The city of Manhattan pulsed up from below in ripples of sound—the issue of car horns, roar of engines, and peal of tires, as I sipped a very red and potent concoction of spirits. And although it had been explained to me that the *rococos* were always looking for new ways to amuse themselves, this focus on my swim was giving me a sharper sense of identity. I felt vines of pride slink up into my chest and shoulders.

Laswell explained his distain for idleness; he moved constantly as he spoke. He was a motorcycle enthusiast, a golf and squash player, a former tennis champion, and was learning to fly airplanes. If he wasn't managing investments or sporting one of his pastimes, he was mastering his mah-jong game. He ran his fingers along the edge of the tablecloth above his lap. When this became redundant, he ran a flat palm on the table, sweeping non-apparent crumbs over the edge.

"Apollinaris White Rock," said a host, suddenly from beside me. He held a long-necked bottle of water in the crook of his arm. Laswell signalled for him to fill our water glasses, and another host brought us plates of soup. The hosts were multiplying and they all looked the same. Seasoned Vichyssoise garnished with lumpfish caviar was announced to the table.

"Bon appetit," said Laswell. "I chose their mightiest dishes for us." He dipped his head and brought a spoonful to his mouth. I predicted that if we were having red meat that he would take his very rare.

I worked around the lumpfish slime, careful not to stare at it too long, or slurp the broth, or say anything prematurely about the swim, when I caught Tad's fine eyes, and we exchanged covert smiles across the table.

Laswell explained that our main course—medallion of spring lamb with *chassewer* sauce—was the *very* recipe that President Calvin Coolidge had been served at the Waldorf-Astoria Hotel. And after a thorough and industrious whittling of his meat to the bone, he stretched himself and rested.

"Shall we confirm some dates?" he said.

He pulled a small leather-bound notebook from the breast pocket of his dress suit and became eerily ceremonial. "I'm told the first week of September is the balmiest time of year in the Channel, but—according to my Jims—we should expect sudden and stormy changes in the conditions."

"I'm sorry," I said, "your Jims?"

He ran his hand in a circle where his plate had been cleared. "My personal advisors—they investigate into matters for me. I'm afraid you won't be making their acquaintance. I keep my confidentials under wraps, you understand."

"Sure." I blinked at him. "Of course."

"You'll leave for Gris-Nez via ship mid-August," he said and panned everyone at the table. "All aboard?"

I'm sure my face was awestruck, and Higgins nodded, as though he had heard all of this already, which he likely had. Bobrosky looked detached, involved in all of this through association, but sat pleasantly and silently, sipping the Venetian coffee that had been brought on a silver tray. "All agreed," Higgins said. He lifted his water glass in my direction and Bobrosky lifted his too.

The boy with the finest eyes I had ever seen would glance from the view of the city, to his father, to me—a cyclical shift of those eyes, which I could feel on me when I wasn't looking at him. It sent small hailstorms down my vertebrae. Then, when there was a silence, Tad said, "You do *know* the English Channel is the coldest shipping lane in Europe."

"Sure," I said. "Otherwise it wouldn't be known as the Everest of marathon swimming, now would it?"

"Everest," Laswell interrupted. "Now, that would be something."

Despite Tad's fine, charming face, and his soft and considerate voice, I was still aware of the fact that a boy of his experience would not understand the tedium of public service, or the exclusion from most parties, or having not been to school past the age of fourteen. He would not understand the exhilaration of possessing a line that could open new and wonderful doors. The hot drive to get somewhere else.

Bobrosky's green eyes landed on me. "Reporters had a field day after Ederle's failed attempt last year. Articles about women forever remaining the weaker sex made the papers from London to New York." He was sedate, scrutinizing. "What did you make of that?"

Laswell resumed his circuit of running his fingers along the edge of the tablecloth, sweeping invisible crumbs, listening for my response.

"Ten times more men have failed the Channel than women," I said. "You don't have to go very far to find stories about man's inhumanity to women."

Bobrosky lifted his water glass. "Sadly," he said.

Higgins cleared his throat. "The argument is full of holes as far as I'm concerned. Particularly in the case of swimming," he said. "The average woman moves much more naturally in the water than the average man—never mind a woman's high tolerance for pain."

Peter Laswell clapped his hands together. "Savvy Swimmer Assaults the Sleeve," he said, filling the pause that had swept over the table.

I had read in Michael's naval book about u-boats that the

Sleeve was the translation for what the French called the Channel—la Manche—and I was inwardly proud for knowing this. "Now, there's a zinger for the newshawks!" Laswell was saying. "Don't you think, Bobrosky?"

Laswell looked to Bobrosky for validation before assuming a ceremonial demeanour again. "I should explain, Savanna, why Mr. Bobrosky is here. He is my partner in business, indeed, but he's also got his fingers in the movie business. As part of our agreement—while I am not seeking any percentage of any future endorsements you receive, I'd like to stake the film rights to your story. The movie biz is steaming—producers are frothing at the mouth for stories like yours." He rubbed his palms together. "We can hash out movies in further detail another time. But on the subject of Trudy Ederle, the Jims tell me that she may—mind you, this is not widespread knowledge—be planning a second attempt."

I felt a burn of alarm in my ears and chest, as though Bobrosky, who had just lit up a cigarette, decided suddenly to extinguish the burning tobacco on my solar plexus. I looked past everyone on the rooftop and became transfixed on a half-erected skyscraper opposite the patio. A row of precariously seated workmen were pulling lunches from small carry-boxes. Higgins nudged me with his foot under the table, breaking my freeze.

Laswell was explaining, "All I know is that a coach of hers was sniffing around town, looking for a backer. Her previous funders cannot, or will not, support a second attempt. Hearsay, of course, is that the Women's Swimming Association fears they would be throwing more of their *boffos* out the window in vain." He laced his fingers, stilling his hands. "Personally, I do not believe she is cause for concern. I gather that in her hunt for backing, she has also divulged a mid-September date for her supposed rematch with the Channel. Between the difficulties she will have getting a sponsorship, the psychological wreckage of already having failed, and the sheer fact that she is slating for mid-September, unaware of our plans—the

Jims have led me to feel completely at ease. If the Jims tell me not to worry," he winked at me, "I don't."

"But what if Ederle discovers our plans for the first week of September?" I asked. "We are, after all, having a press release—she is bound to catch word."

Laswell looked at me patiently. "I understand your concern," he said. "Let me assure you that odds are off Ederle will find any funding again." He opened his hands, releasing his flurry of fingers. "Fact is, this press release will work to our advantage. See it this way: if word is out that Laswell and Associates is sponsoring you— the first girl to swim across the English Channel—other sponsors won't be interested in doing the same. Nobody wants to back the same thing as their neighbour. We're all looking for something new and electrifying. This press release simply puts more obstacles in her path. You see?"

Higgins didn't appear ruffled by any of it, which had a calming effect on my nerves. "We must also iron out the fray with respect to the gala," Laswell continued, "which I suggest we hold in July, on the tenth, say—a grand celebration of your swim. Savvy Swimmer Assaults the Sleeve!" He sat back and rested his arms on the sides on his chair. "How fine to see our city's youth strive for such mighty ideals." He turned to look admiringly at his son, who was gazing casually around the restaurant. "As for Tad, he has begun his studies this year—Political Economy and Business at Columbia." Tad acknowledged his father's approval with a look of near embarrassment.

A newsman and cameraman were led to our table by a host, and before I could truly ready myself, there was a burst of flash powder and the smell of magnesium. It was during the press flap that Higgins assumed a more significant function, responding to questions of dates and plans. I smiled stupidly around the table while the camera flared out of the corner of my left eye. An avalanche of questions were put: How much did I train each day? Would I be swimming around Manhattan to prepare? What foods would I consume during the swim? What foods would I *not* consume? Do I put restrictions on my intake as it was? Who would be on my steamer? What colour was my swimsuit and cap?

On Saturday I found the article inside folds of newsprint; a slim column with a photo of our fancy lunch. Mr. Bobrosky had been cropped out of the shot, and the image contained a formal-looking Higgins, Peter Laswell beaming directly into the camera, and his son lounging in his chair. Tad's dark eyes were looking across the table at me, and I was looking a little bewilderedly at Higgins. As I dissected the picture, I couldn't recall that precise moment at all.

Laswell's zinger had been modified to *New York Girl to Assault the Sleeve!* The article told of my six years of Amateur involvement in swimming and my high rankings at the Olympic Trials, but that I had not qualified for Paris due to a cruel and unusual JD. There were exaggerated references to my hours of training and it was declared that I would be swimming around the entire island of Manhattan in August, which was a mix-up, as I recalled Higgins explaining that I would swim the twenty miles from lower Manhattan to Sandy Hook—a swim I knew Trudy had done as well. The article testified that hot chocolate would be my primary food throughout the swim, and that my suit was jockey-red. A predominant section was devoted to the history, success, and generosity of Mr. Peter Laswell.

I clipped the article and photo from the newspaper, and pinned it to the wall above my stacked mattresses. I took careful interest in Tad's expression.

Maizee came immediately to the flat late Saturday when she knew I would have returned from the tank. She was attending workouts more and more sporadically; Higgins had not yet heaved her off the team. My eyes were red around the edges, but I felt loose and weightless. She rang my flat from outside, and I peered out the window. "Oh, my God!" she said from the sidewalk. "I saw your pic in the paper!"

I went downstairs to let her in, and we climbed the narrow flight of stairs back to the flat, where she flung herself onto my unmade bed. "Tell me about the spiffy luncheon." She rolled onto her side and stared at me. I told her all about the *wards*, the multiplying hosts, the lumpfish, Laswell and his elusive pair of Jims, and the looks I had exchanged with Tad. "I can't believe it," I said. "It's all coming together."

I could see that she was on the cusp of asking me something. "Did you ask about the party? If I can come with you?"

I'm sure she could see the colour momentarily drain from my face.

"You did ask about me—didn't you?"

"Everything was so official, Maizee. So much happening all at once, and we didn't discuss the party at all other than to agree it would be planned for the second half of July. I'll ask Higgins tomorrow."

She picked up the wand of mascara from the bedside and twirled it around with her fingers. Her eyes were round while she pouted. "Do you think I am wrong to be quitting the tank?" she asked me. "Because I'm so bored I could die—and now you're getting invitations left, right, centre, and upside down. All because of *swimming*."

She pulled the mascara brush out from its container.

"It was only one lunch, Maizee, and it's only going to be one party," I said. "Boredom can't be your only reason to do something. You know that."

"Aren't you bored? Everyone is *bored*. Everyone is so bored that one of these days the city will wake up in bored hysteria. I wish something would happen. Why the hell do you swim, anyway? What reason is there other than sheer desperation against bone-cracking boredom? Tell me, please, I'd love to know."

"You of all people should know the answer to that question. I know you do. Don't you suppose I should follow this?"

She examined the mascara brush. "Hell," she said, "how *old* is this stuff? You could have scum growing in here—time to change your tubes." She put the wand back on the table with a sigh and turned her examination to my face, looking peevish.

She pulled the pillow from the top of my bed, rolled onto her back, and placed it over her face. Her small and muffled voice came from under the pillow. "My mother said she'll make you a dress."

ELEVEN

I HELD the clipped photo close to the lamp beside my mattresses every night. Sometimes I woke up startled by a warm glow that seemed to centre at my navel. A new humming sensation moved through me as I performed my bake house tasks with more punch than usual; the higher spirits at work bewildered my parents.

I was prepared to ask Higgins if Maizee could be my guest at the party when he told me Laswell had invited us to join him for appetizers at the same spot where we had shared lunch. "He wants us to sign a contract that outlines his intentions to fund your swim and secure his entitlement to the film rights," he said. "I've scoured the contract and it's all to the letter. I assume he needs the documentation of donation for tax reasons, but don't ask me about those loopholes."

I used more of my savings toward a second dress, which was again a silky, sleeveless crêpe de Chine, smoky mauve and tubular, with an ecclesiastic purple band low at the unstated waist. It would go with my sleek black lid and T-strap evening heels. My *French* heels—almost three inches high. I had rarely worn them because the additional height made me wobble. I was able to patch together an ensemble with relative ease; the colour scheme and time of day would suit the smoky kohl I planned to rim my eyes with. Maizee appeared as I was cranking up for the signing. She sat in her armchair in a horizontally striped chemise, legs crossed, head rested against the back of the soft chair. "Why didn't you take me with you to choose your new dress? You know I love to shop."

I was inserting two silver earrings that dropped an inch from each lobe. "I had to grab it quickly. Higgins only told me yesterday about the signing."

"I was home all day yesterday," she sighed, "and I need to buy some new bub reducers." She grabbed her round breasts in both hands. "*Not* the rage."

"Sorry," I said, distracted by the surrounding mess. Everything was in disarray—stockings, cosmetics, lids, and sundry items tossed all over the room.

"Did you ask about the party?" she pressed.

I couldn't find my kohl amidst the piles of laundry, books and beauty supplies strewn around the small room, and once again, my nails would not be manicured—looking *just so* was an awful lot of work, and I'd only had to undertake the ordeal twice. I could feel my percolating frustration with Maizee's jip-fest erupt.

"No! I haven't asked about the party, Maizee—I'll raise it at the right time. I am not in a position to be asking for favours. Lay *off.*" I was pulling apart a bag of miscellanea: a sewing kit, skin balms, lip balm, a bar of soap, a bottle of Aspirin, and finally, I found my container of kohl.

Maizee was looking at me angrily from the chair, the sides of her eyes crinkled into a squint, her lips closed tightly, breathing through her nose. We stayed that way for a moment, stock-taking.

"I don't get you any more," she said.

"Why? Because you can't make fun of me right now? For once? Now that I may have some success."

"Parley-*voo?* That's a hot one—I don't make fun of you! Why don't you want me to come to the party?"

"I've been trying to *explain* to you that I can't just *ask* for personal favours already. The man is backing my travel and all the race expenses! I am the one who is supposed to be *graciously indebted*."

"Yeah, well, you don't seem excited if I come at all," she said. "Since when did I become such a drag on you?"

"You're not a drag on me."

"Sure, well. Who cares? I don't."

"I said you're not a drag on me."

She shook her head. "You know, sometimes I just want to gather you up in a little box on my shelf and play with you whenever I want."

An awkward silence bore down on the room. I bugged my eyes at her.

"What did you just say?" I asked. "Are you on dope?"

She looked embarrassed. "That's not what I meant."

I sat beside Higgins, across from the Laswells; hundreds of glass windows reflected late afternoon, and from the streets there was the overlapping rumble of cars. I had been shaken by the standoff with Maizee, but the whirling change of scene helped divert my thoughts. I was thinking that Theodore's being there could not have possibly been necessary until Peter Laswell explained, during our initial exchange of pleasantries, that his son was working as his junior assistant for the summer. Tad looked fine in his linen suit, his complexion warm in the light. Seeing him again, there was the slim, crackling storm down my back. The table was adorned with fruit and cheese platters, cucumber sandwiches, stuffed mushrooms, and greasy pieces of fish. Everything was making me salivate, it seemed, which was almost alarming. A host appeared with four balloon glasses of drink. We all raised glasses, sipped, and I recognized the combination as sweet gin mixed with lime juice and the effervescence of soda.

Peter Laswell passed a document across the table. Higgins signed without reading, having scoured through it already. I passed over the fine print—it was not very long—which confirmed the funding, the travel dates, and production rights. I signed along the dotted line underneath Higgins's signature.

"I have decided to slate our party for July seventeenth after all. I expect a grand soirée—music, hors d'oeuvre, dancing." I hoped he didn't mean *ballroom* dancing. Then I remembered reading how socialites like Laswell had started frequenting the outskirts of Harlem to experience true jazz—true, spastic jazz with all its rattles and drums and horns, its impossible rhythms and smoking pace. He looked at me as though I might, at any given moment, pull a tambourine out of my sleeve and start shaking it, and when I simply sat there, a frozen-smile pan, he turned to engage Higgins into talk about Florida and the phenomenal real estate down south.

I noticed that Higgins didn't let on to Laswell about his own sunny-slice dreams. He didn't mention the pile of leaflets he was building on his desk at the tank; leaflets I caught him stroking absent-mindedly in some of our meetings. Laswell explained his plan to sail the Caribbean Sea the following winter—that he was making arrangements for his cruiser's transport from the Hudson River Yacht Club. Even though Higgins didn't reveal the slightest flicker of jealousy, I thought we were both a little green as we sat there listening to him reel off his assets.

I watched Higgins and saw his early social graces, his posture and delicate, carefully paced manner while handling the greasy mackerel and soft oozing cheese. I wanted to eat at a faster pace, taste everything, and have more drinks—but instead I sat, sipping chastely, and slipping an occasional grape into my mouth.

"Tad isn't as partial to golf and sailing," said Laswell. "He's a *bird* enthusiast." He motioned toward his son, who shifted uneasily in his chair. "He's all for the colourful types—seems to be building a bird sanctuary of sorts in the garden house—parakeets and cocka-tiels, isn't that so? He's got some exquisite ones with brilliant faces, quite something, really."

When I lifted my glance, Tad looked embarrassed and rolled his eyes, and I almost burst out laughing. We listened to Higgins and Laswell banter about Harding's booze-filled cabinets and the hypocrisy of it all. When the discussion started to eddy, as political banter often does, I looked at Tad again. He had an elbow propped on the table, resting his head on one hand, and with his free hand he was circling the rim of his balloon glass with a fingertip. A vague, high-pitched tone rung out from his glass. He yawned, and when the sun was at its most swollen, and we could both sense the close of our visit, he winked at me. We all rose to our feet and I teetered in my shoes; Higgins and Laswell clasped hands firmly.

"Thank you, Mr. Laswell, for—everything," I said.

"Pleasure's all mine. Keep up the splendid work. We'll be seeing you at the party in two weeks."

"Oh." My mind stung with the thought of Maizee's prodding. "At risk of fishing for an invitation out of turn, would it be all right if I were to bring a guest?"

Tad's eyebrows lifted.

"There is a girl, she swims with me, and Higgins coaches her too."

Higgins frowned. The subtle sort of frown that you recognize in faces you know very well.

"Why—is she a very good friend of yours?" asked Laswell.

"Yes," I said. "The best."

"Well, by all *means*. I don't see why not. The more the merrier. Please, yes—do bring her. Shame on me for not suggesting you do so sooner," he paused, reflective, added, "you are, after all, our *debutante*, so to speak—our guest of honour."

He clapped Higgins on the back.

As Higgins and I descended in the elevator, there was only the metallic grind of hinges and cables. He turned to me with an incredulous look on his face.

"What are you looking at me that way for?" I asked, thrilled.

"I should have warned you it is very gauche to seek invitations that way."

"Here we go with the gauches again," I rolled my eyes. "I'm not fresh off the bean cart either. San fairy ann, hoss. Or should I call you Emily Post?"

He looked at me, perhaps a little slighted.

The lift man pretended not to be listening.

"I'm sorry," I said. "Listen. You remember when Maizee used to haggle with you in practice, bartering with you to get out of the hottest pepper sets? Remember you said I should ask if her mother would make me a dress for the party? Well—you know Maizee's antics as well as I do. Well enough to know what she'd want to wring out of the deal."

I could see Higgins picture Maizee in his mind—and a small smile pass across his face.

TWELVE

THIS MORNING the water temperature was fifty-five degrees Fahrenheit, and the wind pushed breakers onto the beach, dragging swimmers onto the embankment. Foreseeing heaps of grease-smeared, beached contestants, some Wrigley men in khaki sweaters, including Solomon, assembled a wide swimming lane away from the surf near the marina—but the water there is slick with boat oils and not many have used it. Last I heard, the number of registered contestants is down from four hundred to one hundred and seventy.

That is not why I am headed toward the Wrigley Ocean Marathon headquarters, a.k.a. the WOM—a small canvas hut at the base of the hill of tents. I still don't have a boatman to navigate my course across the channel. The WOM hut has been erected over the course of the past week as race day approaches, and several reps are stationed there, providing first-aid service and general help to the swimmers on the hill. The hut is reminiscent of how I imagine medical tents in the war, but smaller.

Outside the tent I find Rhea James and Ella. The girl is stationed on a tree stump with her leg elevated while a Wrigley man I don't recognize is bent over her foot. I stop and hover beside them. "Everything all right?"

They all turn and look. "Savanna," says Rhea. "Good to see you again. I don't believe you've had a proper chance to meet my swimmer." She puts a hand on the girl's shoulder. "Ella, this is Savanna—the contestant I was telling you about."

Ella's expression is miserable, and when I take a closer look at her foot, I see the Wrigley man is stitching part of her toe with a needle.

"Oh," I say. "What happened?"

The girl shrugs. "I cut my toe on a clamshell at the beach, stung like a dirty bastard in the salt and wouldn't stop bleeding."

"A clamshell?"

"The size of my goddamn head," she says.

A bubbling of laughter escapes my throat as she demonstrates the size of the shell with her hands. "Stung like an Angels' Tit," she says.

"Language," Rhea warns. But she has a way with delivery that doesn't rasp the nerves, and there's something appealing about her manner that I can't quite put my finger on. She has pulled her dark, silver-flecked hair into two low, braided knobs that poke out from under the back of her woollen lid.

Ella has a boyish figure with long calves that run down to where her feet are rested on an inverted pail. The Wrigley man is daubing some sort of alcohol on the stitched toe and she draws her foot stormily away from him in shock. "Damn!"

Rhea looks at her fiercely. "Ella!"

Ella makes a face at the Wrigley man who is fussing over her foot. "Are you quite finished?" she spouts at him. "It's just a cut."

"Stiff upper lip," says Rhea. "Almost done."

The Wrigley man looks at her pensively. "If the pain gets worse we'll need to change the dressing," he says. "You don't want an infection."

Ella rolls her eyes and crosses her arms. "Do you s'pose you have to tell me that?" She shakes her head and stares moodily at her foot. "Jezuzz."

The Wrigley man has finished bandaging Ella's foot and she shoots him a rotten eye. "Why are you all wearing olive drab, anyway?" she asks him. "It's so, I don't know—*military*." He doesn't answer her, starts cleaning up his supplies.

Rhea turns to me. "Taking care of that skin of yours, I trust."

I nod, thinking briefly about the leftover booze I had poured onto my sides that morning with the intention of keeping the wounds clean. "Yep."

"Good."

She looks at Ella, who has returned to gazing unhappily at her big toe. "Well," Rhea says resignedly. "We've got charts to look at."

Ella pushes herself up and off the stump, and as she gathers herself to leave, she gives me a peculiar look, but it's only a flash and I don't have enough time to read into it. Before I can give her fleeting expression another thought, she grins an entirely amicable grin. "On y va," she says. "Watch out for the clams."

The Wrigley man that stitched Ella's toe is rather clean-cut for an islander. I'm still hovering beside the WOM while he disinfects his medical widgets and assembles them into a case. "Can I help?" he says.

"I'm afraid I might have a problem."

He sweeps open the entrance-flap to the large canvas enclosure. "Come on in."

Inside the tent it smells of moth-eaten blankets and manliness, pierced by the rep's excessive use of cologne. "What might I be able to help you with?" he asks me.

"I need to arrange for an observer and boat for the race," I say, sitting on the edge of a squeaky cot.

The rep sits on the cot across from me and presses the pads of his fingers into a pyramid, resting his elbows on his knees. "Most contestants have had their convoys arranged already—our fleet of volunteer boatmen has run dry I'm afraid. It's only four days until the race."

I study his clean face, his delicate features. "But I need a boat and an observer—what am I going to do? I was told when I first arrived that there was a surplus of solicited boats and pilots willing to volunteer their time and vessels. And how could there be a shortage after two hundred of the original contestants have dropped out and gone home?"

"A miscalculation," he says, considering me. He separates his pressed fingertips and brings a hand to his face, rubbing his chin with it. He reaches for a clipboard and rests it on his lap, flipping through a document. "What is your name?"

"Savanna Mason."

"You're the girl who came here from New York unsupervised," he says matter-of-factly.

"How did you know that?" I ask him; pinpricks spread into my hands and feet.

"It's our job to be informed."

This so-called miscalculation strikes me as completely absurd. He is surveying his document, flipping through several pages that look like a list of names. "It appears you are the only contestant to which no observer or boat has been assigned—you should have registered upon your arrival. Arranging for a boat and observer is the swimmer's responsibility. You've been here, what, almost ten days already?"

"Nobody told me I had to register upon my arrival—it wasn't stated in the confirmation letter you sent me—what am I supposed to do now?"

He presents a copy of the WOM entry form and reads: "Each contestant must furnish his own boat or tender, which must be large enough to accommodate one official observer appointed by the committee."

It is possible that I did not read the entry form thoroughly enough before returning it. "I don't remember reading that," I say. It is possible that I was still drunk when I hurled it into the mail. "All I know is that I was told that Wrigley was able to solicit a whole bunch of boats and volunteers for the event. Everybody has told me this."

He's rubbing his face again with his hand, looking nervous.

"I will have to ask one of our representatives if he will volunteer his time and boat for you. We were hoping to have him stationed on the hospital ship as part of the medical corps, but I'll see what I can do."

"Who are you thinking of?"

"What does it matter to you? Nobody has a choice with respect to his observer." I can hear the annoyance in his voice. "Your official observer is appointed by the committee." He holds up the entry form as some sort of reminder. "You might consider this a favour."

"Which representative—if you don't mind too terribly much?"

"His name is Solomon. You would be in good hands, he's a doctor. He's also got a first-rate sense for the water. He'll set a fine course for you—if he agrees, I might add."

The pinpricks spread into my face and my lips are cold. "No," I say. "Not Solomon. Is there someone else with a boat? There has *got* to be someone else. This is an *island*—everybody has a boat."

It seems absurd, this panic. But Bea had made another cryptic reference about Solomon, something about his having been exiled for doping problems or a botched surgery—something sinister, that was for certain—and that I ought to stay away.

The representative looks at me, brow furrowed and a little taken aback. "Excuse me, Miss Mason, but may I remind you that you are in no position to be choosy."

"There must be someone else—please find someone else with a boat."

He places his clipboard beside him on the cot, leans forward. "Why? What have you got against Solomon?"

"Because. I don't want him to be my observer."

"I am afraid that under the circumstances that's not a good enough answer. Perhaps you simply will not participate. Perhaps Solomon wouldn't be interested in all the extra work involved—it could be twenty hours in a skiff, you know. And we're short on oarsmen—he may have to double up and serve as your oarsman *and* your observer."

"I heard he isn't really a Wrigley representative," I say. "I heard that he's an imposter."

"An imposter? That's outrageous. Where did you hear such a thing?"

"Please find me another boatman—there has *got* to be someone else."

"We have taken great care in the selection of our representatives. They are men of good judgment, and I will not have you throwing ridiculous rumours around. I will check into this conundrum of yours, Miss Mason. But I make no promises."

I pace back up the hill, opening and closing my fist, fixed on the path. The sign of the fig: closed fist, with thumb between index and middle fingers. I'm going through my rituals in my mind—I still never cut my fingernails on Fridays or throw stones in the sea; I always get out of bed right foot first, and put the left shoe on before the right. I never completely rake out my fire before retiring—a few embers should always be left—and I never eat my fish out of order, always beginning at the tail and moving toward the head. All of this precaution does not appear to be serving me well at all. Out of habit, I knock on a tree trunk as I pass: good spirits live in trees, and knocking on anything wood calls upon these spirits for protection against misfortune. All of these rituals are always there, buzzing in my mind, like a hive.

When a sharp pain in my chest crops up, and I reach to feel cold perspiration on my face, I sit down on a boulder off to the side of the path. I thought these spells would go away once I left New York—I thought the island would calm my nerves, but my hands are trembling and I close my eyes to focus on breathing normally. I wait until the trembles pass before I start walking again.

My fists are clenched as I walk through the hillside of camps.

I decide to deviate off the path and find the Canadians. Maybe they know of someone with a boat.

George, Hastings, and Doc O'Byrne are stationed at their orderly camp—their celluloid tent is large enough for three and their fire is blazing. There appears to be coffee boiling in a pot and slices of bacon frying in a pan. I approach them. "Hey," I say, and all three of them turn to look at me—Hastings and George smile and stand up. Doc looks back at the fire, remote and seemingly disinterested. They're all holding sticks with punctured pieces of bread at the tips to toast over their perfect fire. While my clenched fists are hidden under my sweater-sleeves, my face must bare the alarm.

"Everything all right?" asks Hastings, taking a step toward me. "You look ill."

"Yeah," I say. "Listen. Do you guys know anyone on the island that has a boat, any observers that haven't been assigned yet—anyone?"

"Eh," says Geo, wincing. "I was wondering if you were going to have trouble. Have you gone to see them at WOM yet?"

"Yeah. There's nobody left."

I am an empty treeless plain and everything is about to fall apart again.

"Nobody at all? Seems impossible considering so many people have dropped out."

"That's what I said," I say. "There might be one, but I don't want him."

"Well," George says sheepishly. "I think you ought to take who you can get."

Hastings interjects, "What's wrong with the one they might have? Does it really matter who does it?"

"Oh," I say. "Never mind."

Doc O'Byrne turns and looks at me as though I have just taken their fatty-fried bacon, dumped it on the ground, and am standing on it; his small eyes are narrowed so thin I can only barely tell they are open. "Perhaps if the women were going to wear their effing swimsuits there would be enough boats." He looks exasperated, face purple with rage. "Revolting," he says—a low, belligerent hiss.

My already shallow breathing quickens, and a current of electricity passes through me—so cold it feels like ice and fire at the same time. My ears burn. I walk past George and Hastings, pushing them off to the side to stand in front of Doc, who has turned back to his blackened piece of bread. "What did you just say to me?"

The drippy little man turns back to the warfare he has just set off. "I said *revolting*. Should I explain what that means? Re–*vol*–ting," he repeats. "Very unpleasant—disgusting. Your coming here on your own like some sort of bachelor *savage* is one thing. It didn't take long for you to get hauled out of the water because you simply shouldn't be here in the first place—and the *idea* that you think you can go expose yourself at a sporting event is appalling, it's an effing *outrage* is what it is. Never mind the *nerve*—prancing around the island without an effing chaperone—you're an effing disaster waiting to happen."

The Canadians are floating out of the corner of my eyes, saying things that I can't hear against the roar in my head; they are trying to calm the situation—but I am already wound and ready to spring. Despite the boil in my chest and the weights that seem to have attached to both my arms, my self command is *gonzo*.

I see dishes caked with sourdough, I hear my parents' chorus of *why why why:* why would you want to do *that?* What if you *fail?* I see the dismissive faces of bake house clientele looking through me, I see Higgins's face after I blew the Trials, I see Peter Laswell's porcelain teeth, and I see Tad's shirtless back in the morning light. I hate myself just thinking of what I let happen, revolted by my own naivety. And before the Canadians can do anything to stop me, I've brought my hand to their business agent's face with a hard whack.

"I'll tell you what's *revolting*," I say, searing mad. "You calling yourself an effing business agent! What exactly *are* you, anyway? Some sort of con*bag?* Grifting forty per cent of Geo's money if he wins—forty per cent! For *what?* Feeding him oranges and roasting bread on a stick? Yeah, well—I smell a *rat*. And, hello? Who said anything about swimming nude? You can go to hell in a hand basket. Nobody asked you."

He's staring at me, entirely paralyzed and without words, holding his hand to his cheek. George and Hastings stand there with their bread-sticks elevated in awe.

Pacing back across the hill my mind is reeling, my fists are opening and closing uncontrollably, and I'm talking to myself, I am officially going mad, I must appear no saner to onlookers, should there be any, than that bottle-collecting palm reader reciting his words, his *dits* and *dats*, humming and talking to people that aren't there. I'm shaken by my own ability to hit someone, I have never hit anyone before, I wasn't even angry before he laid into me, I hadn't been thinking about him at all. I bring my hands to my face and feel cold moisture. I run past my campsite and down the sandy bank toward the beach where no swimmers are training in the cold, I peel off my clothes, all the way down to my skivvies. My breathing has become erratic with panic, and I don't know what has brought all of this on, all of this over a delay in securing a *spotter* boat? I haven't been feeling much of anything for months and now this absolute storm has cracked open.

Breakers are crashing onto the shore and there is no lifeguard on duty—I know from my recent exposure to the ocean that if I get past the breakers I can swim out into calmer water, and I sprint the two hundred yards of beach, run into the shallows, and plunge into a wave. Suspended and temporarily deafened in the underwater roar, I ascend to the surface and break into swim. I swim out toward bitter, grey nothing—*stroke, breathe, stroke, breathe, stroke, breathe*—nothing but overcast, salt, and the odd ropey branch of kelp floating on the surface.

Numbness swells around me, takes over, insensibility. Limbs move, pushed forward, not by feel but by the muscle's capacity to remember—by conditioning. I swim out, past the orange buoys, past outlying rocks, coasting through slate-grey water. Farther out, the waves turn to rollers that exist without wind, stirred by some magnetic force at the ocean floor. Liquid silver traces my finger-tips with each forward extension—stroke, stroke, stroke, *breathe*. A whispering glide in between arm strokes, a crisp smack of cold air when I turn my head to inhale.

Swimming wild, I am a tiny speck in an enormous ocean, haunted with life and fear and fossilized secrets. I swim in and out of cold spots, in and out of fog. And as I move through a soft patch of mist, a harbour seal undulates over the surface of the water beside me and slides under, disappearing into the darker depths. Moving through the water I start to feel that power again—the catch and roll of my stroke, the beat of it, the pull and the push—a brush of recog-nizable emotion that turns over in my stomach.

Stroke, stroke, stroke, *breathe*. My parents were kneading slabs of sourdough and curling thin, cinnamon-covered strips of pastry when I told them about the gala. I invited them to be there, even though I knew they wouldn't come. "A charity invitation," my father said sourly, "to the great ball of disillusion." He was wearing the most miserable of fatherly expressions, flinging his whisk and setting pastry mix into the air. "I'll tell you what I don't like, Savanna—you're a prop to these people, taken up in a society bobbing contest that seems perfectly absurd to me, and you—don't—see—it." Liquid yolks of egg splattered onto the wall behind him. While my father ranted, I half listened and watched my mother, who may have well been deaf by the way she stayed out of it all, carefully curling pastry strips into cinnamon buns on double-papered pans. I think of Bea. *Divorce rate is one in six,* she said the other night. *Fact.*

In preparation of the soirée at the Laswell mansion, Maizee and I cranked up at the flat. Her mother had asked for my measurements and constructed stylish gowns for both of us. The colour of my silk was "champagne." Maizee called hers "pink murder." Both gowns were long at the waist with racier necklines than any daytime or afternoon frock. They would expose our calves, arms, shoulders, and even some of our backs.

Maizee had also brought skinny scarves that matched our gowns and long gloves. She said that dressmakers didn't usually make gloves, but that her mother had ordered some patterns. To boot, she had absconded with two strings of pearls from her mother's relics. The real pearls were so much nicer than my phonies.

The invitation appeared to have appeased her frustration toward me, and despite a residual dusting of tension, we shimmied happily to the tinny jazz that crackled out of the wireless. We slid garters up our legs and flattened our chests with reducers.

"I was a *heel*," she said finally, attempting to blot her freckles out with a rose-skin powder. "I hope you don't despise me."

I was scouring my stockings for small holes. "Of course not."

She put down the powder and started to apply her kohl, intensifying the effect with a sheer layer of Vaseline over each eyelid. The goal, she explained, was to achieve heavy-looking eyelids. "Too much of this stuff, though—and we'll look like Pro Skirts. Your father doesn't want to come to the party?"

"No."

"Why not?"

"You know, ever since Trials—it's all a big bowl of laughing gravy to them. Except they're not laughing. You know what I mean."

She shrugged. "Maybe he's jealous."

"What?"

She rolled her eyes back while her makeup set. "This stuff makes my eyes water. What I mean is—put it this way, your papa never thought your swimming was going anywhere. Even at Trials. And by something actually coming of it all—like now—his predictions are wildly off the mark. And you aren't exactly carrying a torch for the family business the way he wants. Not to mention your brother. I mean, *hell*—that's got to roast."

She scuffed her hair with both hands. "Well." She turned to study the old eyelet trim around my pillowcase. "I have a confession."

"A confession?"

She hesitated, staring at the pillow.

"I made the gowns myself," she said finally. "It wasn't my mother."

The gowns shimmered in the evening glow that swept in through my south-facing window. Dust was illuminated in the visible slats of sunlight. I watched her and wondered if she had really intended to tell me at all. She picked at the eyelet trim with her painted fingernails. "I couldn't very well ask my mother to do it. She would have asked too many questions—and they don't make necklines like this in rosy Pollyanna-*ville*."

I looked down at the intricate yet simply constructed folds of silk. "You made these? You made the scarves and the gloves?"

"Yep." Pride and colour rushed her face.

"Oh, my God," I said, a long drawn breath. "They're mag*nif*."

"I know," she said. "We couldn't very well go to this affair looking like a couple of Greenwich Village socks. This isn't some kind of Broadway beer garden."

I was struck by her confession, and also by the insight she was still spouting about my father. "I've been helping my mother a lot more since I broke training, you know, and that's what your parents want from you. Think about it, Savi. You've got Higgy, and you've got this Greenback, both of whom—pardon me for saying—want to help the poor baker's daughter. You get it? So it's a kick in the teeth for Daddy—makes him feel like a dud, maybe—or maybe I'm way off beam. What the hell do I know? Don't listen to me—we have a *gala*!"

I fiddled with my silk-covered fingers, shocked that she could actually make evening gloves when she came to sit beside me on the bed. "I didn't mean to say that I didn't recognize you any more that day." She blinked her kohl-irritated eyes. "Maybe we're all a little bit green."

I felt my arms embrace her before I knew what I was doing, and we stayed that way for a while, the crush and rustle of our silks, loose hair on each other's shoulders. She drew a silky cream cloche from one of the armchairs and fit it snugly on my head. It had a wing that swept down over my right cheek. "This lid will knock their spats off!"

The evening was thick, humid, and misted with a film of ruddy light. The air smelled grassy with hints of charcoal that drifted out from the courtyard grills. Our gowns and scarves hung from our bodies like thin liquid, the soft brush of silk made me feel almost naked, and a wash of tingles spread over my skin like the anticipation of a thunderstorm. We found Higgins standing watch on the mansion's front landing where torches burned. It was a great brick manor covered with garlands of ivy and treed in from the sidewalks. Maizee spit her gum into the immaculately pruned hedge. "Pippy tux," she said.

"My, oh, my," Higgins said. "The regal rags have arrived."

I spun around to show off my gown, a little unsteady in T-straps.

"That's the stuff," he said, grinning from ear to ear, and we climbed the narrow rise of steps to where he was standing. We were all delighted to see one another. He adjusted the empty sleeve where he had delicately pinned the linen, it magnified his missing arm. At his wrist, his silver cuff button glinted in the purpling dusk. We all stood happily at the top of the stairs, grinning at one another before a doorman appeared, inviting us inside. "Please," he said. "Step this way."

I could hardly breathe at first sight of the vestibule, the gleam of the decor—marble floors, polished mahogany furnishings, tall mirrors, and the pulsation of music coming from somewhere in the house. Small exotic trees with twisting stalks occupied the corners of the room. My palms began to feel clammy and my new and only pair of garters were constricting the blood flow to my legs. The three of us followed the doorman past some large and fragrant lily bouquets into a reception hall where we were shanghaied by a tuxedo-slick Peter Laswell.

"Clem!" he called. "Miss Mason!"

He greeted Higgins and went for my hands, but wholly delighted by the moment's thrill, I did not squirm with the hand kiss. The summer had deepened his colour; he radiated. "Look at you," he said, still holding one of my hands, stepping back to get a better slant. "Lovely gown, lovely gloves—absolutely *mighty*." He released my hand and turned to Maizee, who was at my side, surveying the room with a look of marvel. "And this must be the very good friend you told me about."

"Yes," I said. "Mr. Laswell, this is Maizee Sullivan."

He took her hands and kissed one. "I understand you are a swimmer as well."

Maizee laughed. "Sure," she said. "If you say so."

Laswell threw his head back and exhaled a laugh. Higgins moved to stand beside Laswell and they blocked my view of the room. An enormous chandelier hung from the ceiling, frosting the room with a warm, electric glow. Gelett Burgess called this type of half-light *meem lighting;* it reflected off the cocktail that Laswell had his fingers curled around. An orchestra was playing slow jazzy songs somewhere in the vicinity; brass and piano streamed and whirled in musical eddies. Laswell's attentions swerved back to me.

"The guests, my dear, are simply enchanted by your story. You're the star of the evening—our mighty shining star." He clenched an athletic fist and shook it. "Once you have had a chance to tour the hall and mingle," he said, opening his splay of fingers, "I will say a few words, and Clem will follow with a speech at the platform where you will pose for the cameras and say a few words as well." He raised his cocktail. "Until then," he motioned to the room, "enjoy."

Higgins excused himself and slipped inconspicuously toward the food. An official-looking man in a polka-dot necktie came over and tapped Laswell on the shoulder. They engaged in a hushed bull session and I wondered if he was a Jim. Laswell turned to us regretfully. "Do excuse me, orchids. My attentions are being called. Please, taste the food."

"Seems keen, your Greenback," Maizee whispered when he was out of earshot. "Live wire, methinks, but keen." For a moment we took everything in; the lily-filled crystal, crushed velvet, silver candlesticks, tiaras, and feathery headpieces all blurred into a weirdly glorious eyeful. "It's like a coming-out ball without the stupid receiving lines," she whispered. We both caught sight of the very long, glass-topped table that showcased an extravagant spread of gourmet foods. Maizee stared at it like an animal. "There goes Higgy—hitting the paté."

We started to move toward the food, sliding through a kaleidoscopic tunnel of sparkling fashionables that I had no background for whatsoever, guests who touched my arm and said, *How wonderful, divine, admirable.* Society ladies drifted like the music around the reception hall and the gents gathered in scrums of man-talk.

"Hold up," I said, stopping our progression to the food. I thought I had caught a glimpse of substance reminiscent of that shoal of lumpfish caviar I had navigated around at the fancy lunch. There were oysters on an enormous bed of ice, laying dead and slimy in their shells. "I'm not ready to eat," I said. "My nerves."

Maizee dropped her shoulders and pouted. "Mal a l'estomac already?"

I brought my hand to my guts. "Just a few minutes, I'll be fine."

She gave the food a sidelong eyeball. "All right," she breathed. "But we *are* tasting that stuff before it's all gone. Got me on that? Where's the hootch, anyway—everyone's got punch."

In headlong pursuit of a punch station, our eyes passed over the gilded walls, chandeliered ceiling, Romanesque arcades, and landed on a huge window that was catching the last of sundown on a vaulted ceiling. It poured amber onto a staircase that curved to the second story. While the party was contained in a lower hall, it was apparent the rambling house had a great number of rooms. I imagined drawing rooms, libraries, conservatories, parlours, fireplace rooms—all sorts of secret staircases and hallways that connected the niches and dens.

"Come on, Savi," she said mischievously. It was clear she had a slinky idea. "Let's go upstairs."

When the coast was clear in the reception hall, we darted up the wide flight of stairs, gold with sundown, and peeked into the first room at the top. It was empty of people, dimly illuminated by meem lighting. We entered cautiously, and gathered quickly that it was a display room of sorts—the walls were covered with photos; trophies occupied the ledges and shelves. Maizee clutched her rope of pearls in a small fist. "Nifty chambers, Mac."

She walked to a mantle of trophies and took one into her hand. "Tennis," she said. "Your backer was a tennis champion." She put it back down on the mantle with a clang.

"Careful!" I hissed. "Let's go back."

"Not yet," she said, picking up another shining cup. "Golf," she announced and put it back down noisily.

"Quit it!" I hissed again. "What are you doing? Higgins will flip his lid."

She held a large bronze award in her hands, a sculpted racehorse. "He bets on bangtails!" She thrust her chin at a row of racehorse trophies before putting it back, the base screeching against the mantle. "So he plays it on the ponies," she said, and dusted her fingers over the sculptures.

She swung her hands behind her back and moved toward the wall of photographs. "Come, looksee," she said. Annoyed and reluctant, I walked to where she was standing.

"Jack of all pastimes, your Greenback," she said and pointed to a wall of photos showcasing Laswell's tournaments and sporting adventures. In many of the shots he seemed to be on top of something—a mountain, a horse, an elephant, a camel, an iron motorcycle. In one photo he was precariously perched on the wing of a grounded airplane. There were images of him hunting, fishing, swinging golf clubs, even *dog* sledding—and it occurred to me, did he not have a wife?

"Evening," came a voice from the gallery's threshold. Maizee squealed. I froze. We bounced to face the doorway and saw Tad, who stepped casually into the room. He was with another young chap, and they were dressed in suits. They both had punch.

"I see you found the showroom," Tad said. A sly smile passed across his face.

I looked sideways at the row of bronze-plated bangtails to my left.

Maizee shrugged, as though our presence in the upstairs showroom was the most natural of all places to find us. "I can't *believe* you live here," she belted out, walking blithely toward them. I followed her, trying to calm my nerves.

I realized she would have recognized Tad from the photo in the newspaper and because of what I had already told her.

"Maizee, this is Theodore," I said. "Peter Laswell's son. He goes by Tad. Tad, this is Maizee."

"Good evening, Theodore," said Maizee. "I saw your pic in the paper."

The youth who stood beside Tad took a drink and moved forward, and Tad introduced him as Robert Bobrosky.

I paused. "Don't I know a Robert Bobrosky?"

"You met his father at the luncheon, my father's associate—this here is his son, Robert Bobrosky *Junior*."

"Oh. Of course. Pleased to meet you."

Tad touched my arm. "We've been looking all over for you."

"Oh, I'm sorry—we really only just got here it seems."

"You look *smash*," he said.

From a downstairs hall, we heard the piano pick up a faster kick and Maizee clapped her hands together. "Oh," she said, "I'm all *for* this music." She began to shimmy, almost suggestively, beside me. She tilted her head back to look at me from under her lid. "Let's get back down there. This music is hot!"

We all returned casually to the downstairs hall and stood beside the food.

"Try the punch?" inquired Tad, who was holding his glass at the stem. He nudged Robert to fetch us a round, and Robert returned almost instantaneously, double-fisted with drinks.

"Thanks, Bobo," said Maizee, taking up her punch. Robert Bobrosky laughed.

Tad smiled and took a sip. He was clean-shaven, and I could see the creases where his clothing had been pressed. He wore a black suit with a white tie, and from his breast peeked a red pocket square.

We examined the spread of delicacies, suspiciously unfamiliar and slick. Maizee and Bobo stationed themselves at a fondue table with skewers, dipping pieces of bread into a pot of melted cheese. Tad must have noted my uneasiness about the food, because he touched my arm again and brought me to a different table where crisps were fanned out beside a dark paste. "Olive tapenade," he said, "knock-out."

We spread the tapenade onto wheat crisps, and when I brought the paste to my tongue, everything I had ever imagined about places where olives grew passed before my closed eyes: olive and fig trees growing along cliffs overlooking a blinding turquoise sea.

"I knew you would like it," Tad said.

When I opened my eyes, Maizee and Bobo were bouncing to and from various stations of food. They were now in front of the enormous ice-bed of oysters. Maizee was slurping a tiny piece of sea meat from a barnacle-encrusted shell. Tad leaned into me. "Oysters?"

I scowled.

"Okay," he said. "What about oyster *fruit?*"

"What do you mean? That slime is nauseating."

He grinned, one hand in his pocket, one hand curled around his punch. "I have something for you," he said.

He pulled a hand from his dinner coat pocket and appeared to be cradling something in his palm. He thrust his chin in the direction of the oyster station. "I was in the kitchen earlier tonight, shooting the breeze with a few of the cooks when a shucker scored an oyster fruit. I thought of you right away." He opened his hand, and glinting from the creases of his fine-looking palm was a tiny pearl—iridescent and raw.

"Oh," I said, startled. I stared at the tiny pearl, and at the fine hand that was holding it. "I don't know what to say."

"Please," he said. "Have it—a lucky token for your swim. Fresh from the water, discovered in the kitchen only hours ago." I held the pearl between my silk-covered fingertips, elated by the gesture, and Tad was beaming.

Then came the sound of someone hitting a dinner gong, and a drove of guests moved toward the elevated platform where Peter Laswell motioned for me to join Higgins at the podium. Maizee and Bobo were suddenly beside us again. Laswell was beginning his welcome and his guests crowded like magnets around the stage, rapt.

"Thank you," I said to Tad, and I slipped the pearl into my long glove, safe in my hand, sealed in silk.

The gong sounded again and Maizee squeezed my arm. "Off you go," she said. "*Toot sweet*—go on, now." I moved away from Maizee, Tad, and Bobrosky—and shuffled in my silks, en route to the podium where Laswell was completing his greeting.

"And now," he said, "ladies and gents, friends, associates—a word from Savanna Mason's expert coach, Mr. Clem Higgins."

There was a spattering of applause. Higgins approached the lectern and everyone stared at the place where his arm should have been. I stood beside him, my champagne dress gleaming in the meem.

Higgins began to speak. "Above all, I would first like to thank Mr. Peter Laswell for his generosity." The music had been halted, and the audience was still. "Peter's enthusiasm has been nothing short of remarkable. Savanna's dream of becoming the first woman to successfully swim across the English Channel is coming to bona fide fruition because of his belief in her. Without his support, his vision, and—once again—his swell generosity, we would not be standing here today."

A series of flares exploded to my right, and I turned to see a cameraman partially obscured by flash powder. Higgins paused—for effect, I wondered—before resuming his speech. "Thomas Edison once said that opportunity is missed by most because it is dressed in overalls and looks like work."

A ripple of amusement passed over the shining congregation of socialites.

"It has been a great delight working with this fine young sport standing before you now." A rumble of approval punctuated his statement, and he paused calmly as they became quiet again. "Savanna Mason has constitution and *heart*—has earned her stripes with flying colours in the competitive world of amateur swimming. I have never seen such keenness, such *perseverance* in all my years of coaching."

At the back of the crowd, Maizee stuck out her tongue. Bobo stood happily beside her. I saw Tad looking poised and listening, watching me intensely with his loud, penetrating eyes. I stood still, on exhibition, my heart pumping quickly, and squinted into the crowd while Higgins completed his run of my credits.

"I tell you, ladies and gentlemen, this young sport is *made* to move through water. She *knows* she can do it, and she will." Upon his closing statement there was a great smatter of claps and Maizee released a catcall from the back of the room.

Higgins looked at me, smiling, and the clapping grew louder, and louder as he guided me to the lectern. At the lectern, the harsher light made it more difficult to see everyone. I drew a deep breath and words began to scramble in my head, the applause dissipated, the reception hall hushed, and—blinded at the platform—I began to speak.

It was a blur as I thanked Higgins for his kind words, and thanked Peter Laswell for his generous sponsorship, his belief in me, and for the swell party. Then I froze and stared blankly ahead, fixating on the large metal disk of a Tam-Tam at the back of the room. "Thank you, ladies and gentleman," I said, "for being here tonight. I am so honoured and thankful to be here, sharing this evening with you."

I became clammy again, swallowing and saying nothing, and when the awkward lull had successfully closed in on the room, someone began smacking his palms together. The guests took it up noisily and I scuttled away from the lectern, prematurely, as though I thought it might suddenly catch fire. The gong was struck with a soft mallet again, more camera flares popped and burst in my wake, and the orchestra resumed its shuffle. Within moments I was back on the marble floor of the hall with Maizee, Bobrosky, and Tad, feeling as though the speeches hadn't actually happened yet.

The muscles in my face ached from smiling. I held my jaw in my hand and pressed.

"You didn't thank me!" declared Maizee, shimmying to the music. "Why are you holding your face that way? Quit it—you'll smudge your powder."

I let my hand drop to my side. "Oh, my God," I said. "I was *awful*. I completely forgot how to speak English. I was a clown up there."

Maizee rolled her eyes.

"I don't even remember what I was talking about," I pressed.

"You and your nerves," said Maizee. "You were grand up there. It's all happening, Savi. You're really going to do it."

I brought my hand to my face again.

"You charmed the room," said Tad.

Bobrosky nodded in agreement.

"Quit it." Maizee came at me and removed my hand from my face. "I said, you're smudging your powder."

Tad and Bobo laughed.

My face muscles were forced into smiling again. And my worries about the speech slackened. "You don't need powder," said Tad.

It was as though the room had been misted over from the instant I had entered it, and now it was coming into clear focus. Had I not noticed all the faces staring at me? I was unaccustomed to this emphatic approval and interest in my swim. There were no self-doubt incarnates in the room that night, at least none that could puncture my elation, and I started to feel as alive as I had ever felt in my entire life. I pedalled backwards through my thoughts, to the moment I was shanghaied by Laswell. When he and Higgins were standing before me, blocking my view, I had been caught up in the overall gleam of the room, naive to the fuss that was occurring among the guests. I—the *guest of honour*—then drifted inconsequentially upstairs on a sneak and later toward the glass-topped food table, oblivious to a group of fashionables that were waiting to see which items I would or *wouldn't* put in my mouth—a group of fashionables, to whom, my inadvertent snobbishness was taken as mature sophistication. I recalled the tips of their fingers brushing against my arm, their words: *wonderful, admirable, divine.* I recalled the pride in Higgins's voice, and the regard of the guests. And when I blinked, perceiving the party in a new, astonishing light, I saw the fiery look on Tad's face.

After the party I was elevated off the ground by new fervour; Maizee, Bobo, Tad, and I went to a nightclub, also in the uppers—a little after-hours joint that Tad and Bobo said was a swell spot for dancing, and for a celebratory round of drinks they defined as "reliable." A cabbie drove us along a street of stylish brownstones, and from the curb, the building where there club was supposed to be hidden had scant appeal. It was dark and rather dull, and struck me as a vacant old thing that was waiting to be refurbished to match the more elegant dwellings along the narrow street. "I don't know about this, Tad-*pole*," joshed Maizee in a low voice. They took us around the back and down a series of wrought-iron steps to a doorman in the shadows. Tad and the doorman exchanged a few easy words, and we were welcomed into a cozy, brick-walled nightclub that was swollen with the auditory spice of real jazz music. Positioned in a velvety corner, there were four flared-bell horn players who had been brought in from Harlem. I knew this because they were negro, and all the good musicians were negro and lived in Harlem. Maizee gazed around at the overstuffed chairs and couches before turning to Tad. "I take it back. This is a corking spot. *Who knew*—you'd never know it from the outside."

"That would be the idea," Tad said.

Bobo explained to us that this was the latest and greatest of the secret clubs frequented by students looking to escape academic boredom—lose themselves in drinks, music, and, from what I could gather, dark-corner seductions. By students, I presumed he meant the Ivy League set with scratch in their pockets. "Juice joints come and go quickly," he said. "Dry squad round every corner looking for a joint to crash."

Maizee listened to him intently. "Stringy ferrets."

The place was smoky and dark, sultry fabrics lined the walls, and we found a velvety grove to sit where my three compatriots collectively lit up ciggies with three separate matches. "Bad luck to light three cigarettes with the same match," Maizee had declared, and Bobo accommodated her warning like a gent. Though he seemed to be a man of few words, the two of them were peppy together while we waited for a host; she thrilled to every word he *did* speak, and he listened to her talk about making the gowns and gloves, delighted. He didn't recoil from her superstitious ideas. "I pricked my finger a dozen times making this," she told him, holding part of her gown in a fist, "means something extraordinary is going to happen while I'm wearing it."

A host came to take our drink order and Tad watched me with those huge brown eyes. "The juleps here crash an A," he said.

I agreed to a julep, and his eyes brightened when I asked about his birds.

"Sometimes I want to go to South America and study birds," he said, turning his eyes to the table. "Other times I think I could settle into business or advertising—new religion and all. I don't know. For now I'll follow my fancy, you know what I mean—see where I land."

"Where did you get your birds?"

"Lower 'hat. But it was Paris that really got me started."

"Paris?"

Our juleps arrived. We touched glasses and held them close to our chests.

"Yeah. There was this Frog who walked the Quarter with a parrot on his shoulder and a flask on his hip. It was funny, you know, the hip flask in France where it doesn't even matter. But anyway, I kept seeing him at different terraces pouring booze into his coffee drinks and sharing the paper with his bird." He leaned forward, all grins. "He taught it to *curse* the host if the service was punk."

We laughed. "My brother would like that story," I said, took a drink.

"Yeah? You've got a brother?"

"He's in Paris, actually."

"Oh, yeah?"

"Writing a novel."

"I can't imagine writing a novel." He smiled and we stabbed the ice in our drinks with stir-sticks, pushed the cubes around our glasses. "I can't sit that long," he said.

He was so polished, so handsome, his eyes were hot, and his hair smooth with some sort of emollient. He was, perhaps, what I'd never thought of any man before: *beautiful*. It was *so* out of style to be thinking in such terms—but I was mesmerized. The little pearl was burning a hole in the centre of my hand.

"Tell me more about Paris," I said.

"Lemme see," he said. "Well, the art moderne is very big. The artistic types have taken it up wholesale—and of course the terrific markets and cafés." He stopped a moment, looking thoughtful. "I would travel more if I could."

I couldn't see what was possibly stopping him. "Well, why don't you?"

He jarred, struck perhaps by the challenge in my tone.

"My father's got me pinned, expects me to finish uni—you know how it goes."

No, I had no idea how it went—school, university, opportunities that were not in my grasp. But *he* was in my grasp. Right there at the table.

"Maybe you could join on the boat," I blurted, "for the swim or something."

He paused, slackened, and rested a finger on my hand. "I'd be delighted."

We sighed over our glasses before draining them, and Tad ordered us another round. "My dad calls you his diamond in the rough, you know. Your swim really got his attention. And you should *see* the folks he turns away—flagpole sitters, marathon dancers—*especially* the atom-splitters. He's got some sort of beef with modern science."

I thought of the photos in the showroom. I wondered about his mother.

"What about your mother? I don't think I met her tonight."

"Oh," he said. "No—I don't imagine you did."

"Oh!—"

He was immediately assuring. "No," he said. "Not the flu."

I breathed a sigh of relief.

Tad looked matter-of-fact. "She dropped the pilot a few years back. Went out of bounds, off the reservation, you know what I mean? It's not official—domestic smash-ups never are."

"I'm sorry," I said. "Touchy subject."

He smiled and took my hand. "You know, let's you and me not worry about that stuff. Too moony. This is your night. And frankly, I was old enough to get it."

Our drinks arrived and we leaned into each other to touch glasses again. "You know what the Prohibies say, don't you?" he asked. "That it's impossible to stop liquor from trickling through a dotted line." I laughed and raised my glass. "To success," he said, an enormous smile spreading across his face. He reached to touch the silk that was draped over my thigh. "Perhaps sometime I could show you my birds."

"I'd love to see your birds," I said, sipping my fresh julep.

Maizee was in the grip of talk, explaining to Bobo that she was quitting the tank for good. For a while we listened to her complain that Higgins never believed that she had a bad knee. "He told me breaststrokers don't have *bad knees*." Her colour was up as she ranted. "He said if I was going to pull a muscle, it would be a *groin* muscle." She was throwing her curls, *carpe diems*, and silver-polished finger-nails around. I could see she was out for a flutter; this time I felt it too, the eagers—that rush.

My skin burned. I was keen to have this boy close to me. I anticipated the electric crackle and singe when we touched. After our second round, he smiled and put down his glass, moved from his seat and held out a hand. I knew it would be impossible to dance in my French heels; they were killing my feet, so I took them off and tossed them under our table.

"Get hot!" Maizee called to us, smiling—which is precisely what we did.

We stepped and kicked in four-four time, swinging arms from our elbows and crossing hands. The pearls around my neck flew with the fast pace, and when our brows and palms were coated with moisture, I took off my lid to shake out my hair. He pulled me to him. *Stay close*, he said. *I don't want to lose you.* We moved closer, the forward lean, careful not to whack arms as we gyrated to the rhythmic shuffle. Toes in, toes out; beads of sweat trickled down the sides of our faces, and we flopped, breathless and reeling, onto an overstuffed couch to have another drink.

When we took it up again on the dance floor, the brass quartet started playing a flat Charleston—a *flattie*—it was almost a Slow Fox, and we grew increasingly bold—legs intertwined, torsos pressed together. "You know what they call a close dancer, don't you?" he asked, wiping sweat from his forehead.

"A *smudger*," I said, laughing—and he smiled his gleaming white grin. As the night moved toward morning, body heat and summer humidity pressed against the walls of the small nightclub. Maizee and Bobo had been dancing too but were now cuddling, talking, and sharing a drink on a soft bench.

I was on fire, my eyes fixed on Tad's as we stepped and swayed, looking into each other's faces without conversation. A dark rumble was working its way into a roar in my head—the way pressure creeps along a fault line—toward the electric crash of his hand on my cheek, neck, shoulder—his lips pressed against mine. A hot current moved from my mouth to my ribs, hands, navel, and conspired between my hipbones.

His kiss was a tumble into the colour red; it was the untidy, chemical, unfamiliar kiss that would change everything. With his mouth on my neck, my fingers through his hair, everything whirled: the crush of my champagne silks against his flannel suit, the crush of my hair against his cheek, the soft, velvety press of lips.

The musicians were closing in on their last wailing song, Tad's mouth was at my ear—his firm body pressed against me, and he whispered, "It is absolutely against your better health to repress your desires." His voice aroused my every cell, and all I could think about was the thrilling sear of skin against skin.

Everyone knew it was the girl's responsibility to set the parameters on how far a whirl could go—which liberties could be taken and which could not—but the pleasure principle had won the tug-of-war. I could scarcely remember how I had achieved such a remarkable state of undress in an upstairs bedroom with the beautiful son of the rich patron who was funding my swim across the Sleeve. Dawn was on the cusp of breaking outside a single-paned window, and early morning light streamed onto Tad's smooth, exposed back. He turned to me, sun pouring golden onto his face. The black pupils of his eyes constricted. "And what might you be doing tomorrow?" he asked.

The subsequent exhilaration and introduction to the finer things enjoyed by the higher hats made me edgier about the bake house, especially when it was bustling with a Friday rush and customers were ferrets.

There was a rumbling about Johnny Weissmuller having won the annual three-mile Chicago River Swim. Despite windy river-chop and some snags with his navigating spotter, he had come flying toward the finish line where Hawaiian ukulele players had stationed themselves on a barge, welcoming his record-breaking finish with "Claphands—here comes Johnny!"

I was in the whirling throes of an affair with Tad after the night-club, and we met up whenever possible—in between training and my hours at the bake house. We spent our time together in his garden house that was unused on his father's property beside the mansion. It was secluded in trees and ivy, which made concealing the affair from Laswell Senior uncomplicated.

After an ordinary day of routine in the bake house, accustomed to my father's ongoing stonewall, I met Tad on the front steps of the garden house. He stood there, offering me an afternoon drink. We sat surrounded by the sunny, manicured garden, and he held my face in his hands and kissed me.

It was not at all smart or *modern* to fall in love, I knew. Girls were most desirable if they were casual, thrill-seeking, marriage-evading chums. *Pals.* But I wanted more of him, I knew that I did—

and I sensed that my blithe attempts at projecting an impression of lightness were not entirely convincing.

"I don't want to stop kissing you," he said. His touch had such an effect on me, and while I had intended to insist we go somewhere else—for a stroll or to a movie—I was swayed by his mouth into the garden house where we kissed, and ran our fingers along each other's spines all afternoon.

THIRTEEN

WAVES COLLIDE onto the shore below me; the sky is bearing down on the island like a dome. Low smoky clouds have blown in from the mainland where a forest fire caught just outside of Los Angeles. The moon keeps getting fatter. I wasn't even drinking when I took a run at that ass—I haven't talked to anyone since it happened, and it appears that the first person I am going to see is the lunatic bottle picker. I can hear him clinking up the path toward my camp, and my panic has turned to exhausted deadness again. I stare at my fire as it struggles to breathe, and feel the sting of damaged tissue under both arms where my undershirt has done a number on the skin.

His bottles cease clinking, and while I can't see him, I know we are both standing there, observing the strange, dark horizon. He drops his bag to the earth and at least a few bottles shatter. When I turn to him, he is beaming. He's fluttering his long, skinny fingers to the rhythm of what I can only guess are his thoughts, counting, reciting. "Remember?" he says and slaps his hand to his chest. "Loot."

"How could I forget."

He moves to stand beside me and points to the harbour where boats creak and bob in the rougher water, ocean sloshes against hulls. There is a metallic rattle of halyards knocking around in the wind. "Ack Emma," he says, pointing. "*Ante meridiem.*"

"Yeah—whatever," I say, and move back to my boulder beside the fire.

Now he blinks at me in the dark, points to the tent. "Swell bivvy."

"Sure," I say. "You too."

Here we go. This time he collects a few branches and weeds for the fire and throws them into the pit. He perches opposite me, holds open his palms, and points with one hand at the lines all over his other palm, points to me. "Understood," he says.

"Listen. I don't *understood* anything you're talking about."

Crouched into a ball, he rocks back and forth and starts reciting those words. He speaks quickly and softly, and I can't make it out until he points to the harbour again. "Ack Emma."

"Okay—I give up. You've lost your marbles somewhere along the line."

His rocking pauses. "Frontline," he whispers. "Funk hole."

Before I can shoo him away with a stick, he whisks white powder from his corduroy pocket and throws it onto the embers. The fire takes immediately and he scurries up to collect more branches. "Flint," he tells me, beaming again, and returns with a heap of kindling he drops onto the flames. He resumes his crouch, long arms wrapped around his knees, mumbling: *Red or grey she does not know—red for fortune, grey for woe. Red or grey, red, grey, red, grey.*

"There you are," comes a voice from the path, and Solomon emerges out of the smoky dark with a shiny dog—the whippet type with the skinny legs. Wind pushes the tall grass around my camp into a single rippling sheet, and the dog scrambles down the bluff in a cloud of lifted sand. Solomon's appearance doesn't seem to induce any significant change in my dulled emotional state. I feel nothing but pain under my armpits. He's looking at the palm reader, who's holding his hands to the fire and talking to himself. "I've been looking all over for you," he says.

"What?" I say.

Sol looks at me. "Excuse me," he says. "But I was talking to *him.*"

I see that the bottle picker is not acknowledging him at all. "He's not even looking at you," I say coolly.

"Has he been bothering you?"

It takes a moment before I say anything more.

"He calls me 'bint' and he always wants to read my palm. But he brought flint this time, so I've been putting up with it," I say. "Why? Is he dangerous?"

We're both watching him—he's fluttering his fingers and humming.

"A bint is a young woman, and no—he's not dangerous," says Sol. "But I understand that *I* am something of an imposter."

We peer at each other in the dark. "Yeah—well, aren't you?"

He looks bemused. "What sort of imposter am I?"

"Why did you say those things to me at the saloon? You're not really a doctor."

"Fact is, I am a doctor—and I see symptoms in you that concern me."

Flaming threads of heat move down my arms. "Symptoms in me that concern you? Oh, who are *you* to tell me I have symptoms? Don't lecture me, Sol. I don't have any symptoms." I gesture toward Loot. "This one's got symptoms."

"I'm sorry," Sol says. "I didn't mean to make you defensive."

"People get defensive when they're attacked. If you're really a doctor, you should know that. And why do you sound so old, anyway? You don't look forty. But you sure sound it."

He looks at me, deadpan. His features reveal nothing.

The bottle picker reaches for his leaking sack of glass and drags it to his side, opens it, and peers inside.

"What's with his bottles?" I ask. "And I think he lives around here, I hear him in the scrubs."

"The grocer gives him a deposit for the bottles—the island reuses the glass. It's an arrangement we made with the store. Keeps him busy."

"I don't get it," I say. "Why does he live in the woods?"

I look toward the dark brush; small round birch leaves flicker in the wind like silver coins under the low, smoky sky.

"He's not the hottest mixer in town."

"No, really? Why does he want to read my palm?"

"Let's go back to you for a minute," says Sol.

Loot interrupts and repeats to Sol, parrotlike. "Back to you, Ace. Back to you."

"What about all his words and sounds? I don't get it. This senseless spate of *ack, beer, Freddie, Johnnie*—I can't remember them all, he says them so fast. And what's a bivvy? He says I have a swell one."

"Your tent."

"He makes theses sounds, like dah-dah-dah-dit—it sounds like Morse code."

"It is Morse code."

"Oh. What's a funk hole?"

"Those were excavated openings on the front walls of trenches where soldiers could rest when they weren't on duty."

Crickets whir in the grasses as I close my eyes against the dark and listen to the roar of waves. How could this not have crystallized sooner? Trenches. The war. He went crazy in the war. *Loot*, and suddenly it dawns on me. "He was a lieutenant," I say.

"Shell-shock," says Sol, lighting up a cigarette that glows orange at the tip. "An acute neurasthenic condition from shells and bombs exploding too close. The human brain can't handle the impact."

"Just because you answer questions like a doctor—an *old* doctor—doesn't mean you are one."

"Would you like to see my papers?"

"Why do you care what I think of you?"

"Good question," he says. "Why are you so suspicious of me?"

"I don't like unsolicited advice, not to mention unsolicited *diagnosis*—I wasn't asking for anything. Thanks to you, my control over my symptoms isn't working since the saloon."

He lifts an eyebrow. "I'm sorry? Your *what*?"

"Besides," I say, dismissing his challenge. "Even if you do have papers, you botched up a job, which negates them."

"I beg your pardon?"

"Someone died because you went into surgery after you'd been drinking, or doping up on coke."

"What are you talking about? Where on earth did you hear that? Not the albino reporter, I trust. Now there's a piece of work. She's down at the WOM every second day with a new story about someone. And while you probably don't want to hear this—she has attempted to have you pulled out of the race twice since you've been here."

"What! Bea? She wouldn't do that."

"She is attempting to get the women contestants disqualified from the race so that she will have a better chance at the female purse. She sees you as a threat."

"What! What did she say?"

"At first she said you weren't following the rules—refusing to grease up, trouble-hunting, and what have you. Today she came to us having heard about the trainer you socked in the nose, and said that you were off the track, in no psychological shape to swim a channel."

"I don't believe you."

"Well. After the incident, there was discussion amongst the committee as to whether or not you should be pulled from the race, but I insisted we let it slide," he says and takes a drag from his smoke and exhales. "You're welcome."

"I don't believe you."

"She calls you *the hermit*," he says.

"What?"

"Perhaps you might consider that I *am* who I say I am."

"Nobody is who they say they are."

I feel as though I am going to throw up.

"Get me on this," I say. "That drippy half-pint had it coming. He didn't think I knew the definition of the word *revolting*. He spoke to me as though I were some sort of idiot."

"I see," says Sol. In the dark I can perceive his warm, sweater-layered torso leaning back against a boulder—his hair curling out from the sides of his cap. "Perhaps it wouldn't have bothered you so much if you truly believed that what he was saying was ridiculous."

"What is that supposed to mean? That I got in a lather because I think I might be an idiot? He's taking forty per cent of Geo Young's prize if he wins. He's a scummy old drip who hates women."

"Hm," he says.

I regress to questions about him. "I was told the locals don't know why you came here."

"A lot of the locals think there must have been some sort of personal failure for me to have come and decided to stay here. Apparently city folk only stick around when they're trying to escape."

"You're telling me you didn't come here to get away from something?"

He stands there, quiet for a moment.

"I came here for the fishing. Best in the world."

"Yeah. *Sure.*" Returning to the Lieutenant: "Why does he always want to read my palm?" I ask, again, attempting to shake my mind of Bea's betrayal. "He keeps saying I forgot something—he chants this riddle about red and grey, and I don't know why he keeps saying it."

"Maybe he's trying to tell you something."

"I thought he went mad in the trenches."

"Doesn't mean he isn't trying to tell you something—some people see things."

"Oh," I say. "Some people see things? Some people *see* things?

Don't tell me he *reads* people. Doctors aren't supposed to believe in that stuff."

He shrugs.

"What's a *goggle-eyed booger with the tit*? He said that to me the first time he came to my camp and I nearly knocked him clear off the cliff."

"It's a British gas helmet. The wearer had to breathe in through the nose from inside the helmet and breathe out through a valve held in the teeth."

Loot starts laughing, whispering surreptitiously to an invisible person beside him.

I sigh. "Does he see people that aren't here?"

"Yes," says Sol, flicking ashes away from the wind. "NYD."

"What does that mean?"

"Not yet diagnosed," he says.

"How do you know all of this about him?"

"Savanna, listen. I understand you're set that I not be the one to navigate your course. And, believe me—it's no skin off my back to take the day off, you understand—this event is one monkey short of a circus as far as I'm concerned. But you're in a jam, and I wouldn't want to see you have come all this way for nothing."

The wind picks up and roars through the trees, branches rub up against one another, creaking, and palm leaves click and rattle like bones. It isn't *his* problem I'm in a jam.

The hill of camps is a fire-flecked haze. "What?" I ask. "Like some sort of charity?"

Freud says biology is destiny. I freeze momentarily when I realize I sound exactly like my father.

"Not charity. I'm the last boat available for you. You can't swim without an observer. You know that."

"You didn't answer me when I asked you how you knew all that stuff about the lieutenant."

"Are you going to accept my offer or not?"

Loot perks up again. "Ack Emma!" he says and points to the harbour. The whippet reappears at the edge of the bluff.

"Why does he point to the harbour like that? He was doing it earlier."

"He's associated the harbour with me because I live down there on my boat, *Emma*."

I look at the harbour and think of Bea. "How could she do that to me?" I say under my breath.

"If you still don't believe me, think about it. How much did she actually have to drink the night she was getting you ginned?"

"It was her idea to get more booze at the saloon."

"Sure. But did she actually *drink* any?"

I look at Loot, who is flattening out the dirt beside the fire pit with his white hands. "Tell me why you defended me against the committee."

"Don't take this the wrong way," he says, dropping the end of his cigarette to the earth and rubbing it out with the bottom of his shoe. "But you seem so sort of alone out here. And your shell is as hard as a rock."

I empty my lungs of air. Loot is carving SOS into the flattened dirt beside the fire with a broken piece of glass, and I can barely hear his croaky whisper: *You forgot it.*

FOURTEEN

I OVERHEARD in the dressing room at the tank that one in four college girls "had experience." We all knew what it meant—and it could leave a mark if it happened too early. I also knew that there was nothing stupid or *blaah* about whirls any more. Tad crashed an A in geography.

The swim was fast approaching. Maizee and Bobo were spending as much time together as I spent with Tad—but the four of us seldom went out. They went to Broadway shows and shared meals while Tad and I always seemed to be within a hundred yards of the garden house. Maizee was different about Bobo than she had been with her earlier trysts; she referred to her past affairs as *juvenilia*.

I had never seen Maizee so relaxed and content; her mother was granting her more freedom to design gowns that were selling in department stores. Her superstitious tendencies seemed to be dissipating—no more did she hold her breath when walking past the cemeteries at risk of breathing in the spirit of someone who had recently died, nor did she avoid the laburnum trees along Gisby Street. She still picked up pennies and knocked on wood, but never made the sign of the fig any more or rescheduled her manicures to avoid Fridays. She said it had all become too paralyzing. She officially quit the tank, which by this time surprised nobody. In between Tad and the tank, I ran from table to table in the bake house, cradling dishes in my arms, cleaning ashtrays, washing counters, and baking trays of rolls: finger rolls, shell rolls, ring rolls, plume rolls—you name it.

The only friends that Tad had introduced me to, save Bobo, were his birds. He kept them in a spacious cage in a bright room inside the garden house. When I was first acquainted with the garden house and bird sanctuary, a certain miniature parrot naturally fluttered onto Tad's shoulder and nuzzled into his neck. "These guys are called pocket parrots. This one is an anomaly though," he said, while the bird rubbed its metallic-blue crown on his chin. "They're not usually this affectionate—they're supposed to be mischievous little rascals." The bird was beautiful, its tail glimmered with iridescent feathers, and it didn't seem to be going anywhere. He showed me his lutino cockatiels with their spiky head feathers and his peach-faced lovebirds. The lovebirds were the most striking, emerald-green with bright red faces. "You're awful quiet today," said Tad to the fattest-looking lovebird. "What's eating you?"

The red-faced bird looked at me sideways and said, "What's eating you?"

I laughed out loud, and Tad was delighted. Again the bird repeated it, "What's eating you?" which made us laugh again, louder, and finally it squawked: "Don't take any wooden nickels!"

Having met up with Tad after swimming one evening, and having inadvertently fallen asleep, I was jarred awake by the clamour of a trash-collecting truck on the street outside. I could hear the chatter of birds and a distant car engine snarling, and I jumped from the bed. "What time is it?" I shook him. He came to, goaded by my shoves, and rubbed his face.

"For God's sake," he said, bothered and unsmiling. "What's on fire?" He reached for his wristwatch on the bedside table. "It's only nine."

"Damn!" I said and whipped on my cotton dress and sandals,

moving swiftly around the room to gather up my clothes, dashing in and out of the washroom. I was a week away from the twenty-mile training swim from lower Manhattan to Sandy Hook.

"I missed half my training—Higgins is going to *kill* me—and if he keeps me late I'll miss pie prep at the bake house."

"Pie prep?" He looked at me blearily from the bed. "What's that?"

"Pies always sell out on the weekends. We have to make a surplus on Fridays," I said and moved toward him to say goodbye, but his affection was pat. He had turned mercurial on me, and it caught me off guard. His exquisite eyes were frigid. I paused.

"I'm sorry," I said. "I didn't mean to wake you."

He softened and brought a hand out from under the summer quilt to touch my face.

"I'll talk to you later," he said quietly and rested his head back down onto his feather-stuffed pillow. "I'll ring you tonight."

I had no choice but to rummage in my satchel for a nickel and flag a jitney to get myself to the tank, where I threw myself out of the back seat of the cab and ran into the tank facility, up the crumbling staircase, through the main glass doors, down the hallway, and skidded to a halt outside Higgins's office.

He was not there. I looked both ways down the hall, breathless, expecting him to materialize from around a corner—but only warm, humid air drifted in from the tank. I checked the clock on the foyer wall—he was always at his office between nine and twelve, but I couldn't find him anywhere in the building, and not knowing what else to do, I walked anxiously to the bake house to make pies. The summer humidity was close and thickening as I walked passed walls of brick row homes, wrought-iron balconies, and through flocks of warbling pigeons. Moisture was already beading along my forehead. There were people sitting on their front steps, smoking, watching.

My father gave me a sidelong glance as I crossed the parlour where customers were gathered with their biscuits and squinting blearily at their coffee. He was stationed at the long wooden table in the centre of the kitchen. The kitchen was misted over with flour. I took my apron from its metal hook and tied it around my waist. He watched me with uncharacteristic interest, and didn't even turn around when rhubarb started boiling over on the stove.

My mother was in the backroom where we kept large burlap sacks of flour and sugar; she was completing the weekend inventory—I could see her shadow projected on the wall.

"What are you looking at?" I said to my father, flippant. "I'm not late."

I walked across the kitchen, turned off the gas-heated element, and moved the pot of rhubarb to a cooling shelf. He was still looking at me.

"What are you looking at me that way for?"

He cleared his throat. "Have you seen Higgins this morning?"

"No. I got there late and couldn't find him anywhere. Why?"

"Oh," he said. "I see."

"Why? Is he all right?" I asked.

"Oh," he said again. "Yes. He came here looking for you earlier this morning when you did not show up—I knocked for you upstairs but figured you were on your way to the tank."

I could feel heat radiating from the pot of molten rhubarb I had just placed on the cooling shelf beside me. "Well. Why did he stop in?"

I watched my mother's shadow projected on the wall outside the storage room where she was doing the inventory. I could see that she had stopped her work and was listening to the talk I was having with my father. While she had always stayed out of everything to a ludicrous degree, I still thought it strange that she was hiding in the backroom. The smell of boiled rhubarb wrapped the three of us in a sweet, suffocating tent.

"I—ah—gather you haven't seen the headlines," my father said.

"Headlines? What headlines?"

He released a gold-medal sigh. "I'm not sure what's worse," he said. "You not having heard the news on your own or my having to tell you." His tone was eerily soft, sending spikes of panic through my bones.

He reached for the *New York Times* that was rolled and stationed at the end of the long wooden table. He handed it to me, and I opened the newsprint, spread the paper out. I had to close my eyes and read the large bold headline twice through, blinking:

Britain and America Thrilled by Great
Achievement of New York Girl Swimmer.
Channel Exploit Thrills the City.

Something inside me rolled over. I knew my mouth was open, and colour must have drained rapidly from my face; I looked at my father, who was staring at a large slab of sourdough. The article started on the front page, and there was a series of photos:

Gertrude Ederle, the first woman swimmer to vanquish the English Channel, has all the qualities that go to make up the kind of heroine whom America will ungrudgingly and freely worship and honor for her splendid accomplishment. The record of her 19 years shows her to be courageous, determined, modest, sportsmanlike, generous, unaffected and perfectly poised. She has, in addition, beauty of face and figure and the abounding health that is the natural result of the normal life she has led of her own volition.

My blood raced and my ears were on fire, but I forced myself to read the rest of the spread. Her official time of fourteen hours and thirty-one minutes was more than two hours faster than any man before her. The article dragged on about her glorious past achievements, her gold and bronze medals in Paris, her hearty German bloodlines, and how she quit school in the tenth grade to focus more on her training. Apparently, throughout her crossing, her father had been coaxing her with a new convertible fliv if she should finish. She ate candy bars fed to her by her coach. "I knew I could do it," she was quoted as saying after the swim. "I knew I would, and I did. All the women in the world will celebrate."

"What?!" I shouted, having seen enough, and I threw the newspaper back across the flour-coated table. Time froze. My father stood motionless, still staring at the slab of dough on the table, and my mother's shadow was unmoving on the wall.

The back door opened and Higgins walked into the kitchen, charging the room with movement again. I could see the relief in my father's face upon his arrival, and my mother poked her head out from the backroom, looking anxious.

"Impossible!" I shouted at everyone. A small group of customers, drawn by the drama, began to line up for biscuits at the front counter where they could better survey the standoff. But Higgins was alive to the issue and ushered me out the back door to the small veranda where no customers were loitering.

"Where were you this morning?" I was shouting. "I was there just after nine!"

"Where were *you?*"

"Laswell said she wouldn't get funding. *You* said she wouldn't get funding—and even if she did get funding, she wasn't leaving until the middle of September!" I searched his face for answers.

He was trying to have me sit down on one of the benches back there, but I couldn't sit—I paced around the veranda, breathing quickly and shouting at him.

"Savi!" he said firmly. "I just got off the phone with Peter Laswell."

I continued to pace, opening and closing my fists. My imagination soared with what this could mean.

"Calm down!" He forced me to sit on the bench with him. "Breathe—in—out, deeply—there—you need to calm down. You follow? Calm down."

I sat with my arms crossed and tried to control my breathing. "I'm doing it anyway," I said. "I don't care if she's done it first—I'm swimming the Channel. Faster than she did. This is impossible!"

I was waiting for him to say *that's the stuff*, but when no reassurances came, I slammed my fist on the bench. "Did you not hear me? I said I'm going ahead with it anyway!"

His big, round eyes were quiet, and he dropped his head into his hand.

"What?" I asked him.

He stared blankly at his hand. "There is no funding."

"What?"

"You recall the contract we signed. Your funding was endorsed on the assumption that a girl had not yet succeeded—now it has been done. You know they never want to back the same thing as their neighbour. There were conditions, and the condition in your case was that the swim had not yet been successful for any girl."

I stared at him.

"There was nothing devious in that clause," Higgins kept on. "We had no reason to believe Ederle would be in Europe before us—never mind succeed."

"Are you joking? Sure we had reason to be concerned! Was I the only one who saw it? For God's sakes! It was the WSA, right? Her sponsor?"

"Actually they were not her sponsors. As it happened, two newspaper publishers funded her in exchange for the exclusive rights to her story."

"Which ones?"

"The *Chicago Tribune* and the *New York Daily News*."

"The *New York Daily News*? The *New York Daily* News? How could we not have heard about this? Tell me—how is that possible?"

He paused. "I gather they kept it quiet. Save face if she didn't make it."

"Impossible!"

"I'm sorry," he said, looking morbid. "I'm so sorry." He pressed his hand to his chest, and I couldn't bear to look him in the face. "I trust you believe that."

For a while I fixated on the timepiece that Higgins pulled from his pocket and had rested in his hand. The time ticked smoothly, precisely, around the watch face. It was from Switzerland. He had told me this in one of our meetings. It had been given to him at the Antwerp Games. It was a TAG Heuer. I had rarely seen him without it.

I buried my face into my palms and could feel Higgins's hand on my shoulder.

"Can't we do *anything?*" My breathing had become erratic again.

"I'm afraid there is nothing we can do. It's been done." His hand clamped around my shoulder, punctuating his words: "Remember what Elmer Davis said about rich men ruling the world—this is not your failing, it's one of life's blows. If it makes you feel any better—which I'm sure it won't—by accepting the sponsorship from the syndicate, Ederle had to forfeit her amateur status."

"Big *deal*," I sobbed.

"It means she will not be competing in Amsterdam." His hand was still rested on my shoulder. "Perhaps you might return to your hundred-metre event, focus on the next Games. You'll bounce back, Savi," said Higgins. "You're a rubber ball."

You can't down the spuzzard; he is elastic, and bounces up after every failure. Charged with humiliation and fury, I walked downtown, through the dark corridor streets in between skyscrapers, to Laswell's tower where I knew he kept his investment office. I took the elevator to the ninth floor, glaring at the lift man, who stood there and looked at the floor until the cables snagged and the elevator jarred to a stop.

He slid the wrought-iron door open for my exit and did not eyeball me for a tip.

I had never seen this floor because we had always met at the bistro. The hall where I stood was spacious. To my right, I saw a glass door with an elegant sign that said *Laswell and Associates*; I moved toward the door, opened it, and proceeded to follow a hallway, which took me to a reception desk. A big blonde receptionist looked up from her desk and gave me a very obvious once-over.

"Can I help you?" she asked suspiciously, as though I had clearly taken a wrong turn somewhere down Broadway.

"I have a meeting with Mr. Peter Laswell," I said.

She pulled a leather-bound appointment book from a shelf on her desk and began to peruse the day's engagements. "Name?"

"Savanna Mason."

She crinkled the sides of her eyes as she scanned the page. "I don't see your name here."

"I must speak with Peter Laswell at once," I said impatiently. "It is urgent. Would you please tell him I am here for our meeting."

The receptionist rose to her feet and disappeared around a corner to my right without saying anything. From around a corner on my left, a man appeared and was walking toward the reception desk staring at a document. "Good morning, Mr. Bobrosky," I said without enthusiasm. His eyes leapt from the document, noting the absence of the typist and the presence of me.

"Miss *Mason*," he said. "We spoke with Clem this morning."

"Yes."

From the right, the annoyed typist now stood in the corridor. "Miss, Mr. Laswell will see you." I followed her down the hallway to a windowed corner office that overlooked Manhattan; Bobrosky was on my heels. Laswell stood behind a large mahogany desk, and Bobrosky moved to stand beside Laswell. "I imagine you have seen the bannerlines," said Laswell sadly. "Looks as though she was one step ahead of us."

"Three weeks ahead of us, Mr. Laswell. I would like to swim the English Channel anyway, even though I will not be the first—I *will* be the fastest."

He peered at me, brow furrowed. "Now, why on earth would you want to swim the Channel now? The story's had the biscuit, I'm afraid."

Had the biscuit, I thought ironically.

He slanted his head in bewilderment, estimating, looking at me as though I were a complete idiot, which was exactly how I felt. "There isn't the same punch and originality in a second swim."

His walls were plastered with certificates and various credentials, photos of motorcycles and racehorses and boats. This was the calmest I had ever seen him, my patronizing patron, fingertips stuck to his desk, unmoving—eerily still and unflappable.

"Here is the way it will go," he said. "The Ederle swim will be the big wave for a few weeks, the city will make merry over it, and then swimming will be replaced by a new mountain to climb, a new dance, or a bunion derby—ocean swimming will not be a new thrill. You understand?"

His eyes lit up and glimmered as though he were remembering a fine sunset. My heart leapt from its socket at the faint, pulsing thought that he had struck a new idea—a new idea that made my swimming the Channel interesting again. "There's talk of a nonstop trans-Atlantic flight taking shape for the spring," he said, zeal returning to his voice. "The Jims heard a fly boy letting the cat out of the bag. Now *that* is what people will want to hear about. I am sorry for the flop, Miss Mason. Truly."

"The Jims?" I hissed. "Your snooping Jims must be a couple of bozos if they didn't have a pulse on Ederle."

Laswell was openly taken aback. "I hope you realize that this unexpected appearance of yours is terribly uncouth. I'm rather disappointed; I expected more diplomacy from you, Miss Mason. I thought you were a finer sport. Robert and I explained the agreement to Clem this morning. He was to review it with you."

Bobrosky looked uneasy.

"He did," I said.

"Why are you here, then, making a hash out of this, if you have already been told there is nothing we can offer you?"

"Because I want to stay true to my swim. It's been months of preparation. And I thought if I were to swim the Channel faster than Ederle, maybe while the story is still hot, that you would still be interested."

"That reminds me," he said. "I gather there's already a second swim about to launch any day now. A *Mrs Gade Corson* is gunning to be the first mother to cross it."

"The first *what*?" I was horrified.

In his eyes I saw the flat absence of emotion that I had seen in Tad that morning, and I began to feel my lips tremble with miniature, involuntary convulsions of anguish.

"Oh," said Laswell, hardening his face. "I absolutely cannot have you regressing to a six-year-old in my office. This is not something to cry about—you understand?"

For a moment he seemed suddenly and mysteriously reproachful with himself. "Once again," he said finally, "I do not want to squelch your hopes, Miss Mason. You'll find something else to chase after. I'm sure you will. I have a sixth sense when it comes to reading these matters."

Read this, Windbag, I wanted to spit. But I was frozen in place, shaking and chilled. My hands and feet felt numb. "This is a busy office, Miss Mason. You must adjust to the changed circumstances, put a new face on the matter, and carry on. There is nothing left to discuss."

Laswell nodded at Bobrosky, who had been standing, silent with his hands behind his back. "Bob, will you see that Miss Mason finds the door?"

I was being streeted. I stared at them, strangely dissociated, nauseated and tingling. I was unable to respond.

"Those of us in the bond business are accustomed to how quickly the best-laid plans can fall apart. You win some, you lose some—a person ought to always have as many irons in the fire as possible."

I turned to follow Bobrosky out, but as I was about to pass through the doorway's threshold, Peter Laswell added, "And Savanna. Best not to come around the garden house any more."

I thought of Tad's icy mitt that morning. And it was only then that I looked down and saw that I was still wearing my apron.

On the same veranda where I had been sitting with Higgins that morning, I crushed cardboard boxes by stomping on them with the military heels of my unfastened ammo boots. The boxes always had to be flattened before being carried out to the trash. I piled the beat-down cardboard neatly beside the door and wiped flour from my face with the back of my hand. My task was accomplished all too quickly and I went into the bake house, making a beeline for the cold room. I could feel my father's eyes on me.

"Savi," he said quietly.

I stopped short in front of the refrigerated room.

"I tried to warn you."

I didn't answer him. We stood quietly in the flour-covered kitchen.

"Michael is coming home," he said. "They're staying at the house. A family supper will be in order—two or three weeks from now."

"*They?*"

"I understand he's met a girl. He wants us to meet her. Her name is Ida."

I looked at my hands. "Yeah?" I said. "*Terrific.*"

My father sighed.

I picked dried bits of dough from my arm hairs.

In my disordered flat, I leaned back in one of the big, old armchairs. The heels of my hands were sore from the day's kneading and pressing of dough. Dusk was settling in like a swollen bruise outside the open window. A poisonous spell of heat had possessed the day, and even at night the air hung hot and thick in the room.

Even though there had been a passing roil toward hysterics at Laswell's office earlier in the day, I had successfully swallowed the wad of emotional sick down into my insides. And now that I was alone I wanted to crack the wad, release it, but it was stuck. Outside the open window, engines roared and sputtered fumes, a siren wailed. I could hear the steps and voices of people walking, filling the street, setting off a contest of horns; taxis, jitneys, and flivs were at a noisy standstill outside. I covered my ears with my hands.

River smells blew in from the Hudson docks and tobacco smoke rose up from the alley. I still had not heard from Tad. I kept the little pearl he had given me in a small dish beside the bed. It glinted under my lamp. I couldn't move. I stared out the window, numb and very still. Twilight soaked up the remaining light like a giant, sleepy eclipse. There was a cigarette box in between the cushions of the armchair, a box Maizee had left there by accident many moons before. I lit a cigarette and, in my underwear, stared at the sky well into the small hours as I pretended to inhale the smoke.

FIFTEEN

TWO DAYS until the race, and the island hotels are full of tourists. I wonder if the invisible people that the Lieutenant talks to are spirits; Maizee used to say that Indians shot arrows into the air to drive evil spirits away. I think about the Pimugnan Indians who first settled here in camps, maybe like this one. The island feels charged—magnetic forces of tides shifting and surging in the silent death underneath the ocean. Bea must know that I am aware of her betrayal, because she hasn't come around at all—and when I went to her camp to wring her skinny little neck she wasn't there. Riled surf washes up the shore below my camp; wind shakes in the trees, and what is left of my fire turns to smoke—the wind is extinguishing most of the fires on the hill. The moon is a sliver short of full, and I know I should be sleeping, but in a fit of insomnia I descend down the sandy path, slink past the dark campsites on the hill, and walk toward the main street of town. Once there, I pace up and down the boardwalk with my arms crossed. There's a man leaning against the general store, smoking a cigarette, and my heart slumps in its socket when I see that it isn't Sol. But I am not looking for Sol. Of course not. What would I be seeking him out for at this hour? My insides are unspooling—all these stupid pieces of memory and betrayal all out of sequence—I hate that feeling, that wobbling loss of control—hate it. I continue to pace the length of the main drag, attempting to put my thoughts in order. A few late-night stragglers wander toward the casino, ducking their heads against the wind and holding on to their lids. Waves crash against cliffs in the distance, and there is no faint sway of music anywhere, no barking sea lions; the roar of wind feels ominous. I sit for a while on the boardwalk, leaning on a post as though it were holding me up. Balls of parched, uprooted sage roll by.

Head down in the wind, I am walking again, along the path that leads to the harbour glowing with mast lights. My shoes hit sodden wood when I arrive at the labyrinth of docks; the wharf is filled with the sound of creaking planks, and water laps against bobbing hulls. Rigging jangles, halyards clang, and boats lean in the seaside wind. A nearby vessel revs its engine, coughs out fumes, and the silty smell of diesel weighs the air. I walk the planks of wood searching for his boat, and I find it—*Ack Emma*—moored away from the clumped middle section of the harbour; the vessel is a boxy fishing boat. Hanging from log poles, tackle sways, and attached to the stern, a dinghy floats in the dark water, clinging to the hull of the boat like an aquatic burr.

He is awake, lantern throwing light on the cabin table where he is seated, studying a tidal chart. There is something about the way he looks up at me that makes me ache. He stands there with surprise, hatless in his pyjama pants and rumpled sweater, hair tousled in all directions. Wind cuffs the side of our faces; the wharf creaks; water sloshes. "Uh," he says. "Are you all right?"

"I didn't plan on coming here," I say, and a strong push of wind rattles the harbour again. "I don't know. I just don't know. What I'm doing. My mind is reeling."

He peers at me in the dark.

"I would be losing sleep too if I didn't have a navigator yet."

"Yeah," I say. "About that."

I am unable to maintain eye contact with him and look at his dog instead.

"I will still do it," he says. "I told you I would." He folds the tidal chart into a square.

The whippet is fast asleep on deck, curled into a gleaming sphere. When he hears us, he looks up, ears like little radio locators, and unalarmed goes back to sleep.

"Where did the dog come from?"

He tells me it came from the city, that he had gone to see a dog race overtown—island-speak for the mainland—and not only was this one not winning, it had fallen asleep at the gates and when the starter's gun woke him up, he chased his own tail. Sol caught wind that they were going to shoot him and decided to take him home.

There is an oil lantern at the stern and another at the bow; the light drips a warm luminescence onto the cabin top. "Listen," he says. "Do you want some tea or something? You look a little wrung out." He reaches an outstretched hand to help me over the gunwale on board. The boat shivers. We stand on deck, and I adjust my foothold to the new sway of water underneath me. A gale-force wind pushes against the boats and the island.

"Here." Sol unhinges the little screen entrance, pushes open the wooden hatch, and disappears into the doorway's shadow. A rich glow burnishes the cabin quarters below. He pokes his head out from the meem. "It's warmer down here, out of the wind." His dusky face is not entirely at ease, but his tone seems comfortable. I count the rungs from deck to quarters as I climb down and settle onto a bunk that has been folded divanlike into a long, upholstered seat. The modest cabin is full of mannish paraphernalia—fishing books, clay pipes, and clothing all neatly kept in designated spaces. All the mantles have small lacquered railings so nothing gets tossed about in rough seas; lanterns throw a gleam onto the wood. I pleat my legs underneath me.

In his hand he holds a tea caddy full of dried leaves. He fills a kettle with water from a jug and puts it on the gas stove. I have grown perpetually aware of the smarting pain under my arms where my suit has chafed. I cross an arm transversely across my chest to press the flat of my hand against one of my sides.

"Suit burns?" he asks me.

"The wool scratches the skin off," I say. "Somehow it's worse in the ocean. The chafes weren't so bad in the tank."

"Yeah. We've had to bandage up quite a few armpits over the past couple weeks. Do you want me to have a look?"

"No, thank you. That's all right."

He pulls a box of miscellaneous objects from a shelf and rifles through it, finds what he is looking for, and turns around, holding a roll of white gauze.

"The race is two days away, and it only takes a moment to treat the skin—to help it heal faster." He places the gauze and a second roll of medical tape on the saloon table between us and reaches for a plant on another ledge. He has to manoeuvre his hand around thin wooden guardrails to free the little plant before he sits down beside me on the upholstered bench.

"Aloe," he says and holds up a second container, "and zinc oxide for the broken skin."

"I can apply the medicine myself," I say, and when I pull off my wrap, my muscles are twitching.

"Do you still believe I'm an imposter?"

"No," I say.

"I was an attendant in the war. That's why Wrigley solicited me to watch over the swimmers and help out at the beach."

I scan the mannish paraphernalia for relics of his experience in the war—dog tags, medals, pins, anything—but not a single telling item reveals itself.

"Is it because of the war that you know so much about the Lieutenant?"

He gets up and stands beside the kettle, turns up the gas stove, and leans against smooth wood. "How about you let me fix up your skin? It's an awkward angle to get at yourself."

With a resigned sigh, I lift one arm and with the opposite hand delicately pull my sleeveless jersey down to reveal a line of red welts along my rib cage. "You see what I mean?" Another push of wind-storm rattles the boat.

He sits beside me again to examine the damage. "Oy," he says, "that doesn't look good." He inspects the affected skin. "Looks inflamed but clean—you're lucky the salt water has been keeping it clean."

"And the booze from the saloon."

"Oh," he says, a little startled, "how resourceful."

The jersey I am wearing has been stretched out over time and the armholes are too big. He brings a thick branch of aloe vera toward my wounds; I can tell he sees where my skin gets whiter toward my breast, and he looks quickly back to my shoulder. My eyes rove around the cabin, orbiting to the lantern, plaid curtains, bookshelf, miniature sink, mugs, hissing kettle, and telescope.

Maizee always wanted a telescope. At the peak of her fascination with star alignment and how it could potentially influence her life, she researched astrological signs and their corresponding planets, and she told me my planet was Saturn. "I'm not going to lie to you, Savi," she said. "Saturn is the planet of cold rationality." And quoting from a cheap drug-store magazine, she said, "You're a defensive lover and sullenly obstinate, moosoo. Your sign is often too hard-boiled to make a good partner."

She told me there were eight moons that moved around Saturn, and that it was the second-biggest moon, Rhea, that had the most planetary influence. Of course *she* was a Libra, and *Libras* were ruled by Venus—the planet of love, beauty, and social grace.

"How come you don't want to tell me how you know all that stuff about the Lieutenant?" I ask Sol, seeing no war mementos amidst the shelves or hanging from hooks. "Were you in the war together?"

His steady hands touch my skin. He squeezes the aloe stem; its juices brim out of the green spear and he covers the swollen area with a thick film of the plant's medicinal jelly. He seals it with a layer of sticky zinc. Last, he applies a square of gauze and tapes it down. "I don't like to talk about the war," he says softly. "If you don't mind."

The kettle starts to scream, and it seems like all one movement as he gets up, removes the shrieking boiler, and shuts off the gas. I watch him pour hot water and settle two mugs onto the saloon table. The tea steeps; the wind seems to have temporarily calmed. He sits back down beside me, and I twist my torso so he can doctor the other side. He smells minty, like tooth powder. After applying both the plant gel and thick white cream to the broken skin, he tapes another large square of gauze to my side. I slacken my arms and rest elbows on knees.

"Those welts are very swollen," he says without looking at me. "They could get infected. You should tend to them three times a day over the next few days. I can do it—or you can have the dressings changed at the WOM. Do be sure to have the dressing changed."

"There," I say, "just then—you sounded old again."

"I did?"

I assume a paternal tone. "Do be sure to have the dressings changed."

He surprises me by laughing at himself. "Ah."

"The man I hit," I say. "He said it's revolting that the women contestants are considering swimming the race with axle grease in place of a suit. There's been a lot of nasty talk. The Temperance Union is raging; they're calling Charlotte Moore Schoemmel a vulgarian. What do you think? Is the idea really so reechy?"

"Well," he pauses. "Naturally, a sporting event ought to uphold its guidelines. And while wearing a swimsuit may not have been explicit in the contract—one would think that it goes without saying."

"Some of the women say the grease will be just as modest—*more* modest, in fact, than wearing a suit. They say the grease is thick and dark enough. Do you think it would wash off?"

His cautious expression seems to soften. "I don't know what

to say," he says. The sides of his mouth curl into a peculiar smile. "Except, well—new territory."

"*Terra incognita*," I say.

He takes up his tea. "So, she pours booze on her wounds and knows a little Latin," he says. "Huh."

I reach for the steaming mug and bring it to my face. "I'm not sure what to do. My welts are worse every time I go for a training swim. You said yourself they look bad. That's from swimming only a few hours a day. The channel will be more than ten hours long." I pause to sip. "Besides, I can't get disqualified—the mainland city council threw out the union's protest. *Nude Swim Okayed*—I saw it in the papers."

The mug is too hot and I have to put it back down on the table. The wind gathers force again, throwing lanyards, tackle, and ropes into another fit of racket.

"Tell me," he says, leaning back against the upholstered folded bunk. "How did you hear about this? What made you travel all the way from New York for a gum-sponsored sea derby?"

"That's a long story."

"If you have nothing better to do," he says. "I'd love to hear it."

"You'd *love* to hear it, would you?"

"I would."

"A four-finger gin would be swell."

He pushes the mug across the saloon table closer to me. "Have more tea." I lean back against the bench and begin with Michael and his beating it overseas, Trudy Ederle and the Olympic Trials with Maizee; I tell him about the bake house and my flat upstairs; about my one-armed coach and our plans for my swim across the Sleeve, about my Greenback and the silk-stocking affairs. I decide against telling him about Tad and the garden house. "A few weeks after everything fell to pieces, Trudy was welcomed home by the most ostentatious parade in the history of mankind. I felt like I was socked in the stomach."

I stop talking and stare at the mug of cooled tea in front of me.

"Fresh tea?" He's already reheated some water and steeped a new batch; he tosses the old tea into the miniature sink and gives me a fresh brew. "Go on," he says.

I tell him about the stomach-turning parade. "A few weeks later I had to have dinner with Michael and his fiancée, Ida. Michael had been away for years and he didn't know anything about anything when we sat down at the table. If it hadn't been for Ida," I say. "I don't think I would be here at all."

That supper with Ida had been an agony. I lapsed into stony silence while Michael told colourful stories about living in Paris; about the odd jobs he had acquired—clerking at a popular bookstore on the Left Bank and baking croissants in the south of France. Of course I was happy to see my brother; it had been a long time. But old jealousies loomed and his timing astounded me.

Ida, his *sweetpea*, sat across from me at the table. She was stunning in her blue dress trimmed with black braided satin; she had the features that one would expect to find in Maizee's European *Vogue* mags: nice cheekbones, wide eyes, and that genteel, elegant quality that you're either born with or you're not. Immediately, I didn't like her.

Our parents had taken out the good silver and old, fragile china; the linen was curiously spotless. I watched Ida cautiously—the way she moved, ate, spoke. Words flowed from her; she had that way with delivery, that gift for sounding clear and interesting no matter how dull the dialogue. She used her hands when she spoke—her fingers moved gingerly with her words. Palms up, down, side to side; the cadence of her talk moved in time with her hands that opened and closed like delicate butterfly wings. And Michael had this smitten look on his face. He was always kissing her head; I had never seen him gush like that. It nauseated me.

"Say." Ida rendered a bright smile from across the table and settled her attentions onto me. "I hear you're a swimmer." My fork fell onto my plate and clattered. She smelled like lavender. I wanted a drink.

"Yeah," I said, shoving potato into my mouth. Michael leaned toward me, his hair combed and slicked back with water.

"Come on—tell us about the Olympic Trials, Savi," he prodded.

I swallowed my food and smoothed out the exceptionally plain black tulle I had decided to wear for the dinner. I had pulled my hair back like an equestrian and wore no paint. "Why? The Trials don't mean anything," I said, reaching for the wine. "Besides, that was ages ago, and you weren't even *there.*"

I poured myself wine and grasped my fork to keep eating, but Michael was quiet, which compelled me to go on. "You've missed the best train wreck of all time," I said. "But it appears our parents have not briefed you on that—qelle surprise."

I shoveled a forkload of food into my mouth without looking at anyone.

Ida watched me. I could feel it. I saw myself as unbearably gritty next to her—a colossal eyesore. "Savanna," she said, and her half-sleeve of bangles clanged against the side of the table. "Anyone who can make it to the Olympic Trials has clearly got talent. You should be very proud. Speaking of which—did everyone hear about that New York girl who just swam the Channel! How absolutely fantastic! It's been all over the radio. She must be about your age, Savi—only nineteen, can you believe it? Nineteen."

My parents sat there, frozen stiff.

"Hm," my father said.

"Oh, dear," my mother whispered. She looked at Michael. "We didn't get a chance to tell you."

Michael held out his glass. "Tell me what?"

His teeth were purple from the wine.

"You're supposed to hold your glass at the *stem*—not the bulb," I snapped.

"Red wine," he said, leaning back in his chair, "is a *warm* drink—you can hold it at the bulb." He sounded arrogant.

Even though it was *Ida* who had committed the big jip, I was furious with Michael. "Your teeth are black," I said. "Maybe you should clean them or something."

He rubbed a napkin over his teeth and turned affectionately back to Ida, baring them for her approval. Our parents asked them about France. Time passed, but their ignorance had me reeling, trapped in a tailspin of seething meditations. I grew increasingly drunk and could hardly recall the taste of the food that I had just finished inhaling. At some point Michael and Ida had pulled their chairs close together and they were holding each other's hands. Michael stroked her hair every once in a while, and when I started to listen again, the talk had been redirected to their engagement. Michael was raising his glass—again. Candles flickered. "We want to tie this knot as soon as possible," he said.

I fixated on their hands, intertwined in a ten-finger knot.

"I've been reading Oscar Wilde," I announced suddenly, tossing back what was left in my bulb.

Michael's eyes lit up. "You have?"

"I *have*," I said. "Would you care to hear my favorite quote?"

Everyone looked a little nervous, except for Michael, our literary night light radiant with gleeful expectancy.

"'Some bring joy wherever they go'," I said loudly.

"'Others—'" I looked directly at Ida. "'*Whenever* they go.'"

Everyone stared. I had successfully paralyzed the table, until Michael turned his head in a low swoop, and Ida looked at her lap.

"What in God's name has got into you?" he hissed. "You've been kicking me in the face all night. You leave Ida out of this, whatever *this* is, exactly."

I scraped the last of my potato from my plate noisily and reached for the bottle. I held it out to him. "*More* wine?"

I topped up his glass without looking at anyone. Then I

brought my dinner plate right up to my face and I licked it. I thought of Laswell's remark about regressing to a six-year-old and considered shattering the plate against the wall. I couldn't take it any more. My family was behaving as though absolutely nothing at all had transpired, as though the solar eclipse that had just slid over my entire life wasn't anything—and now my brother was marrying a beautiful, talented *lounge canary* that he met in effing *Monaco*. I had to leave the table. I slammed down my plate and fumbled with my napkin before pushing back my chair and storming clear out of the house.

My head was spinning, but all I wanted to do was swim. The outdoor tank was flat and still before me, and lights burned underwater. I stood on the edge swinging my arms from side to side. My skin tingled. I stood, breathing. Four lampposts cast a glow at each corner of the tank. I shook out my hands and stretched. Took a deep breath, and threw my arms into a starting plunge. The water covered my body, a cool film of bubbles slipping down my skin. There was nothing but the musical slosh of water in my ears, my breathing, my stroke, the turn at the wall—my simple song bag. I knew that I was swimming slower than I thought because I was canned. I could see my shadow projected on the tank wall when I turned my head to breathe, dusty light inside the water.

After what seemed like a while, I heard a voice, but I kept swimming. The voice persisted and it sounded an awful lot like my name being shouted. I brought my head fully above the water and saw Michael standing on the side of the tank, his body a dark silhouette against the lampposts. He covered his eyes with his hands.

"Savi! Put your clothes on this instant!"

I treaded water.

"I want to talk to you right now."

He peeked, but seeing that I was making no effort toward my clothing, he spun around in the other direction and planted his hands on his hips. "Put your clothes on!"

Just then another shadow emerged from the darkness surrounding the tank. The distinct outline of a woman. Ida, doubtless. She was carrying the magnum of champagne from the house; we hadn't got so far as to open it in celebration of their knot-tying intentions. She said something to Michael, but I couldn't hear what it was. I felt like an animal that people were trying to coax from a tree branch.

"Savi," she said, "mind if I join you?"

"Yes," I said.

Michael threw up his arms. "Have you fallen completely off the melon wagon?" he demanded, still facing the other way. I leaned my head back so that water spooled into my ears and their voices were obscured.

Ida started to remove her clothing.

"What are you *doing*?" Michael asked her. "She's having an *episode*."

They bantered back and forth, but I couldn't hear it. Michael took his English driving cap from his head to shield his eyes from my stark bareness.

She continued to undress. I saw a silky pink garment wrapped around her bust and laced on the sides. My head was high enough to hear their voices again. I heard Michael muttering, "Good Lord."

"Michael," Ida said. "Why don't we meet you at the house in a little while? It'll be all right. Leave the fliv, though, would you?"

I had hugely spoiled their announcement to my parents, not to mention the entire evening. A hot mix of outrage, liquor, and shame churned my insides where the wad was still sitting like a fist of clay.

Michael threw his head back and walked away into the darkness; Ida slipped out of her garments and into the water. I looked away. I tried to ignore her, floating on my back with my ears just barely exposed to the air. Whatever she was trying to pull had caught me off guard and I stayed where I was without saying anything.

The water grew agitated, and when I looked sideways, I saw that Ida had shoved off the wall and was trying to swim over to where

I was floating. Clearly, the girl was not at home in the water; she couldn't swim her way out of a paper bag. She had to work hard just to keep her head from going under. Maybe if she wasn't so weighed down by all those bracelets it wouldn't be so bloody hard to swim, I thought dryly to myself. She paddled like a dog, splashing erratically, distress crinkling her determined little face.

And while I had been set on the idea of prolonging the resistance indefinitely—watching her, so uncomfortable and out of her element, I started to feel wearied by it all. The weariness turned to alarm when she swallowed a gulp of water and started to choke. Then panic started to spread over her popeyed face, and I felt that smouldering burn in my chest, like someone was extinguishing a cigarette on my middle rib, and I swam over to where she was whipping her hands just under the surface of the water and breathing fast. I reached out and seized the circumference of her skinny arm.

"Stop," I said. "We can get out."

She seemed to noticeably calm once I had a grip on her arm, and the choking settled. We paddled to where she had arranged her clothes in a neat pile with the magnum. She clung to the sidewall, relieved, and caught her breath. "Thanks," she said quietly, the tenor in her voice sounded almost ashamed. I pulled myself from the tank and spread a wrap on the stone for us to sit on. She slid out and we sat on the side, dangling our legs in the water.

For a while we sat without words. The air was heavy and warm.

"Here," she said finally, dragging the magnum from beside us. "Your father told us everything. Bloody *hell*. I had no idea when I brought up the Channel. I'm sorry. It's a difficult rumbling to avoid."

"You can say that again."

She held out the oversized bottle. "You first."

I had to hold the bottle with both hands and crane my neck back to drink.

Sitting with her then, both of us damp, our bare skin glowing in the dark, I was filled with a strange and unexpected relief.

"How did you know where I was?" I asked.

"Michael knew," she said, taking a swig. "I don't know how." She didn't sound as cordial any more. I liked that better.

I held up the bottle, knowing it had been intended for the celebration of their engagement. "We shouldn't be drinking your handcuff hooch," I said.

She smiled. "My what?"

"Engagement bubbles," I said. "Listen, I didn't mean for this. I'm sorry about the ing-bing."

She slouched forward, moving her legs in the water like egg beaters. "Well, I had it coming," she said. "I feel like an idiot."

"No," I said, feeling drunk and holding my head in my hands. "I'd never take you for an idiot." I rubbed my face and sat up again.

"Well." Her face was quiet. "If you say so."

Humidity hung low over the park. City smells were always the strongest when the air was thick: gasoline, barbecue and tobacco smoke, rotting garbage—but it was less peaked in the uppers and especially in this private green space, where the smell of freshly cut grass surpassed the urban reek. I reclined so that my back was flat on stone, the way Maizee used to lie down on concrete rooftops as the sun came up, asking for painkillers. Ida did the same.

The sky was dark; clouds moved eerily past the moon. There were no stars.

"Starless nights are ill-omened," I told her. "They bring out the worst in people."

Ida looked at the sky. "Here's to that."

"Don't get me started on moons."

She moved her eyes from the sky to the bottle, and I curled up to hand it to her before having more myself to keep my inebriated haze from waning. "Listen," I said, weirdly and drunkenly confessional, "I don't want to excuse my episode or anything, and I don't presume you want to hear this, but there's more."

"More?"

"I was in a whirl with my backer's fine-looking son," I told her and crossed my arms. "And I haven't heard a word from him since the morning Ederle's swim hit the papers. He threw me over like yesterday's trash."

"Oh." She put her hand over mine, and while my reflex was to pull away from unsolicited affection, I stayed still, bracing myself against the spins.

"I know," I say. "I must be really stupid or something."

"Savi." Her voice was like velvet. I guessed that's what Michael had meant when he talked about her fantastic pipes. "That's a horrible story," she said. "You've had a hell of a patch."

"Crushed under the heels of the Lies-wells," I said and moved to raise the bottle in honour of my stupidity. "I made an ass of myself."

"They sound like a pretty rotten set."

"Society puppets."

We both took another drink, beating our legs in the water again.

"Well," I said. "Clue numero uno: we never talked about much—not really." The bottle clinked as she put it down. "And you know—I think he hid me away like that, you know, from his friends and stuff 'cause he was embarrassed. He never cared a snap of his fingers about me."

I tried to snap my fingers, but they were moist and snapless.

I didn't tell her about the congealed wad of pent emotionalism in my gut. It was there, even as we sat, dangling our legs at the side of the tank. Sometimes it started to creep and boil into the cavity where my ribs came together, but always at the wrong time, so I had to cram it back down. And the wad never wanted to crack when I was in private. I didn't understand.

"Oh," she said again. "Hell with him, Savi. Hear me? *Hell with him.*"

One of the lampposts flickered and burned out. Ida smiled faintly, hunched her small shoulders, and squeezed my hand.

Having spent years sleeping badly, I got myself some sleeping dope from the peddlers at the tank. I started to swallow one chalky tablet every night to lure myself to sleep, and there was no longer the constant hum in my muscle that I had grown so accustomed to. I corked off like a dream. I didn't show up for work, choosing instead to lie motionless on my back and stare at the ceiling of my flat. But because I lived above the bake house, people came knocking.

"Lemme alone," I said through the door. "Go away."

"What's wrong? Are you not well?"

"I'm ill. Lemme alone." And their footsteps would descend down the narrow staircase to the ovens and pans where Michael was taking my place while I was idle. Michael and Ida were planning to stick around New York for a few months, and they were staying at the house. They took the fliv for drives every night to park it somewhere and coo at each other; the parental ignorance was shocking.

I stayed in the flat, wearing my oversized blue pyjamas and feeling sorry for myself. I ate walnut meats from the fruitcake ingredients and listened to newspapers thud against the door under my window. If I was not lying on my back, I slouched across the room to the armchair and watched the sky outside. The wad was nauseating; I was trying to think of ways to release it.

Higgins had decided to leave the city for an open-ended hiatus in Florida. Maizee was already engaged to Bobrosky after only two months of courting. They were planning to get married in Spain in the winter, and she was busy teaching herself Spanish. "Me he perdido," she said, "means *I am lost*. Cuanto es? *How much is it?* Mas vino, *more wine*—say it like vee-no."

I hated the city and felt trapped inside an insular, suffocating balloon glass of engine fuel and sun-baked trash. I found my only solace in the philosophical realization that daydreams were better left unlived, where they were safe inside the cavity of my head— protected from the grand delusion of reality.

Late one evening I got lit, and then I got hungry, and, peering out of my fog, I snuck down to the bake house after hours. I knew, as always, where my father stowed the brandy that was saved for the seasonal demand of fruit and pound cakes. I had already achieved a pleasant edge from an entire bottle of cheap wine, and, thinking primarily of sustenance, I slipped inside the cold room looking for eats. Disheveled in my pyjamas I perused the shelves under the electric drone of the lights.

Cheese. I would make myself a good old cheese sandwich with sourdough bread. There was tomato, onion, lettuce, and cheese, all there, easy to snitch. The light wavered and I could see my breath. As I groped for sandwich fillers, I was startled by a sudden ringing of the service bell in the kitchen: *ding ding ding—ding ding ding.* I jumped, shocked, and dropped the large white onion that I had been cradling like a polo ball in my hand. Everything was supposed to be locked up—it was past eleven o'clock.

I skulked out of the cold room and flicked on a lamp. My eyes adjusted. Waiting beside the ding-bell, in the dark kitchen, stood Ida. She moved forward, smartly put together in a crimson dress that matched her snug lid and carmined lips; her eyelids were silvery with Vaseline and kohl. Traces of lavender wafted about her. She took off her gloves. "Your father gave me the key," she said. "He asked me to check in on you. And I found something that might interest you, besides." She thrust a newspaper in front of my face. Tiny letters danced on the page.

I fumbled with the paper and gave her a sidelong eyeball. "Page eleven," she said with authority and—noting my scrabbled coordination—reached across my body to unfold the paper. "Let me," she said.

She took a seat on the counter and dangled her legs. I wobbled and was thinking about food. My stomach churned.

"Ederle," she read. "And the Wrigley Proposal. That's the headline. Last week, William Wrigley Junior," she lowered the paper. "The chewing gum, you know?"

"Fine for digestion," I said. "Fine for the teeth." I braced myself against the wooden table across from her—of course I knew Wrigley Chewing Gum. *God.*

"William Wrigley Junior offered English Channel super-heroine, Trudy Ederle," she dropped the paper, and gave me the spiel without reading, "five thousand dollars to swim across the San Pedro Channel in January. When Ederle threw down his offer, Wrigley upped it to ten thousand—but still—no dice. She didn't take it." Ida waited for me to find something to say, and when I stood there saying nothing, she kept on. "Her grounds—in case you're interested—are because she has decided to take up vaudeville. She's going on tour for six months with a former teammate, a diver called Riggin. Oh, and there was some mention of ear damage."

"Ear damage? What kind of ear damage?"

"She has quite possibly damaged her hearing permanently."

I was looking at Ida's shoes. Why were there four pairs of shoes hanging off the counter like that? The room was moving. Four shoes that buckled over the tops of four separate feet. Shimmery stockings. The overhead lamp flickered, I squinted at her, trying my best to keep listening. There was a disc of diffused light around everything.

"Okay—listen," she was saying. "It says here that the San Pedro Channel is a twenty-two mile stretch, says it's longer and tougher than the English Channel; tides and deep currents make it longer. Something here about rollers and cold that grabs. It's never been crossed before." She paused and took a breath. "You would start on Catalina Island and swim across to the breakwater at Point Vincente. That's just outside of L.A."

I wavered in the horrible sway of things, transfixed on the four shiny shoes.

"As for Ederle's decline, Wrigley has settled on a twenty-five-thousand dollar jackpot, and he has opened the race up to everybody—on or about January 15—and a *second* amount of fifteen thousand will be awarded to the first woman finisher."

I reeled and the kitchen smudged into a nebulous, blotted painting.

Ida threw the paper across the counter. Attempting to control the spins, I smoothed the newsprint with my hands and gazed up at the two girls, my future sisters, propped on the counter. They were duplicates and they were looking down at their shoes, tapping the toes together. "What are you looking at?" they asked, and it echoed in my head.

The overhead light glinted off their pale hair.

Ida pulled me up to my flat. It was an abominable sight. She scanned the clutter strewn about the floor and shook her fine, pretty head. Surveying the empty wine bottles, melted candle wax on the table, hurled stockings, and spilled chocolate powder, her eyes landed on my vial of sleeping tablets. She dropped me in a chair, marched across the room to the bedside table, and took them up in her perfectly manicured hand. "What is this?" she flashed.

There was no reason for me to answer because she was already reading the label out loud. "Veronol. Where did you get this?"

"Oh," I said, feeling very woozy from the drink and the sedatives. "You know. Got it from some peddlers at the tank. Terrific stuff—never slept so good in my *life*." Ida looked at me fiercely.

"Get dressed," she said. "Put your suit on. We're going to the tank." She held the vial up so I could see it clearly. "Do you know where this is going? It is going in the garbage. No wonder you look like death warmed over. Now get a move on."

With awkward fingers, I put on my tank suit and followed her down to a little breezer parked outside. How she had access to a breezer while staying with my parents was not clear, but I guessed it had something to do with her family's scratch. We drove with the top down and the air was magnificent—dry, crisp, thrilling air. She drove to the outdoor tank that we had swam in the night I ruined supper. "Out," she said.

"No," I said. "I—don't—think—so."

"Come on, Savi. Let's go."

"Stop bossing me. I'm through with the whole works. It's stupid and I hate it."

"No you don't. You're upset and feeling sorry for yourself. What about the Wrigley Race? You've saved enough money for a train ticket, haven't you?"

"Rah—rah."

"There's no race fee."

"I said I'm *through*. Something will go wrong. I'm cursed."

"Oh, really?" Ida narrowed her turquoise eyes. "Cursed?"

"Why did you bring me here?"

I started laughing hysterically and leaned against the seat. The outdoor tank was glowing in the dark—bright blue and empty as usual.

"Go," she said. "You haven't swum for weeks. Go and pull yourself together. I will wait for you here." She crossed her arms and waited.

I sighed, stopped laughing. "No."

"Savi. Out of nothing, nothing comes."

"Oh yeah? Says *you*. Says *I-D-A*. Besides—I've heard that before."

"Shakespeare."

"Oooo. *Shakespeare*."

We sat in the car without a word for more than twenty minutes.

"I'm never good enough," I said. "Everything I do is stupid, everything I touch falls apart." I pulled a ginger ale bottle of my father's whisky from my satchel and brought it to my mouth for a swig.

Ida was furious; she grabbed it from my hand in a flash, held it up. "You little—look at you! Where did *this* come from?"

I belched. She poured my drink onto the street outside the breezer.

"I was once told," I said, pressing my forehead against the windshield, "that I had a physical intelligence."

We sat in the car without another word for another stretch of many minutes. I would *not* get back into that water. I was wrecked. Finally, after what seemed like hours, she turned the key in the ignition and we silently drove back toward the bake house.

On the ride home, the wad started to roil; I felt it creep into my rib cage. The crack was inevitable, at last—I would be released. I sat very still in Ida's car as we rumbled along. I had to protect the rising simmer from any turbulence or distraction, so I kept my forehead pressed against the side window and concentrated on staying still.

On the sidewalk after being let out, I fumbled eagerly with my keys. I wanted to get into the bake house quickly, entirely game for the fruition of my burgeoning nervous breakdown. I burst inside, heart pounding and charged, ready for the escalation. It was going to happen—the gush, the relief. I stood in front of the kitchen, tingling with anticipation under the electric drone of the lights, and waited.

But the wad had retreated. "What?!" I shouted at the basket of day-old rolls beside the cash register. "No!" I paced in circles around the long wooden table at the centre of the kitchen and wrung out my hands. I stopped, focused again, waited for it to stir—but no. "Daaamn!" I slammed my hands down on the counter and stared fixedly on the black-and-white checkered floor.

And then, suddenly, I was blasted by a thought, an idea that in my stupor was nothing short of genius. The onion. That freakishly large white onion that had rolled from my hand when Ida rang the bell. The memory of it leaving my palm and hitting the cold-room floor was a slow movie-reel in my head. Yes, yes, yes—this gorgeous white sphere would put an end to the churning volcanic pressure inside me. Absolutely cymbal-smashing *brilliant*.

I cut the onion in half and impatiently carried my gibbous half-moons up to the privacy of my flat where I set them down with the ceremonial air of a regalia-wearing religious type. I positioned myself in my special place on the hardwood floor, and proceeded to break apart the layers of onion with my fingers. I smeared the juiciest pieces over my eyelids. My eyes watered, burned—stung like acid.

I laid myself down with onion parts over both eyes, folded my hands over my rib cage, and waited for the wad. Come on, you little bastard, I summoned. Come on. But the wad was not roiling. The wad was not *interested*. I was not accomplishing the release—my glorious nervous breakdown. No, clearly, it was not in my stars—just like the rest of it.

I look at Sol. "I woke up the next day with a flaming infection in both my eyes. And I wasn't exactly going to tell the doctor about the onion ceremony. I showed him the aged and crud-ridden mascara that Maizee had pointed out to me months before. Any case, *post hoc ergo propter hoc*—after this, therefore because of this." I look at his miniature sink. "Blaah."

I think back to the fire of leaves that punctuated the hard set of knocks; the crunch under my feet along sidewalks; blackberry and pumpkin specials at the bake house. "I had to leave. After Christmas I announced to everyone that I was leaving for California, I packed up the bare essentials and I got on the rattler. Before I got here I hadn't swum in four months."

He leans forward, and for a moment I think he's going to put his hand on my knee like Tad, and the thought makes me curl up, but he retreats a little inside himself and I'm relieved. "Onions," he says, and he seems quietly beside himself, but in an amused sort of way. He lets out a muffled laugh, "I'm not sure I know what to say."

"That's okay. You don't have to say anything."

"Ah, well," he says. "Four months without training, pretty brave, I might say—or mad as a hatter."

I look at the small clock on the wall of his cabin, and it's almost two in the morning. "I should go," I say. "I've stayed too long." The boat is still pitching a little with the wind. The storm whistles.

"You're welcome to sleep on that bunk if you like," he says and points across the saloon table. "I'll stay on the other side."

"Ah—thanks," I say. "But no."

He stands, slowly, to put our mugs in the sink. Wind beats against the boats, a raucous of ropes and halyards hitting wooden masts and metal.

"Well. If you get back to camp and your tent has blown away, you can sleep on the bunk. It folds down, it's not a problem." He's talking and he's asking questions I think, and I hear *Ida*, and *Ederle*, and *New York*, and despite efforts to keep my eyes from closing, I fall away, underwater, to the roll and slosh under the hull.

I fall into a dream that I am swimming upstream, up a mountain, stroking through cold, rushing water that isn't very deep. I am underwater and can see the creek bed perfectly; smooth stones and crayfish pass underneath me. I swim up the mountain and don't need to breathe.

Red or grey she does not know, red for fortune, grey for woe. Red or grey bint does not know, red or grey bint does not know. To either side of the creek, there are dugouts. My dream turns to images of the Lieutenant in the trenches. I see him wandering an endless, treeless plain—barefoot and chanting.

SIXTEEN
JANUARY 15, 1927

PALOS VERDES Point. Originally, the race was to start from Avalon Harbor, but rumour circulated that Avalon was too small a bay to accommodate the flotilla of boats involved in the race. We've all been transported to the isthmus, the skinniest part of the island. Morning fog and low clouds are lifting, dissipating, and the hot sun heats up the sand and rocks along the beach.

Sol has painted my body with grease head to toe over top of my wool tank suit. Even my face is painted—with just enough ungreased skin around my eyes to put my goggles on. "Be-smeared!" he says and throws up his hands, palms out, launching black globules of axle grease into the air. He pulls off his surgical gloves and lights up, cupping his hands away from the wind. He is wearing nothing but his ridiculous bag-pants, which he tells me are called *Oxford bags*, and his lean, tawny frame glints in the morning light. He flakes cigarette ashes into a glass jar and watches the commotion of surrounding swimmers and trainers fussing and cranking up along the shore.

Fifty more swimmers scratched out of the race this morning. The number of contestants has been confirmed at one hundred and two, and along the beach there is a long string of red poles planted into the sand—a starting place for every swimmer; there are only thirteen woman contestants left in the race. Each pole has been marked with a number, and Sol and I are stationed beside my official number—seventy-four. Cameras flash small bursts of magnesium powder; concession vendors shout deals in slick and rolling volleys. They offer hot cider, coffee drinks, and gingerbread; the air smells of caramel. Jazz echoes over sand; wind riles the tiny grains into swirling eddies. In the dunes farther back, juniper bushes sit like gnomes in ground fog; children collect smooth pebbles and conch shells where the tide has washed up ocean debris. I watch, a little outside of my grease, dazed. "I told you," he says, "one monkey short of a circus."

Catalina's official steamer, the ss *Avalon,* is anchored five hundred yards off shore having transported a host of Wrigley men, observers, and newsmen. The ferry blows the half-hour whistle. Thirty minutes until we race. My knees shake, my mouth feels dry; Sol watches me carefully and with his greaseless hands tucks my stray hair under my rubber cap. "I'm off to the convoy," he says. "This is it—all good?"

The Lieutenant is wandering the beach displaying his yellow grin, white hair standing on end. He's got his corduroy pants rolled up to the middle of his calves, his sack slung over his back, and his feet are as black with dirt as usual. He beams and picks up his pace when he sees us at my red pole. "Butter up, butter cup," he says, exhilarated by the bursts of flash powder exploding on every side.

He settles his watery gaze to the side of my head. "Red!" he says and brings his hand to his mouth, hiding the ear-to-ear grin across his face. "Red!"

I look at Sol. "I don't get it."

Sol smiles and lifts his eyebrows. "Couldn't say."

In my mind I turn over the items that have been packed into Sol's dinghy, which is serving now as our convoy: first-aid kit, whistles, Thermoses of chicken broth and hot chocolate, rope, wool blankets, towels, mast lights, signal flares, and rubber feeding tube. Attached to the bow of the convoy is my number—it has been painted onto a thin plank of wood.

Most of the other contestants have two people occupying their skiffs—their official observing Wrigley man and an assigned oarsman. Some of the contestants also have accompanying powerboats hauling family and friends. The powerboats will not be permitted to come within fifty yards of the swimmers once the race is underway.

"I'm set," comes out feebly.

"That's the spirit!" he shouts.

The Lieutenant drops his burlap sack to the sands and his bottles clash. He shakes his fists in the air. "Red!" he screams again, causing nearby contestants looking spooked to slink away from him.

Plumes of sand move over the beach. Gum trees and black coconuts are scattered over the fringes where bulrushes stand upright with their long distracted heads. Spindly palm trees sway and click in the breeze. Sol leans in and wavers right up close to my face. "Bonne chance," he says. "You know your onions inside out."

"You can say that again," I say, and we both smile.

I look quickly at the bright water and the row of skiffs along the shore. "Thanks for doing this," I say, and it feels like a colossal understatement. "Really."

He has gathered all our greasing supplies into a pail. "Don't mention it," he says and starts to move toward the convoy.

I have been coached to meet him two hundred yards directly out from shore, where he will take up position on my left side and navigate my course across the San Pedro Channel. It's all been hammered out.

Cameramen search for Charlotte—who had made her nudist intentions clear as a bell to the press—but they are disappointed to find that she is discreetly preparing her greasy costume hidden inside a small medic-tent. No doubt there will be publicity cruisers in her wake throughout the swim, on the ready to catch as many compromising photos of her as possible. No Sleeves has his swimsuit at half-mast. He doesn't believe in grease any more, having declared to a newsman that grease wore off, and that surviving the cold was a purely psychological affair, a matter of mental stamina, resilience, grit.

Rhea James is greasing Ella, who is gazing calmly at the pandemonium on the sands. I watch them talking and getting ready in what seems to be their own private bubble. They look unaffected by the surrounding flap of cameramen and the thousands of spectators on the planking and slopes behind the beach. Wrigley himself—an older man wearing a captain's lid—stands on a podium decorated with a bunch of flags and smokes a cigar. The official starter, Fred Cady, stands beside Wrigley holding a bullhorn in his left hand and a revolver in his right. Crowds swarm behind the great expanse of swimmers, and still more spectators are being dropped off from steamboat ferries. I concentrate on breathing, and watch the seemingly endless flow of people unroll along the pier; their heads jostle like balls loosely attached to their shoulders. They are dressed in warm scarves, lids, and wool jackets. I fold my arms across my chest, move my eyes back to the ocean, shudder.

Grease-glazed figures toil in clusters on the beach, all different shades of grease—black, yellow, blue, and dark red, almost black—all dripping onto the sand, glistening in the sun. Voices ripple over sand and water. A dark red monstrosity walks toward me, and it takes me a moment to recognize that pan of hers, her albino eyes through the metallic sheen coating her face.

"Hey, Savi," she says. "Who did your grease?"

"You!" I say, flinging my arms out from my sides. "You snake— you tried to have me kicked from the race!"

She looks at me as though she hasn't got the faintest clue what I'm talking about. "What?" she says, pulling her shoulders back. "What do you mean?"

"I heard all about it, you stringy little ferret."

She swings her arms. "I don't know from *nothing* what you're talking about."

"I'm not an idiot, *Bea*."

A highly strung, spindly man anxiously paces the beach wearing several pairs of long underwear soaked in grease. We both turn and watch him without saying anything.

She wheels around, looks at me again, a bewildered slant, and I brace myself for whatever she's about to say. "I was just looking out for you, *Savi*." She adjusts her big motor goggles with greasy fingers. "You just seemed so out of it, and it's only human nature to *care*."

Before her syrupy tone can throw me into a rage, I realize I don't have to respond to her at all. She slackens her shoulders, waiting for me to find something to say, and turns quickly to assess the crowd. "Well," she says. "I don't know what you're so up in the air about. May the best man win." She extends her greasy hand for a clasp.

"Go to hell." I wring out my hands, sending greasy splats onto her goggles. She rolls an eyeball to the sands and starts to walk back to her pole.

Swimmers glimmer in paint, stand a few feet from the shoreline, folding and unfolding their arms. Some of them stretch and do calisthenics with their legs. I can see Sol on our convoy now, waiting to shove off the beach. No Sleeves saunters down to line up at his pole, waving to his entourage.

Behind the skiffs, there are all types of boats crammed to capacity with audience: fancy yachts, boxy fishing boats, tuggies, and cruisers. They are escorting various pods of newsmen, cameramen, and wealthy spectators who want to see the race up close. Some enormous white sails are unfurling farther in the distance where the wind has picked up. From aboard the *Avalon* and *Cabrillo*—the steamers-turned-hospital-ships—live jazz floats out over the water.

The tide washes up and recedes in a curling froth—a haphazard lace of ocean lips, sucking at a fringe of land, humming into me; through arteries and blood vessels, I can feel it circulating. Doc O'Byrne is standing knee-deep in the water with a thermometer in his hand. He shakes his head and shouts to George Young: *Fifty-three degrees!*

Camouflaged in dark blue grease, Geo stands not far from my starting pole with Hastings. Odds are on, I overhear from within the rumbling swell of spectators behind me, no one will get across. Some tweed hats are thrown in the air.

Powerboats have cleared the bay, having been instructed to stay at least five hundred yards from the swimmers at the start of the race. The *Avalon* emits two booming whistle blasts—fifteen minutes until we race. Official observers dressed in starchy white, coaches and oarsmen, shove off the beach in individual skiffs. There will be auxiliary supervising "umpires" in various types of boats who will sweep from one convoy team to the next, watching each swimmer to ensure there is no cheating, no holding on to their escort boats to rest during the race. Any swimmer who has even the slightest flicker of physical contact with their convoy or observer will be instantaneously disqualified.

"You're not wearing a suit, are you?" Bea asks, having turned up at my pole again like a bad penny.

"What?"

"The suits. Remember? We're all going to strip them as soon as the water is deep enough for cover."

"Didn't I tell you to beat it?"

Through the grease coating her face I can see her eyebrows are raised. "Bet you didn't hear that Big Moose is swimming sans wool," she says. "Cuts down on drag."

"Is it the *go* or the *away* that you don't get?"

"Say," she says, peering out of her mask of grease. "Are you feeling all right? You look a little tired."

"Scram."

She swings her arms, shrugs, and skulks back to her red pole. I hop up and down a few times to get the blood flowing in my legs and keep my feet from getting too cold. I had made the decision to slather my chafed skin with Vaseline and lanolin in addition to the final layer of axle grease in the hope that it would protect the wounds.

I find myself lined up along the shoreline now, beside my red pole, parallel with the others. A legless swimmer, Charles Zimmy, is walking with his hands to the embankment next to mine. I had seen him around, riding a contraption with wheels, propelling himself forward with his arms. He's young, my age or so, and he looks up at me, super-charged. "Ninety per cent upper body, baby," he says and winks.

I now have two swimmers pegged ten feet from either side of me. I look down at land, curl my toes into the wet sand, look up at bright sky, look anywhere but at water. Okay, breathe. Swing the arms.

Keep breathing. This is all I hear now, not the surrounding razzmatazz, but the inhale and exhale of air. *Breathe from your guts*, I hear Higgins tell me, clapping his stomach to show me, and I breathe deep, exhaling through my mouth. *Clap hands, jump. Claphands*, the Hawaiian ukulele players sang to Johnny Weissmuller when he swam that three-mile river swim in Chicago last summer. *Claphands—here comes Johnny!* Nerves sheer and raw, on the ready to race. Behind us, on the planking, Wrigley raises his fists, smiling.

There is no true countdown. As much as I try to relax, I am coiled for the gunshot, the leap. I swing arms at my sides, wring out my hands, and concentrate on breathing deeply from my guts. *That's the stuff*, I hear Higgins in my head again. *That's right, Gutterball.* The tide is ebbing out. Cold water sucks back, spools around my shins—chill salt spray mists my legs. *What if my skin starts bleeding early into the race? What if my pump freezes and stops beating?* I try to make my mind as dark and empty as a cave. Breathe. Waves have calmed near the shore, obsidian-smooth, glassy and clear, whitecaps in the distance. Twenty-two miles. *De novo*, that's why. Clap hands again, come on starter, come on Johnny, come on Freddie—*ack beer yorker*—let's go. Icy slaps of wave. Blue, green. This is it. Do this and *exist*. Exist *now*. Let go. *Terra incognita*. Yes. Keep steady, keep breathing.

"Let 'er go, Fred," Wrigley shouts to the starter.

Eleven-twenty-one AM and the gun cracks through the air. Boat horns blast.

Everywhere, thunderous noise, and two Wrigley men elevate Charles Zimmy from his placement on the sand and toss him into the water. I bolt off, running through the shallow tide, running, running with my reflection, a dark window on the water. Waist deep, I plunge; my reflection and body meld. There is nothing but water, nothing but the underwater crash.

The ice comes in splinters against my face, skin blooms gooseflesh, spreads over my body like dye. Swimming out, I have to push away rivals who swim too close. Pull ahead, claim a position. And then I can feel myself cruise fast with the slack water, fluid and connected to it, oblivious to who is in front or behind. Don't think about ranking now; it's too early, much too soon. Gentle swells carry the swimmers up high with their bubbling crests, and I catch glimpses of other heads, arms stroking; then I fall back down and surge forward. Sol's boat reflects the overcast, bright metal against white sun. His silhouette points ahead, showing me where to sight. Follow his shadow, trust him. Heartbeats punch at my chest, against ribs, against tissue. Breathing every two strokes: one two, one two, one two.

As planned, Sol directs us northeast out of the harbour, away from sandbars and outlying rocks. I watch, gasp at steady cold, unceasing frost. Flurries of bubbles cloud my vision—someone's leftover trail. In this first mile I must find my pace and try to hold that rhythm without wasting thought on what the others are doing. Form, not fight. The right tempo now will save me from tying up later. Fingers together, catch of the hand, pull, and push all the way back.

But I'm not ready to settle yet; I thrash ahead, dart for space, reach it, and hold a steady tempo. Ice burn. Wind burn. Sun burn. Think about where you're going; don't stray. Frostbite, that smouldering ice-over, that blue-hot rime that covers and reddens your skin, sets you ablaze, but only you can feel the cinders, feel your skin blister and singe, invisible to everyone else. I imagine the cold will become a type of anesthetic drug soon, and tuck its magnetic swells and currents around me like a blanket. Biology is destiny. Follow Solomon's shadow, trust him.

The water is not very deep. I can see the rocky bottom, imagine the eerie underworld of sea biscuits and scales; urchins, starfish, morbid bottom-feeders, mud shark, and *eels*. I catch a blur of teeming copper fish, gasp, and pick up my pace. Where the fog is lifting, there is an ear-splitting racket from low-swooping seaplanes; some drop flowers and take pictures. Others are on shark patrol. Coast Guard cutters and supervising umpires weave slowly past and around us. I hear the reverberation of their engines and propellers underwater.

Forget about it. The forgetting is what I'm after, that crystallized simplicity, that breath—the surrender that makes way for clarity and momentum. Stroke, stroke, *breathe*. Stroke, stroke, *breathe*. My arms reach for the path of least resistance, catch water, and there is nothing to do but move as swiftly as possible forward. With each pull, each push, the elastic feel of it, the underwater echo, the heartbeat, the being-so-small feeling.

Press and publicity boats glide by, flashing, observing. Noon is harsh light on the water, dreamily misted over by my fogged-up motor goggles. When I stop, I tear off the goggles and throw them at Sol, my head feels suddenly weightless without them strapped on, and I almost knock over the iron canteen he is transferring hot liquid into from a Thermos; it's attached to a rope, designed for easy tossing and reeling in.

"Your eyes will burn without them!" Sol yells. "It's too soon."

"They're all fogged up and leaking!" I scream.

The sunlight burns. Sol tosses the canteen. "Chocolate!" he shouts.

I grasp for it and my hands shake—pulling out the cork stopper is awkward, and I toil for precious moments, losing heat. Once released, I curl my mouth over the iron lip and swallow, some of the liquid spills down the side of my face. When waves splash salt into my eyes, they sting worse than expected, and I tread water, blinking, trying not to let myself rub them with my greasy hands. I gulp as much hot liquid as I can before letting go. But I've lost the cork-plug. Sol reels back the container, and leans over the gunwale with a smoke hanging between his lips and the goggles in his hand.

"Put them back on, Savi. I'll throw them over." He tosses them at me and they hit my arm. I grab for them.

"If I win," I say, jerky with cold, and carefully readjusting the goggles around my head to minimize grease smears, "you quit the smokes."

"And you quit drinking on an empty stomach."

We can't shake on it because his touch would disqualify me from the race. I think of the lost bottle stopper. "Feeding tube next time!" I shout at him, and he nods.

I drop back down and stroke into a pulse: stroke, stroke, *breathe*. I try to lengthen my reach and breathe every three strokes. Words flit through my head—spuzz, pepper, treeless, *breathe*. Sexless, treeless, pepper, *breathe*. I move through the water feeling strong to the rhythm of my favourite Burgess poem:

> *I wish that my room had a floor*
> *I don't so much care for a door,*
> *But this crawling around*
> *Without touching the ground*
> *Is getting to be quite a bore*

It is quickly trapped in my head—over and over I swim to the cadence of the rhyme; Ya-DA-da-da-DA-da-da-DA, *breathe*, floor, door, bore, *breathe*. Arms pulling long, all the way over, reach, all the way back, onward into the green.

I stop suddenly to look behind me, remembering the pod of rivals I had overtaken in the Hudson River, but I can't see anything through my fogged-up goggles. "Almost one o'clock!" Sol yells. "Almost one o'clock! Keep it up, Savi! Thirty swimmers have already quit. Looking swell!"

I can feel his gaze, the drag of his smoke, but I can't tolerate the fogged-up goggles. I tread, muscles tense with cold.

"What's the matter?" Sol shouts. "You okay?"

I reach, trembling, and remove the goggles again, throw them back at Sol a second time.

"Crazy!" he shouts, holding them up in his hand. "You know where they are if you want them back. Okay, Sealegs—let's go," he urges, but a dull ache has me by the back of my head. I drop into position, strike out, breathe.

I wish I knew who was leading. I imagine No Sleeves churning like some paddle-steamer flagship, guiding a drove of water threshers. I have to imagine it. The sun is too bright. I'm blind with the goggles, blind without them. As the afternoon turns rosy on the water, warmer light spills onto my shoulders, and I know there is something growing suddenly wrong about the water—and I know I'm not imagining things; it's still too soon for that. The water is thicker, heavier. There is a peaked smell of diesel. I hold my head above water, flustered, and swim a clean head-up crawl.

"Oil slick!" Sol shouts, hands cupping around his mouth like a bullhorn. "Oil slick!"

I bob, float on my back like an otter. "What?!"

"Oil slick! Watch out. It's not big, swim through it. Come on now!"

It's not big, but it's disgusting. I hold my breath to stroke through the scummy patch of oil and I can hear Maizee in my mind: "That's just *vile*, Savi. Vile. Oh, my *God*." I imagine her sticking a finger down her throat and retching as I slip through the oil, lips drawn tight and blow water out my nose.

She was getting married in Spain, a small ceremony—family only. She had been teaching herself Spanish before I left. Me he perdido, *I am lost*. Lo siento, *I am sorry*. She had chosen a passage from *Tristan and Iseult* to be included in their vows: "May all herein find strength against inconstancy, against unfairness and despite and loss and pain and all the bitterness of loving." Inconstancy. Unfairness. Loss. Pain. Bitterness.

Me he perdido, *I am lost*. Lo siento, *I am sorry*.

After a few hundred yards of keeping my head above the foul water, I seem to have progressed out of the slick. But because I had to slow down my pace, the cold is seeping deeper into my core; the ocean has curled its icy tassels around my every bone. Cold is carving me out, looking for a place to rest, to sleep. Dig deep, keep on digging. As feared, the sores at my sides where my suit has been chafing are bleeding. I don't have to see this to know that it doesn't look good, and I begin to shrink a little from the pain with each stroke, the sting of wool against water-softened flesh—the more I think about it, the worse it seems to become.

Sol's boat looks superimposed on the water, a black shadow interrupting the ocean view. If this were warm water, say—in some jungle somewhere—there might be dead animals floating past. Fish with teeth. Ish Pish the giant fish. Maizee had ordered a Nile-green tank suit from a catalogue during her Egyptian-look phase, when all she wore were tunics with hieroglyphic embroidery and heavy eye-pencil. She had ordered a King Tut over-blouse—"the design of symbols came right from the tomb!" she said, ecstatic. I imagine a school of tiny hieroglyphic symbols passing below me.

My stomach burns for food. And I can't pee until my limbs stop moving; the body can't do both. Or can it? I don't know. Too cold to stop, even for that. Skin hurts. Okay, count to sixty twenty times, that's twenty minutes, and then you can rest for a moment, have chocolate. Right now—keep moving. Stroke, stroke, stroke, *breathe*.

I cruise. No mountains in the distance, no mist, no craggy chunks of island to reach for. Clear nothing. I know that I am steadily ahead of a woman; I can tell she is a woman by the shorter arm cycles, her more elegant turn to take in air. Her stroke looks marginally familiar to me, but of course there is the burning salt making it difficult to see. As practised, I apply my competitive strategy and break away now and again to hold myself securely ahead. I alternate my pace, swim fast and easy—floor, door, bore, *breathe*—attempting to bolt off ahead, leaving her to flounder in my wake.

Twenty minutes pass. Everything looks the same. It's late afternoon, I can feel it. Like a native Pimugnan tells time by a shadow on dry ground, I can read the light on water. Three o'clock, maybe four. I stop, hungry, and tread water.

"Everything okay?" Sol shouts.

When I try to say *food,* it comes out long and quaking. My jaw feels funny. But it appears he has understood me. He nods, waves, and moves to prepare the feeding tube—a rubber tube that I can siphon hot chocolate, water, or soup from. My throat is hoarse, and my hands shake uncontrollably.

From somewhere close behind us, a screaming flare shoots upward, marking the sky with red. A power vessel rushes in the direction of the flare, generating waves that toss both Sol and me into a series of troughs and swells. I spot an umpire boat hovering to our left, surveying, watching that I am taking my food without any artificial support.

Sol extends the arching rubber tube to where I am bobbing at the boat's side, and I place my mouth over the tube's opening to draw out the liquid food.

"Chicken soup!" he screams, repeats himself several times. I wolf it down, try to swallow. The soup burns my mouth, but its heat traces down into my stomach swiftly. "Your legs," he shouts. "Your legs are dropping! Arms look swell. Keep it up."

I try to nod, swallow, and empty my bladder. *Three blew beans in a blew bladder, rattle, bladder, rattle.* Say it three times quickly to deflect the evil eye. Sol reels in the feeding tube and hollers, "Shake a leg, now! You're losing her!"

I glance to the swimmer that is stroking parallel to my convoy and resume; stroke, stroke, stroke, stroke, *breathe*. One two three four—blue came knocking at my door—five six seven eight—feeling like a piece of bait—nine ten eleven twelve.

Swells carry me up and down in a nauseating roll of watercolour. I am insulated inside it—inside a feverish painting, inside twisted colours. Surrounded by press boats and umpires, it is as though we swimmers are trapped inside paintings, have been hung on museum walls, and people stop to look without seeing us there, stuck inside the mural. My sides feel as though claws are scratching down my rib cage.

"Thirty left!" He shouts. I gulp down more heat, so hastily that I throw it up. What stays inside has scalded my throat, squeezes in between my frozen organs. *Zimmy Zimmy Zimmy Breathe*!

The woman I have been pacing beside does not let up. Our arms arc in tandem, and I begin to feel quite angry. Stroke for stroke, we swim in unison. And despite my efforts to pull away as I have been coached, she stays with me, steady—a maddening annoyance to my right. I see her every time I turn my head to breathe. Stroke, stroke, stroke, *breathe*. I kick my legs, whipping my feet up and down the way I used to thrash them in my hundred-yard sprints, but my legs have become heavy. While I have not succeeded in overtaking her, she has not succeeded in surpassing me either. We stay like this for quite some time as I grow more and more infuriated. Finally, I stop and tread water. Sol leans over the gunwale.

"Who the HELLLLLLLL is that?" I slap the water in the direction of the swimmer to my right. I can hear the splash of her arms hitting the water as she continues to plod ahead.

"WHAT?"

"WHO IS THAATT?" My face and tongue are numb.

Sol is a silhouette in the boat. I can't see him clearly; he is but a looming shadow above me. Waves smack up against the sides of the dinghy, and in the far distance I hear voices shouting over water.

Coaches urging their swimmers onward with shouts and whistle blasts. Salt is burning everywhere—skin, eyes, tongue.

"SAVI!" he shouts. "COME ON, SEALEGS. PRESS ON!"

"WHO IS THAATTT?"

"THAT'S YOUR TRUDY OVER THERE!"

"MY WHAATTT?"

"YOUR TRUDY!"

"WHO?"

"TRUDY."

I shake my head, treading water and losing heat. "BEAAAA?"

"TRUDY."

"WHATTT?"

It couldn't be Trudles. Trudy came here? *No.* Impossible. A surprise appearance at the start? That *would* be her style—sneaky ferret. Oh, my God. OH MY *GOD.* Could it be her? Sol is telling me that it's her. What if it is her? *No.* A plant? Impossible! Fierce, hot amazement flips over in my stomach, turning quickly to buoyant, weightless rage.

"YOU'RE LOSING HER!" he's shouting. "LET'S GO!"

She is swimming past me in a series of spattering arm strokes, and I am bobbing like an idiot in one place, shocked. First, I can no longer tolerate the pain at my sides. I grope at my shoulders, fumbling through tremors for my suit, and pull the straps down, pushing the wool suit off my body.

I can hear Sol's voice bouncing off the water: "What are you doing!"

He is saying something else, but I am unable to make it out. My fingers have lost their dexterity, all thumbs, which is making for an extremely clumsy slip-off. Sol is manoeuvring the boat closer to my side—he probably thinks I am drowning. "BEAR OFF!" I scream, floundering in the water beside the dinghy. "I'M GOING!"

I let the woolly mass sink into the dark water underneath me and feel remarkably light, like froth cresting a wave, and in a delirious charge to catch her, I dip, forge splashily ahead, and hear Sol's high-pitched whistle. I stroke forward again—stroke, stroke, stroke, *breathe*. Stroke, stroke, stroke, *breathe*. She has gained on me, but with my renewed leverage, I catch up to her, and again we stroke in unison, stroke for stroke, water reflecting late afternoon, blinding light all around us.

It is her. It's Trudy—I recognize the stroke now and I know it. Olympic Trials, and I could see her hand enter the water marginally in front of my own—that blur of flesh in the corner of my eye when I turned my head to breathe. I know that stroke. Crystal-clear tank water—a far cry from the cold dark of the channel.

The last time I saw her was at that hellish parade in celebration of her successful crossing. She was standing up in a brand-new convertible car while millions of people threw ribbon, chits of paper, and pages from the phone book. It was a riot—car horns, boat horns, sirens—even airplanes. Ticker tape was thrown from every financial tower down Wall Street; rolls of toilet paper fell like streamers from the windows. Perched in her breezer outside of City Hall, Trudy listened to the mayor make a special speech about her courage and physical prowess—and there was even a telegram from the president. Calvin Coolidge called her "America's Best Girl."

Everyone was shouting *What for, Trudy—What for!* The catch-phrase had come from the newspaper accounts of her swim. When the Channel waters had turned rough and a storm was pitching her around like a ragdoll, her trainer had repeatedly asked her to quit. He shouted, *What for, Trudy? What for?* But she had refused to leave the water and abandon her dream. "Hello, Miss What For!" the city of New York shrieked, and they presented their Queen of the Waves with an imperial crown.

Shirking the crowds, Maizee and I bought hot dogs and climbed a fire escape to sit on the rooftop of a Broadway grocery store. From there we could survey the parade from a platform, and I could consider throwing myself off the edge. And in my already crystallized despair,

I saw him. Defying all the odds of coincidence, I spotted him amidst a crowd of millions. There he was, his royal slyness—Theodore effing Laswell—happily walking arm in arm with a young, finely dressed, cloche-and-pearl-wearing sophisticate.

For a while I had entertained the idea of trespassing onto the Laswell property and freeing all of Tad's birds from the garden house. I imagined all their colourful wings soaring up through the sky and into the trees; I wanted them to be free and wild—and I wanted Tad to be sick over it. I never did. I slept and drank the bake house stock of brandy.

I slept and drank the brandy, listened to the scream of car horns, the sputter and roar of engines outside, and stared out the window. And one night after the parade, I took the tiny pearl he had given me from the small dish beside my bed—and I ate it.

Wait. I thought Trudy's hearing had been damaged—I thought the cold temperatures in the English Channel took its toll on her ears. Was this another way of deceiving everybody? Leading us to believe she would no longer compete? That sneaky ferret—it's all coming together now. Not this time, Trudles. Not again.

Twilight washes the sky into mauve, then orange-peel sundown, arm to arm we wrench at water that never ends. There seem to be more hospital ships steaming here and there, plucking swimmers from the water who have cramped up, started vomiting—seasick and exhausted—or gone frost-raving mad. Wherever a red flare spikes into the darkening sky, cutters speed in that direction. At least that's what it seems like. A red flag or flare means a swimmer is leaving the race. With all the boats, it's hard to stop thinking about propellers dismembering you. Forget about it—keep swimming. But through my blurred vision, I can tell there are fewer mast lights and convoys in front of me. Trudy's convoy, light on, stays perfectly parallel to my right. Unbelievable. As darkness sets in, my vision is blotted— like being sprayed in the face by octopus ink. I imagine all the Pacific octopi collectively squirting ink, turning the ocean black. Feel the air temperature drop. But how much do I feel anything any more? Any more for any more?

"How far is it?" comes out slurred and drunk. "How far is it?" I slap my wrist; try again: "TIME!"

And all at once, Trudy's stroke falters. Her rhythm becomes uneven and sloppy. She falls behind, and I lose sight of her. I know she is there, but I can't see her as the sky slides into darkness. The sun descends into the empty bowl of ocean. Sharks flitter like moths out of the corners of my obscured vision.

"EIGHT-O-CLOCK. Fourteen swimmers left! Eight men, six women," he shouts. "Good show!" My heart races, padding fast against ribs. Now I just have to swim through the blindness, the voices, their images all around me in my head.

The hull of my escort boat has become as domed as an immense turtle that gives me the evil eyes of its running lights—one green, one red. I imagine the relief of crawling on its back, curling up and sleeping. Just a couple of chalky tablets and that sweet rest would follow. But this turtle just eyes me. A full moon is rising directly above the calm water, calmer than it has been for hours. The moon leers at me and my white nakedness in inky water. Stop looking. Stop it, *moon*. You big fat yellow ball. You've been building up your tides for days. I can feel you in my middle—pulling and waning, in and out of skin I don't recognize any more, *moon*. Stop glinting at me that way. You lump in my throat, fine sand on my eyelids. I shake my fists at you, yellow!

The sky and water have melted into one big slab of collective darkness. I grasp through liquid outer space, through gauzy shafts of ocean weed. My eyesight has completely failed me; everything is a nebulous blob with evil eyes, changing colour, green to red. Three blew beans in a blew bladder, rattle, bladder, rattle. Bladder, bladder, *breathe*. Bladder, bladder, *breathe*. Breathe blew breathe, rattle, breathe, rattle, bladder, rattle, *breathe*. The water is getting thicker, turning to quicksand.

Judas! I spit at the turtle. Did you say Bacardi? Well then. WELL THEN. Maybe you don't have the bumps after all. My head pounds to the stroke count: one two one two one two one two one. This moon is my metronome. A full moon has influence over all the body's fluids. Conjures outrage and sudden hysteria. Never let the full moon shine directly on your face.

Numb numb numb. Numb: deprived of the power to feel or move. But I *am* moving. Sol whistles. "LEGS, SAVI. KICK!" he shouts. "Kick those pins. Don't lose it, Sealegs. Let's go!" I want to explain to him that my constellation isn't right. Saturn. Saturday, day of Saturn. Never do anything with a utilitarian purpose or leave hospital on a Saturday.

Small wonder nobody lives on Saturn, with all those moons orbiting their icy bodies around. "Titan is the biggest one," Maizee told me. "It has the most eccentric orbit. Rhea is the second biggest one, all water and ice, bright wispy markings—minus two-hundred and eighteen degrees Fahrenheit!" Rhea who? Rhea *James*. No, the moon Rhea, wife of Saturn, Goddess of caverns. Measurer of effort.

Am I in a beautiful delirium? No. Dark and cold and boring, my bones are crumbling. An illusion of deserts, of red-hot sand, of laburnum trees. Dry land melding into poisonous yellow petals and melting clocks, time folding in on itself like earth along a fault line. Onions and pearls, onions and pearls, onions and pearls, *breathe*. I hear music. Charlestonized jungle music strums and wails in time with my arms, my breath, my pulse—my San Pedro song bag. But the wild drum beat and melodic slosh of water is broken by the creak of oars; the screech pierces through my ear canals, scrapes my brain. Cramped shoulders. My hip joints rub against each other like heated flint. A small orange spark glows from the boat.

Red or grey she does not know. Red for fortune, grey for woe. Friend, foe, fortune, woe—row, row, row your boat. I hear the Lieutenant on the beach, screaming. But I am an island surrounded by water with no beach in sight, only the slap of water, splashes in the dark. Trudy? Where are you? I know you're there, you minxy ferret. More red flares and flags, like a war game. Like real physicians in an infirmary, the hospital ships make rounds. I've come to recognize the pitch of their rumbling engines.

A voice shrieks out of the darkness, *It can't be done!* One two one two one two one two I'm not crazy, *you're* CRAZY. Floodlights spill over water. I'm CAUGHT. Okay, you caught me, I give up—but pass the highball would you. A four-finger drink would be swell. Ah—make that seven. You promised. Is anyone even listening?

There are shadows. Boats. The sound of a rifle. I'm sure. A sharp release sets off and a high-pitched wail cracks the water, splashes violently. Stillness. I bob up, panic-stricken. And the thought slices through my haze like lightening splitting a tree: SHARK PATROL. I spin around, frantically treading water.

"DON'T STOP!" Sol yells. My eyes are swollen, rimmed with crystallized salt and minerals. I can't see. "KEEP GOING," he is yelling. "FALSE ALARM. KEEP GOING! IT'S OKAY, SAVI. I PROMISE. YOU'RE OKAY. I MEAN IT."

But the shock has stunned me and I'm not sure what do, how to keep going. I think I see a fin in the darkness, a wedge beside the skiff. I try to shout, but my mouth is now stuffed with cotton balls. Another fin, I'm sure. Sol is shouting, telling me that he is holding out the feeding tube, but I can't see it. I only see the many colours of blackness. The fin.

"I CAN'T SEE!" I scream.

"Savi, over here," he's saying. "That's it, attagirl. What's the matter? What? What's the—no—no sharks. False alarm, false alarm—yes. It's okay now." I can only see cloudy light in the direction of the boat, and Sol is trying to direct me to the feeding tube. "Over here—just a little bit closer, almost, a little more—there you are!" Finally I think I can feel the rubber tube brush against the side of my face. "There you go," he says. "Snack time. Drink up, now."

It's chocolate this time, coats my mouth.

"You're in seventh," he says while I attempt to swallow. "SEVEN!"

The tube falls out of my mouth and disappears. I tread water.

"Can you show me seven fingers?" he says. "Seven fingers, Savi. Hold them up for me."

I don't have any fingers. I tread water, freezing. What a stupid question. And where's the seven-finger drink I just ordered? The service here is punk. You tell him, *bird.*

Sol hangs close over the gunwale. "What's your name?" he says from the edge of the skiff. "Tell me your name."

Another stupid question. I say my name.

"What's your name?"

I say it again.

"There! *Good.* Now—do you see those lights?" I see faint, blurry light burning ahead of us. "Those lights are very close. Let's go, Savi. Keep it up. Let's go get those wise guys—kick those legs!"

I lower again and stroke on. My legs drag like ribbons behind me.

Hello? Is anybody there? There is nobody. Nobody. Nobody here: only pain coming at me in cold silver sheets. Got the icy mitts on me. White like Aspirin. Is that you? Aspirin? Tad? What a riot! An effing riot. You put the *ass* in *class,* mister. No mutton, thank you. Where's my drink?

Now there is Solomon: "Come on, Savi, Sealegs. Looking super. Can you hear me? There, now, you're so close. You see those headlights over there? That's the mainland, can you see the lights?"

No. I don't see the lights. I only see black combers closing in on me, wrenching at water that never ends. *Ad infinitum.* Floor, door, bore, *breathe.* Core, oar, sore, *breathe.*

But then, all at once, there is a streak of light that passes underneath me. A whoosh of bright green sparkles. Darkness. Then, again—a flurry of light to my right. I stop swimming, try to tell Sol.

"What?" Sol is urging. "Do I see what? Savi—I can't hear you. I—can't—make—out—what—you're—telling—me. It's okay. You're okay. No sharks—none of that. Only seals—the seals are harmless. It's okay. Keep going."

Seals. *Seals.*

I tilt my head back into crawl. *Keep going*, I think, over and over again, *don't stop.* I must exhaust my former self, exhaust her out, exhaust all her fist-clenching rituals, exhaust the imprints—all that control I never had, the dread, the failures, the not-being-good-enough. *Keep going.* With each pull, each push, the elastic feel of it, the underwater echo, the heart beat—I reach for it, catch, pull, and I know it's happening—the moult, the absolute being. *Don't stop.*

I hear the ocean breathe inside me. I imagine the streamlined glide of first entering the water—the soaring, weightless sensation of being suspended—free. The first catch of the hand, the first pull, the first push, the loose recovery of the arm; music drums, stretches, constricts. A geyser of renewed force teems through my arteries, my blood and bones. This monotonous repetition of stroking through wild, open water—a primal sense of peace, cleansing atonement, the peeling, stripping, moulting out of myself, out of my skin, an estrangement from all things human, societal constraints, expectations, the disease of materialism, sex. The clearing out of everything, wipe the mind's slate clear—*tabula rasa.*

If a person's life were divided into chapters, there would be an end to them—and the death of my life to date had to be this way, my body baptized by the frothing conviction of the elemental earth. Here, in this cold, dark place of salt and exhaustion. The moult has freed me—and I stroke onward, onward, crawling through the dark, with nothing but my newborn skin. It is beautiful. I am alone in the ocean. There are no boats or flares or flags or music—clear nothing.

I strike out, stroke, kick, pull, breathe, stroke, paddle, kick, breathe. There are splashes in the water. Glorious splashes have riled a brilliant patch of phosphorescence, the green glow covers me, sparkles in the dark, it dances around my body, illuminating my raw skin. I swim, exhilarated, determined and calmly at peace—reaching out to the tiny fireflies. Stroke, kick, catch, pull, stroke, breathe. The splash of each stroke and the entry of each hand is followed by a magnificent comet of phosphor.

Seals glide and swoop in the water underneath me, luminous, graceful protectors weaving here and there. The seals begin to multiply, an aquatic meteor shower of life.

All at once, there are more splashes, erratic and spastic now, and my marine guardians scatter, vanishing into the depths. The radiant phosphor-water returns to thick, black octopus ink. Dark splashes rock my body from side to side, and my elation turns quickly to terror. The splashes are smacking both sides of my face, boxing my ears. The moon, a smudge of white now, pours into the ocean like milk. Stars drip yellow shafts of buttercup smears. I am swimming inside a child's fingerpainting. *All this crawling around without touching the ground.* Water tumbles into me like I'm swimming upriver, it churns, due west; water on a rampage, a crusade of silver and salt that will pour off some cliff somewhere but won't die because water never dies. *Pour out all in the name of Lucifer, fill here, you, fill and fill till it be full.*

Tassels reach up at me like hands. At first I don't notice, but now I am sure there are tentacles, fingers sucking me under, creatures brushing past my arms and legs. I flail, scream.

"Kelp!" is shouted. I don't recognize the voice. "Swim through it!" The voice sounds very far off, droning. A dark ropey mass on the surface grabs at me, running tongues down my exposed body. Somebody help. The water is hissing at me. Salty venom. It doesn't recoil, but hisses again. I can't move through the slimy eel-weed. Beds of eel, fields of them, rippling. Don't, *please.* I try to stroke through another bed of reedy feelers. Dorsal fins are circling, orbiting around me, hundreds of them, waiting. They have eaten my seals.

I am falling, fast. White pebbles pelt me in the face like a hailstorm. They got me, the hands, and they're pulling me down a black vortex underwater toward salt pans, dark bottles, and broken glass. One hundred shades of white; headlights drive at me from the ocean floor, and I cannot breathe. There is nothing but water, nothing but the underwater crash.

No entiendo. *I don't understand.*

Colours turn in and out of each other clockwise: red, orange, yellow, green, blue. And counter—blue, green, yellow, orange, red. I try but don't remember hitting land. Can't recall my fingers grasping at sand. Purple, blue. White light comes at me in shafts, before a wicked pain splits through my frontal lobe. When I swallow, knife-blades lacerate my throat—a startling thrust of soreness. Flames swivel around in slow motion. Try again to remember hitting land, grasping at sands, at roots.

"Savi." A hand is placed on my forehead. Resinous eucalyptus soaked into a terry cloth covers my face. I can't tell if I am lying down or standing or still swimming. I could be dead and levitated six feet off the water for all I can tell. I am afraid of the pain in my head when I open my salt-encrusted eyes.

"Rise and shine, Sealegs. You're on land now, resting. I'm here too. Sol. Don't worry." Worry about what? It's over, isn't it? I must have finished, I just don't remember burrowing my fingers into shore and crawling out. I think I'll stay here, just float a while longer. No salt slivers or plants grabbing at me with tangled weedy fingers. No, this is just fine, *thank you just the same.* The floating colours are rings around my thoughts.

"Here," he is saying. I try to open my eyes, can't. "This will help."

When my eyes finally open, the light tumbles into me, so

brilliant, and so does the pain. It is dizzying. There are two of him in double focus, they are both looking down at me from above. "Yes, it must hurt," they are saying. "It's okay. The exposure is taking its toll. Here, this will help with the pain."

I grasp, but my fingers aren't working, they're curled into white balls. "Don't cry," he is saying. "It's all right, love. Here—let me help you."

He ungnarls my hands and bends my fingers back. All my muscles twitch in fits of spasm. Fingers finally lock around the mug. There is the warmth of another hand, his large hand cupped over mine, helping me hold on.

"Now bring it to your mouth." My eyes are weeping fluid, tears burn rivulets down the sides of my face. I can feel the heat from the cup scalding my palm. Too hot. I'm too salty now, wrecked to the core, ruined. I'll burst into flames, die of fire and salt. The colours dance a painful Charleston. They won't calm down and I can't stop them.

"Sleep," his voice says. The colours turn from brown, to black, to nothing.

Talcum powder scent of crisp linen. Clean laundry, soft against my skin. There is a tepid hush, muted. I hear wind moving through leaves and chirping birds. When I open my eyes, shrinking with the anticipation of a rupture of pain, it isn't as bad; the flaring, stunning surge in my head has subsided to a dull throb. But there are rings around everything, little smudging comets when I shift my gaze. I don't recognize the room. The little tracers follow me, making me seasick, and I vomit into a pan next to my bed.

"Hola." He's still here, sitting on the edge of the cot.

"Where am I?" comes out a croaking whisper. Talking hurts my throat.

"You're being monitored. You were brought back to the island from the hospital ship after nineteen hours in the water. You lost consciousness."

"I don't remember the finish."

He tucks linen around my shoulders. "Helluva try," he says. "Helluva swim."

Too exhausted and nauseated by the smudges to respond, I turn on my side, back faced to him, every muscle yanking.

SEVENTEEN
JANUARY 19, 1927

AFTERNOON SHADOWS are long on the slopes behind the hospital adobe; ferns grow up from the sides of the circular hut. Wind beats against the clay walls; palm trees click, and I smell wild sage brush burning in a fire. Solid earth—a secure foothold. The rustling leaves that I have been hearing glitter pale silvery green against the sky. Sol is outside playing golf with a wooden pole and random stones. He squints into the sun as I sit on the front step of the hut wearing a robe. "Feeling better?" he asks, putting down his pole and walking toward me. My eyes dilate. The shock has settled into a fever.

"Pretty stiff," I say, feeling faint and bracing myself against the adobe doorway. A fresh sweep of wind shakes through the trees and branches again. The comets are almost gone, just a little blotchy now out of the corners of my eyes. He puts a hand on my back, warm and solid, but a boil of residual nausea lures me back to my cot, where I slip back under a sheet into sweet oblivion. I have been sleeping for three days.

I am stirred awake by two familiar voices, Sol, and—Ida? It *is* Ida. She is asking Sol if I am dying.

"Level with me—what did you say your name was?"

"Solomon."

"Listen, Solomon. I need to see Savanna at once."

"She's sleeping. She needs to sleep right now. This is an infirmary."

"You call this hovel an infirmary?"

"Excuse me, miss," Sol sounds firm and collected.

"Ida," I rasp from across the room.

Sol lets her inside the clay hut, and she rushes to the side of my cot.

"Oh, Savi! Listen—I'm so sorry."

"What for?"

"It was all my idea—this madness. They wired us the night of the race, said you were hauled out. Severe cold. Delirious. Oh, thank God, you're all right." She blinks at me. "Oh, Savi. You look a smear."

She leans back against the clay wall. "Michael's here too," she continues. "I insisted on seeing you first; he's outside. Do you want to see him?"

"Sure." She goes outside and moments later they both stand, blinking, peering curiously at my pallid, withered body.

"Oh, good Lord," says Michael. He approaches the side of my cot. "You look like a bloody funeral."

"I missed you too."

He makes me think of the bake house: frosted windows, fogged up by customers and the hot draft of ovens. I can imagine him working behind the counter while I have been away, watching customers stuff their pipes over burning candlesticks, watching that the candle wax doesn't melt and mollify onto the wooden tables. I imagine him wearing my oven mitts, stirring hot pie filling, clearing tables, and brewing pots of dark and powerful coffee.

He appears to suddenly remember that he is holding a package. "Oh," he says, "Maizee sent this with us."

He holds out the package wrapped in paper.

Folded inside yellow tissue paper are two envelopes. One contains a letter that I fumble to open first.

My Savi,

I know that you will not get this until after the swim, but I know
that you will have been successful. Forgive me for cracking into
your flat while you've been away, but I saw an article about
newborn cauls and it said that wise women used to inspect them to
predict the baby's future. If the caul was reddish in colour, it meant
good fortune in that child's life. A caul that was lead in colour
signified a life riddled with obstacle and misfortune. Your caul, my
dear old lemon-pie-face, has been examined by a local expert, and
the consensus is that your little scullcap was red at the time of birth.
It's your bean helmet, Savi. I cannot understand it the way you
understand it, but I thought we might agree to surrender ourselves
from the regimes of our earlier days. I have decided it is a rather
draggy system.

Your Maizee

"What is it?" Ida says, approaching my cot again. "What's
the matter?"

An approaching sound of clinking glass stops at the entrance of
the medical hut, and the clang of his bottles hitting the ground startles
everyone in the room. The burst of glass is followed by a mutter of
words. *Loot.*

When I turn my heavy head to see him there, he is glowing
with elation. He has shaved his face and bathed. His hair is freshly
wisped around his head. He steps inside and shuffles across the room
to my side.

Ida and Michael gasp.

Michael looks to Sol. "Is he allowed in here?"

"It's all right." Sol looks at me. "He's family."

"He's *what?*" I stare at Sol.

"He's my brother."

My voice is still a rasp. "Why didn't you tell me he was your
brother?"

Ida and Michael stand there looking from Sol, to me, to the barefoot man sitting on the edge of my cot. He is clasping his hands around mine.

"You did it. Yes. You did it." The Lieutenant touches my face with a long, skinny finger before clasping his hands on his lap and looking at me with the most open pride I have ever seen. He turns to the others in the room. "She did it!" he beams and turns back to me. "Silly bint."

"Oh, hell," says Ida. "She's crying."

EIGHTEEN

GEO YOUNG was welcomed to shore by thousands of people cheering and beaming their headlights and punching their horns; a blaze of torches, bonfires, and lanterns threw light on the exhausted Canadian as he fought through the kelp and clambered to land, the only finisher, having clocked in at fifteen hours and forty-four minutes. The story remains front-page bannerlines: a thousand dollars here to recommend a chocolate powder, two hundred thousand dollars there to star in a movie. He is the Catalina Kid, the Father of the Marathon Swim, a seventeen-year-old bellhop who hitchhiked all the way from Toronto—*who knew.*

After a series of cold days, the wind is balmy and smooth again, and my fever has passed with all the sleeping. Various salve treatments have helped the chafes at my sides, they're almost healed. Sometimes the ground feels like it's oscillating, but at least my eyesight has been restored.

Ida and Michael are staying at the St. Catherine Hotel, and now they are playing an eighteen-hole round of golf on the fancy turf higher up the island. I am wandering aimlessly around the hill; days before the hill was still a nomadic village of swimmers, but now the tent city has diminished to half as many camps, and people are packing up their folding aluminum chairs and ice boxes. I sit on my boulder and look down at the beach where a wild goat is nuzzling at rocks near the shore. Sol appears from out of the sandy path. "I told you the goats come down the hill to lick the salt off the rocks," he says.

"Yeah, I remember—I didn't like you then."

He grins. "Chinese New Year's party tonight," he says, "at the beach."

"You lied to me about Trudy," I say. "She never made a plant."

"They say the Chinese New Year is a time to reconcile and forgive. I didn't expect you to abandon your suit over it." His grin widens. "Well, not *entirely*."

"Who was that girl I was pacing beside?"

"I don't know. I couldn't see the number on her convoy."

"I can't believe that half-pint is taking forty per cent of Geo's prize."

"Funny you should say that. There's already a scandal on the rise."

"Over what? His contract?"

"It would seem that his *mother* actually signed the contract, George being under the legal age. Appears she signed away forty per cent of any endorsements coming to him for quite some time—he had no idea about the extra clauses, and she hadn't understood what they meant."

"For how long?"

"A year. At the very least."

"That's brutal."

I see that he is not smoking.

"The scandal doesn't end there," he continues. "Wrigley decided to put George's prize money into a trust fund until his twenty-ninth birthday. O'Byrne's filing a lawsuit—breach of contract."

"What? Twenty-*nine*? What a roast."

"Seems his chum, there, the diver, Hastings—well, seems Hastings took a swing at O'Byrne for trying to keep him away from George ever since the race. I thought you might find that interesting."

"Well," I shrug. "Hats off."

"I was wondering," he says, "if you might accompany me to the sands tonight. I understand your brother and his fiancée are planning to show up later as well."

"What about No Sleeves?"

"Who?"

"You know—that contestant that rips all the sleeves from his plaid shirts."

"Oh," he says, remembering. "If you're talking about Norman Ross, he crawled on board his convoy after twelve hours in George's wake and ordered to be taken directly to a hotel—outraged that a *kid*—a Canadian underdog no less—had managed to outswim him so thoroughly."

"I lasted longer than No Sleeves?"

"Six *hours* longer."

"Six hours!" I am amazed. "What about Bea?"

"Couldn't say. But I suspect she had a rather spectacular haul-out. There were a series of mad rushes to the edge of the *Avalon* every time word came that another Venus de Grease was being taken from the water."

I'm sure my brow has just furrowed into a telling crumple.

"Oh, Jeez," he says. "Don't worry—I had blankets around you before anyone saw or could take any pictures."

We stalk through the hills toward the beach, tree frogs sing in the brush, moths flitter as we push back tall grass. In the spirit of the lunar new year, garlands of gold ribbon and paper lanterns have been hung wherever possible; fiery torches have been planted along the sandy path closer to the beach. We arrive, emerge from the trail, and a cork pops and shoots from a fizzing bottle of champagne. Sol presses his palm against the small of my back as we walk toward the foaming shoreline.

There are many people, more, I think, than the last party. Large driftwood fires burn and people mill about, drinking, laughing. An enormous marlin is being baked over a grate down the way. I can feel a thrill in my bones when the wind picks up, carrying the smoke up the hills. That thrill—there it is. We walk toward the glowing party beneath the deepening sky.

There is an orchestra, out of sight, on the balcony of the St. Catherine Hotel; the music is carried over water—it skims the surface, dives under, gathers force, and surges out again like a great flapping crescendo of a hundred flying fish. The intimates of the Wrigleys are here: the slick-haired ukulele player and his identical blonde canaries are wearing designer kimonos this time, warbling "Show Me the Way to Go Home."

We approach a spread of people who appear to be well into the sauce, and Bea is drifting at the edge of the group. She walks toward us in rippling red silks, leans into Sol. "Grub a smoke?" she says, and as he lights her up, she falls over herself a little, wobbly.

"Take it easy," he says.

"California jimson goes straight to the bean." She takes in her tobacco, exhales with her eyes closed. "Year of the Rabbit," she says. "You know what they say about rabbits."

"The bush is worried on account of the hare," says Sol.

"What?" Bea crinkles her flat moon face.

"It's when someone is obsessed with everything outside of her business."

"Ah." She slides a hand down her hip, smoothing her silks, and takes another drag. After another long exhale of smoke, she smiles. "Kung Hei Fat Choy," she says wistfully and turns to face the ocean before drifting back toward her small following who are planting a garden of incense spikes into the sands.

A vendor is walking around selling Orientalia from a tray he has strapped to his body: joss sticks, fire-crackers, portable mah-jong sets, and Tiger Balm. Sol is approached by a city man who wants to know about the fishing on the other side of the island, and I slink out of the crowd toward a series of high sandy banks near the shore, away from the racket. I sit down in the soft sand and listen to the wind in the trees.

"Congratulations," comes a voice out of the dark.

I peer. It's Rhea James. She's wearing a twill dress suit and a long velvety scarf. Red, the colour of festivity.

I rake my fingers through the sand. "Thank you."

"You lasted nineteen hours. That's nothing to shake a stick at. There was a nasty current reeling everyone backwards—the closer you got to the mainland, the stronger it pulled. Never mind the kelp. That stuff went on and on."

"Yeah," I say. "I'm not sure I remember it so well, I was pretty light in the head by then. How did Ella make out?"

"I saw the showdown, Savi. You were neck and neck for quite a spell. Hours. And you carried on to last four hours longer than she did after leaving the water. You've got my attention."

"That was *her*?" I say. "I thought she was Trudy Ederle. My observer tricked me and told me she staged a plant."

Rhea laughs softly. "Clever."

"Yeah. I know."

"Disconcerting about Ederle's hearing," she says, her tenor having turned careful and grave. "Her capacity to hear has always been poor—childhood measles took a toll on the auditory nerves. Her Channel swim only proved to exacerbate the problem. She'll be completely deaf before her thirtieth birthday. That's quite a blow."

I look at her, silent, and wonder how she knows all this.

She crouches down and sits beside me in the sand. We gaze out at white froth glowing along the shoreline, at phosphorescent shimmers in the water.

"I hope you don't resent her too much," she says. "She is, after all, the one who lit the fire under you that ultimately brought you here."

"I don't resent her any more," I say. Then it strikes me, and I straighten out of my slouch. "How do you know that?"

She motions toward the fire-flecked sands where contestants and islanders are laughing and having a good time. "A successful athlete knows how to balance hard work with good times. I have to imagine Clem told you that; he's always been hot on balance and moderation."

"Higgins?" I sit up even straighter and watch her face. "You know Higgins?"

"He's an old friend of mine, from long ago—he speaks highly of you," she says. "You would be surprised just how tight-knit the swimming fellowship is. Everyone talks. At any rate, he was very sorry about everything falling to pieces the last time he saw you. Ederle—the English Channel business. He told me all about it."

"I thought he was in Florida."

"He had to return to New York after the hurricane hit the keys earlier this month."

"A *hurricane?* Oh, my God. Is he all right?"

"Yes. As I say, I heard all about it. Listen. I dug into your history this week, tracked Clem down and cabled," she says, arms rested on her bent knees. "Because there's something I'd like to talk to you about."

Leaves flicker, stars blink. "Okay," I say—a sideways eyeball.

She continues, "I coach a small team on the mainland," and she points across the channel. "At a girls' college in Santa Monica Bay. My program is designed for swimmers who show an aptitude for long-distance swimming. I'd like to recruit you."

"Recruit me?" I say, stunned and tingling. "Recruit me to college? But I didn't go to high school."

She's looking out at the ocean, cool and poised and wholly unperturbed. "Yes," she says. "I know, Clem mentioned. There is an examination; you would have to catch up."

Firecrackers explode in a volley farther down the beach.

"But—" I say, reeling a little. "I don't have any money."

"Not to worry. I'd bring you into the program on scholarship. I only train six girls at a time and I have one space available if you're interested. There's much promise in these marathons and the culture is growing. There's travel. South America. Overseas. Meantime, Wrigley is looking to sponsor another marathon race in August, in Canada. Toronto—home of George Young, headquarters for the Canadian National Exhibition. Lake Ontario. Twenty-one miles. Pyjama-cracking cold when the wind is up. Thirty grand."

She gets up and shakes sand from her twill dress suit. An ironic look moves over her features. "According to the latest market studies, not enough Canadians are chewing his gum," she says and laughs. Her red scarf shines and whips in the wind. "In any case. Do think about it, Savi. I'll be leaving the island in the morning. You can find me at the St. Catherine." She vanishes into the dark and I lay back and stare at the stars, beaming.

When I hear the crush of his Oxford bags, my legs are completely covered by a two-foot heap of beach. "Crazy fish," he says, bending down. He takes off his jacket and sits on it.

"You didn't come here for the fishing," I say.

"Oh, no?"

A few minutes pass and we listen to the surf. The ocean curls around us, a new moon. He rakes his fingers through the sand. "He was getting into too much trouble back home in the city, constantly in the path of the authorities," Sol says. "His condition progressively reduced him to wandering the streets. I had to find a place where he could exist without constant run-ins."

"Why here?" I ask.

"Actually, someone *did* tell me about the fantastic Tuna Club. Said it was a quiet." He pulls a cigar from his chest pocket. "Share with me?" he asks.

Wordlessly we watch the sky and share the cigar. He sweeps to his feet and his pants billow in the wind. He reaches down, offering his hand. And it seems like all one movement, weightless and fluid, I stretch out my arm, can feel the little muscles fan out in my shoulders and back, still sore.

But if I die, drifting with cinders
never finding my way across
never turning over the right stones
misreading the rifts in sand—then, love
bring my body back in a cask of brandy

Lo siento

ACKNOWLEDGEMENTS & NOTES

MY SINCERE THANKS TO:

My family and friends—always.

Shane and Debbie Collins for introducing me to the world of open-water swimming and for casually mentioning the 1927 Wrigley Ocean Marathon, which became the inspiration for this book; Sam Montgomery for his coaching; and all the coaches and swimmers I have had the opportunity of working with over the years. These experiences have doubtless played an inspirational role in the creation of this book.

The faculty and students of UBC's creative writing programs, especially: Keith Maillard for his encouragement and insight at the outset of the project and for his exceptionally generous help along the way; George McWhirter for his keen remarks and pointers; Patty (Fernie) Bass, Shannon Cowan, Heather Frechette, Lee Henderson, Richard Van Camp, Michelle (Ivy) Winegar, and Monica Woelfel; and the grad fiction class of 2001–2002 for their friendship and valuable feedback on early drafts.

Fred Stenson and the Banff Wired Writing Studio 2005–2006; the Alberta Foundation for the Arts for helping me get there; Lynn Coady for her illuminating editorial guidance; Anne McDermid and Martha Magor (agency extraordinaire) for their invaluable support; Lee Shedden for his smart and perceptive suggestions as my editor;

Ruth Linka for her enthusiasm and for (very) patiently answering all my questions; Heather Sangster for her "eagle-eye" proofread; Kelly Pearn for helping me locate the image chosen for the cover; Emily Shorthouse and everyone involved with Brindle & Glass who made this book possible.

David de Vlieger for his enthusiasm and intelligent feedback on every significant revision of this book and for rolling so gracefully with the troughs and swells of the process; for asking how the characters were doing if I hadn't mentioned them in a while; for understanding during intense periods of revision as the fictional cast loitered around the house, monopolized conversations, and left trails of dishes and laundry all over the place before raiding the wine.

And the Catalina Island Museum Society and the Santa Catalina Island Company for providing articles, clippings, records, and photographs of the Wrigley Ocean Marathon at the beginning research stages.

Throughout the process of writing this novel, I read a great number of books—both fiction and non-fiction, popular and literary—written in the 1920s and about the 1920s to get the essential feeling for the time. *Sage Island*, however, is not imitative of any single work or the works of any single author. That said, I would like to acknowledge *Swimming the American Crawl* by Johnny Weissmuller for the insight it gave me into competitive swimming in the 1920s. Johnny's references to his coach, William Bachrach, and his accounts of Bachrach's coaching philosophies influenced and inspired the development of Higgins's coaching style. The phrase used on page 213, "Pour out all in the name of Lucifer, fill here, you, fill and fill till it be full," is from Francois Rabelais's *Gargantua and Pantagruel*, Chapter 1.V., "The Discourse of the Drinkers."

While I stuck reasonably close to the facts surrounding the Wrigley Ocean Marathon, some creative licence was taken. I created a camp of swimmers on Catalina acclimatizing for the race, for one, but in fact many contestants were stationed in hotels around Long

Beach and Santa Monica, where they trained off the mainland. For a non-fiction account of the swim, a primary source was *Wind, Waves, and Sunburn: A Brief History of Marathon Swimming* by Conrad Wennerberg (chapter 6, "Catalina Island: the Chewing Gum Swim").

At times this story plants real people—usually competitive swimmers or coaches from the 1920s—in fictional time and place. In the Catalina sections, please note that Charlotte Moore Schoemmel, Norman Ross (a.k.a. No Sleeves), George Young, Bill Hastings, and Henry "Doc" O'Byrne were real people, but their dialogue and eccentricities are the product of my invention. All other characters, save known historical figures, are fictitious, and any similarity among the people, names, and other events in this book and any real people, names, and events is coincidental.

SAMANTHA WARWICK was born in Montreal and raised in Sutton, Quebec and Vancouver. She received her MFA in creative writing from the University of British Columbia in 2003. Her work has been broadcast on CBC Radio and has appeared in various literary magazines including *Geist, Event, Room* and *echolocation*. Samantha spent seven years coaching competitive swimming between 1997 and 2004, and has participated in long distance open-water swim races in British Columbia, California and New York. She now lives and works in Calgary where she is at work on her second novel.